ONE GOOD MAN

SMALL TOWN ROMANCE

BARRINGTON SERIES

SUSAN MACKIE

Original watercolour painting for the cover by Fiona Hayes *@fionahayesart*

Cover Design by Susan Mackie, Small Town Publishing

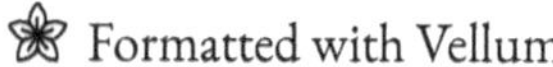 Formatted with Vellum

For all the women who put the needs of those they love before themselves. This is for you.

Susan Mackie

WHO'S WHO IN BARRINGTON

This is the tenth story in the series but it's the sixth full-size book. There are also three novellas and a short story.

While it's best to read the other stories first - in case you haven't, or you've forgotten who's who - here is a cheat sheet for you.

Rose Gordon Hamilton (author and Councillor) married to
Angus Hamilton (Vet) – we met them in **Charlie's Will.**
Own Barrington Homestead and farm & the Vet practice.
Son **Charlie** (school).
Daughter **Harper** (toddler)

Steve Webb, Mayor of Barrington and wife **Rachael Webb**
parents of Debbie (deceased) and father-in-law to **Jamie Tait**
(grazier) – we met them in **Coffee is my Calling.**
Grandson **Warwick** (nickname **Woz**, kindergarten).

Douglas Barlow - retired Solicitor. We met him in ***Charlie's Will.*** Wife, ***Frances,*** is unwell.

Harriet Russell Murray married to ***Drum Murray*** (grazier, Councillor) – we met them in ***A Place to Start Over.***
Own Montrose Homestead and property.
Harriet's office is within Evans Real Estate.
Billie – Drum's daughter (primary school).
Hamish - their son (toddler)

Meggie Hamilton (Angus's sister, in business with Harriet) married to ***Max Masters*** (Vet, Angus's partner) – we met them in ***Meggie & Max.***
Meggie's office is within Evans Real Estate.
Indiana – Max's daughter, lives away.
Tommy – Max's son (primary school).
Debbie-Anne (nickname ***Dee*** - their toddler)

Melanie Mitchell Evans (Vet nurse) married to ***Ben Evans Jnr*** (nickname ***Little Ben***, Evans Real Estate) – ***all books.***
Tiffany – Melanie's daughter (primary school)
Bronte - their toddler daughter

Laura Harrison (farmer, bull breeder) dating ***Ben Evans Snr*** (nickname ***Big Ben***, Evans Real Estate) – we met them in ***A Place to Start Over.***

Nicole Reid Stewart (accountant, BnB owner) married to

Robbie Stewart (builder) – we met them in ***Ragged Mountain Ranges.***
Harry Stewart – Robbie's son
Lucy Reid – Nicole's daughter (high school)

Millie Tucker owns cafe and is in a relationship with ***Finn Anderson*** (Barrington Ridge Estate) - we met them in ***The Barrington Book Club.***
Millie's son - ***Matthias.***
Finn's son - ***Lucas.***

Hannelore Tucker - Millie's daughter. Runs a business inside the cafe called *Say Yes to the Cake*. Dating **Harry Stewart**.

Kristen Laing – works at cafe with Millie & Hanna.
Judith - *Kristen's aunt* - we met her in ***The Secret Reader.***
Runs the ***Barrington Book Shop***.

1

———————

Looking up from her book, itself tattered and much-read, Samantha turned to the train window. Shocked, she clapped a hand over her mouth to keep her gasp at bay. She needn't have worried. The other person in the carriage was an older woman, asleep with her head back on the train seat, snoring gently.

Tentatively touching a strand of hair tickling her jawline, Samantha looked again at her reflection. She wondered how long it would take for this hair, dark and wavy, to feel natural. She didn't look like Sarah anymore. Now she had to learn not to act like Sarah. Unconsciously she sat a little taller and straightened her shoulders.

Evie stirred. She was curled up on the seat with her head in Samantha's lap, the weight of it providing reassurance they were on their way to safety. Samantha gently stroked her daughter's hair, long and curly now her plaits had been undone. She'd asked to cut it shorter too, but Samantha had faltered. And time had run out.

The train slowed, and peering through the window, Samantha could see the lights of the railway station ahead. She shook Evie by the shoulder, murmuring, 'Wake up, Evie, we have to get off now.'

The woman on the other side of the carriage stirred and sat up, smiling at Evie. 'Hello. I think we both had a sleep.' Evie didn't respond and clung to Samantha's arm with her face buried in her shoulder.

The woman continued to speak, and Samantha was reluctant to meet her gaze. 'Barrington. It's home for me. Do you live here, or are you just visiting?' Her tone was curious yet gentle, but Samantha was wound up and struggled to answer.

'Visiting.' She knew her response was curt, but she didn't want to engage with a stranger, no matter how kind she sounded. Samantha busied herself with their belongings. Two large supermarket bags and Evie's small backpack. The woman lifted an overnight bag down from the rack over her head.

Samantha waited for the older lady to get off the train before taking Evie by the hand, their belongings gripped tightly in her other hand. They stepped onto the station platform. A couple tumbled from the next carriage, each dragging a large suitcase from the train. They were laughing and speaking loudly, and Samantha could see their easy affection. She turned her eyes away and walked determinedly toward the exit.

'I'm cold, Mummy.' Evie tried to burrow into Samantha's side, under a fold of her coat. Samantha hesitated. She didn't want to remain on the well-lit platform longer than necessary but stopped long enough to take a knitted jumper from the backpack, pulling it quickly over Evie's head. With her head down, she scurried through the exit, hurrying Evie beside her.

A taxi waited there, its engine running. The driver stepped out and gave her a questioning look, but Samantha ignored him and kept walking. Just ahead, she saw the lady from their carriage get into a car, saying a cheery, 'Hello Kristen,' as she opened the passenger door. Samantha felt her gaze as they sidled past. Behind her, she heard the couple with the suitcases chatting loudly with the taxi driver. They laughed and Samantha sighed to herself. *If only life was that easy.*

Pulling a scrap of paper from her skirt pocket, she paused under a streetlight.

Nicole Stewart, The Courthouse, Copeland Road, Barrington

There was a phone number, too, but Samantha didn't have a phone. They walked for ten minutes until they came to the small town's wide main street. It was late. Nothing seemed open except a pub further down. *Sunday night. Of course nothing is open. Good.* She spied a tourist map on a billboard across the street. Samantha was carrying Evie now, and she strode over to it, their bags bumping against her leg.

With her finger tracing their route from the train station to the main street, Samantha found Copeland Road. She looked at the hand-written address again. There was no street number, so she had no idea how far it was. But The Courthouse sounded like something that would be in town.

Samantha began to walk, her hip and back aching from

carrying Evie, now asleep in her arms, and their meagre possessions. But as she trudged along beside the road, she looked at the waning moon and smiled. *They had each other. And they were finally free.*

2

———————

'DID YOU SEE THAT YOUNG MUM WITH THE LITTLE girl?' Judith peered back at the train station as Kristen drove slowly away.

'Briefly.' Kristen looked at her curiously. 'Problem?'

Judith sighed. 'Something about her. Their belongings were in supermarket bags. Their clothes were, um, badly fitting.'

'Not being well-dressed wouldn't bother you, Auntie Judith.' Kristen slowed, and indicated to turn into Gloucester Street.

'No. It wasn't that. She couldn't meet my eye when I spoke to her. And the child was timid.' Judith sighed as Kristen pulled into their driveway. 'I said hello when I boarded at Maitland. I'm pretty sure they'd travelled from Sydney themselves. It was obvious she didn't want to chat. And rather than make her uncomfortable, I put my head back and had a nap.'

'Not everyone is as open as you, Auntie. If she's from the city, she may not be used to strangers starting a conversation.' Kristen chuckled.

'You're probably right, Kristen. And I am tired.' Judith took her time getting out of the car, her right knee was aching. *Maybe I should see about that knee replacement soon.* Kristen already had her bag and waited while Judith stretched her leg, then walked to the back door.

While Kristen unlocked the door, Judith thought about the woman and child again. Her last image was of the mother hoisting the little girl onto her hip. She placed her hand on Kristen's arm. 'Wait, Kristen. She had no one there to meet her. What if she has nowhere to stay?'

Kristen had the door open but turned to Judith with a little frown. 'Do you think? We can drive back that way and see if she's still walking. But Auntie, do you want to invite a complete stranger to stay here with us tonight?'

Drawing in a sharp breath, Judith shook her head. 'Not here. But we could check, and if she doesn't have somewhere to sleep, I'd be happy to pay for a motel room. And see if she'll tell us what she needs. Maybe over breakfast tomorrow.'

Kristen had already locked the door, and with her arm around Judith's shoulders, walked back to the car with her. 'You're a kind woman, Auntie. But I agree. Let's see if she needs help.'

An hour later, they were home again. They'd driven back to the train station, then along the road to the main street. Kristen had looped around town, and they'd stopped at the park, too, in case they were sleeping rough. Judith hoped not, but there was no sign of them. Perhaps they had family in town after all and were picked up and taken home. She hoped so.

3

Driving slowly, Jamie left Rachael and Steve's straight after dinner. Warwick had fallen asleep on Rachael's lap, so Jamie helped Steve clear the table and do the dishes.

Steve nudged Jamie with an elbow. 'Do you think Rachael tired him out just enough, to have him fall asleep at the right time to avoid doing the dishes?'

Jamie grinned at his father-in-law. 'You betcha she did.' They laughed together as they finished their task.

Warwick had been at their house all day, as he was most Sundays. Jamie dropped by just after five, and they kicked a soccer ball around the backyard together. Even Rachael had joined in. Woz had loved it, galloping around, stealing the ball from his grandparents and kicking it between the two rubbish bins they used for goalposts. Then Jamie had bathed Woz while Rachael prepared dinner. It had been spaghetti Bolognese tonight, his son's favourite.

And now they were driving home to their empty house. It was more than a year since they'd lost Debbie. And Scarlett. Jamie grimaced as he drove across the bridge where Debbie had crashed the car that terrible night. He shook his head as he did every time. *How did she not see the cattle on the road?* But he had no answer. Would never have an answer. He needed to focus on Warwick and try harder to be a good dad. A good *single* dad. He sighed.

Jamie began to accelerate as he left the town limits. Movement ahead caught his eye, and he slowed as he drove past, peering into the darkened tree-lined roadside. *Was that a woman? Carrying something.*

A quick look in his mirror told him Warwick was asleep. Jamie was still driving slowly, and he looked in his side mirror. Nothing. Maybe he imagined it. Beginning to speed up, he looked in his mirror once more. There she was. On the edge of the road again. A woman. Or a girl. Carrying something. *On the side of the road in the dark? Should he go back? Or call the police?* Something wasn't right. But it was none of his business, and he had Warwick to think of.

Except it was his business. He couldn't un-see her.

There were no other vehicles on the road in either direction. Jamie pulled over and turned around. He drove slowly back towards town, and there she was, walking by the edge of the road. She didn't look at him as he drove by, but he could see she was carrying a bundle in her arms while grasping two large carry bags.

That decided him. He drove across the bridge, turned around again, and idled back. As he approached, travelling slowly, Jamie caught a glimpse of her face in his headlights as she looked over her shoulder at him. Young and afraid. She moved quickly from the edge of the road to the verge, but Jamie knew there was a ditch there. She seemed to trip, then fell as he stopped his car well off the road and left the engine running. Warwick was waking up, but he had to check on the girl-woman, and quickly.

He left a window down so he could hear Woz if he cried and ran around the car to where he'd seen her fall. The head-lamps weren't on her, but there was enough light to see her sitting in the ditch. The bundle in her arms moved, and began to cry. *A child.*

Jamie rushed towards her, then stopped. The look on her face was sheer terror. *Of course she's afraid. Get a grip, man; you're a complete stranger on the side of a country road.*

Jamie stopped. He held his hands out in the universal *I have no weapons* gesture. 'Hello. Don't be scared. I'm Jamie.'

He waited, but she ignored him. She murmured soothing words to her child, whose sobs subsided. She looked up at him. *Fear, and something else on her face. Determination?* Her fright-ened gaze made Jamie drop to his haunches. He sometimes forgot how large he must seem.

'Where are you heading? Can I give you a ride?' He spoke quietly, hoping to reassure her. She shook her head vigorously but didn't speak.

From the car, Warwick let out a piercing scream. 'Daddeee!'

Jamie stood up. He held his hand up, indicating she should stay where she was. 'My son.' He darted back to the car, extri-cated his crying child from the car seat, and carried him back to where she was with her child. Warwick stopped crying, suddenly excited to be having an adventure in the dark with his father.

With Woz in his arms, Jamie kneeled a few metres away from her. From them. He tried again. 'I'm Jamie, and this is my son, Warwick. But everyone calls him Woz.' Some of the fear seemed to leave her face.

'Hello.' Warwick tried to scramble out of his arms.

'Hold on, mate.' Jamie kept an arm around his son. He didn't speak for a moment. He sensed she was considering her options.

'Samantha.' She spoke quietly. 'And this is Evie.' The little girl's face was pressed into her mother's shoulder.

'Hello.' Warwick spoke again, more loudly, and the little girl turned her face to look at him. She was no longer crying but her face was pale, and she had dark rings beneath her eyes.

'Where are you heading? Can I help you?' Jamie watched her face. She seemed uncertain.

The girl-woman, Samantha, reached into her clothing and thrust a piece of paper toward him. Holding Warwick's hand, he stepped forward and shone his phone light on it. *Nicole Stewart. Ahh. She's escaping a bad situation. No wonder she's scared.*

Jamie took a step back, kneeling again so he wasn't towering over them. 'I know Nicole. But her place is still a few kilometres further on.' Jamie pointed to the road and was about to offer her a lift but realised it might be difficult for her to trust him. Instead, he added in a quiet, confident tone. 'I can call Nicole if you like. I'm sure she'll come and get you.' He watched her face, then said gently, 'But I'd be happy to drive you there if you're comfortable with that.' She looked away, and he saw tears on her cheeks, yet she made no sound.

Decided, he found Nicole's number and called. 'Nik. Hi. I'm by the side of the road, not far from the bridge. I've found Samantha and Evie making their way to your place.'

Nicole hesitated for only a moment, then spoke softly. 'I'm not expecting them, but I can tell by your voice they need me. Stay with them please, and I'll be there in a few minutes. Thank you Jamie.'

He sat down, still a couple of metres away from Samantha, but let Warwick wander closer.

'Nicole is on her way. We'll wait with you until she gets here. We'll be easy to find with my car up on the road.'

'Thank you. Jamie.' She gave him a tremulous smile, and he felt unaccountably chuffed.

Warwick sat by Evie, then pulled a tiny car from his pocket and held it out to her. She looked at her mother and touched the car. Warwick made *vroom-vroom* noises and began driving the car over his own legs, then Evie's. She giggled.

Nicole drove past, then turned her car around and parked behind Jamie's. She walked quickly down the embankment to Jamie and held out a hand to Samantha. 'Hello. You must be Samantha. I'm Nicole. I have a safe place for you to stay.'

Samantha took Nicole's hand. 'Hello. Thank you.' She cried as she began to stand and then stumbled. Jamie moved forward, but Nicole was quicker.

'Ankle?' Nicole put an arm around Samantha. 'Lean on me.'

Jamie thought he heard Samantha mumble something about tumbling into the ditch.

Nicole turned to Jamie. 'Can you gather up Samantha's things, please, Jamie?' Evie had walked to her mother and held her free hand as they made their way up to the cars.

Jamie gathered the large bags and the little backpack, then, taking Warwick's hand, he followed the women. He stood back while Nicole settled them both in the back seat. He saw there was a child seat and watched as Nicole strapped Evie in, speaking quietly the whole time. Keeping Samantha in the back with her daughter was smart. They'd feel safer. He wouldn't have thought to do that.

Nicole closed the back door and gave Jamie a quick hug. 'Thank you, Jamie. I don't know what their story is yet, but thank you.'

And just like that, they were gone.

Jamie secured Warwick in his safety seat before getting in. He looked at the time on the dash of the car. The whole thing had taken less than thirty minutes, but he knew it was a half hour he'd never forget.

4

———

EIGHT MINUTES LATER, NICOLE DROVE DOWN HER driveway. The headlights lit up the Old Courthouse, and she heard a murmur from Samantha behind her. But when she looked in the rearview mirror, she'd turned to Evie, hiding her face.

Nicole had wondered where to put them before she left. The Carriage Shed was vacant, but it was further from the house. She had decided to settle them into the apartment downstairs for tonight and reassess in the morning.

Climbing out of the car, Nicole opened the back door. Samantha already had Evie unbuckled and helped her out. The child was sleepy and unresisting.

'I'll get your bags, Samantha, and we'll go inside. There's a private apartment downstairs for you.' Lifting the bags and backpack from the car, Nicole marvelled at how little some women managed to take with them when escaping a bad domestic situation. She had no doubt in her mind that was Samantha and Evie's story. No phone and probably no money. Just the clothes on their backs.

Smiling gently, Nicole opened the front door and led them through a hallway to the front door of the apartment. Opening it, a wave of warm air enveloped them—good. Robbie had turned the heat on when she left. She ushered Samantha inside, Evie again in her arms.

They stepped into a lounge area, and Nicole waited while Samantha gazed around. Since she didn't speak, Nicole showed her the two bedrooms, bathroom and country-style kitchen.

'There's milk in the fridge and coffee, tea and hot chocolate fixings in the pantry. I thought you might be hungry, so there's fresh bread, butter, and condiments.' Nicole opened the cupboard doors and pointed to the kettle and toaster as she spoke. Lifting the lid of a Tupperware container, she added, 'And my daughter Lucy baked muffins earlier today.' Robbie and Lucy had promised to stock the kitchen when she ran out the door after Jamie's call. *Bless them.*

Finally, Samantha spoke. 'Thank you, Nicole. Really.' Her eyes were over-large, and she looked about to drop from exhaustion. But she had a quiet strength, too, and Nicole wondered what it had cost her to escape.

'I'm sure you're tired. I'll leave you now and will pop in tomorrow morning.' Nicole walked to the door. 'You can lock this after I leave. But I promise you that you're safe here.'

Samantha simply nodded and followed her to the door. Nicole stepped back into the hallway and heard the lock click behind her.

Upstairs, Robbie handed her a cup of tea, and they sat on the sofa together. Nicole sighed. 'I don't really know anything yet. Samantha and Evie. She's maybe four or five. I had no warning they were coming, so I don't really know how they had my details.' She snuggled against Robbie. 'But I'm happy they're here. And thank you for getting the flat ready so quickly.'

Robbie set his cup down and put an arm around Nicole's shoulders. 'That was Lucy, actually. She flew into action the moment you left. She's studying in her room, but I think she's waiting to talk to you, Nik.'

'And Jamie. He understood it was better to call me than insist he could drive them.' She shook her head sadly. 'He's a good man. More sensitive than some.' Robbie nodded his agreement.

Nicole finished her tea and stood up. 'You're a good man too, and I love you Robbie Stewart.' She kissed him quickly on the mouth.

Robbie gazed at her with warm eyes. 'Love you too. Now go and see Lucy.'

Lucy was at her desk, overlooking the horse paddock. It was too dark to see the horses, but she was staring out of the window. She turned when Nicole stepped into her room.

'Robbie said you prepped the flat. Thank you, darling.' Nicole sat on the edge of Lucy's bed.

Turning to Nicole, Lucy smiled, but her eyes were moist. 'That could have been us, Mum.'

'It may have been us. Before. That's why we must help when we can. We know how hard it is to leave. And I suspect

Samantha and Evie left suddenly. They don't have much with them. Not even a phone.' Nicole patted Lucy's knee. 'But they're safe now. We'll let them settle in and then see what more we can do to help them.'

'Alright, Mum. Goodnight.' Lucy leaned forward and hugged Nicole quickly.

'Goodnight, Luce. Love you.'

5

——————

Evie stayed awake just long enough to eat a chocolate chip muffin. Samantha carefully laid a towel over the bed and stood Evie on it while she undressed her. She was grubby. They both were. They'd spent two nights sleeping rough, one in a park rotunda and last night in a sheltered corner of the train station. She wiped Evie's face, hands and feet with a damp facecloth, dried her quickly, and popped her into bed in her singlet and underpants. Evie closed her eyes, turned on her side, and was instantly asleep.

Looking longingly at the bath, Samantha decided a quick shower was best for tonight. She'd had a cup of tea and a slice of toast while Evie ate but wanted nothing more than to go to sleep herself. But before that, she needed to be clean. She didn't want to mess up the crisp white sheets on the double bed she'd chosen to share with Evie.

As she peeled off the layers of clothes, Samantha wondered

if she should fold them neatly, but they needed washing, so she tossed them on the bathroom floor. Her ankle was throbbing, and she could see it was bruised. Experience told her it was a sprain and would mend in a few days. She limped into the steaming shower in her undies and bra, then dragged them off and left them on the shower floor while she washed her body.

Her ribs were aching and bruised. She couldn't look at the weeping sore on her left breast, a cigarette burn. Samantha shuddered. But the pain between her legs was the worst. Despite the sting of the soap, she washed carefully. She knew how painful an infection could be. She left conditioner in her hair while she soaped and scrubbed her underwear. She'd hang them to dry over the bath and wear them again tomorrow; she had no others. Maybe Nicole could help her get a few things before they moved on.

Samantha tugged on a shapeless long-sleeved T-shirt. Once white, it was now grey with age, and she combed her hair out, wincing as she did. She ate a muffin while her hair dried, then finally gave in to exhaustion and climbed into bed beside Evie. She removed the snowy white pillow from the bed and folded up her old coat, using it instead. She wasn't sure if the hair dye would run, but she didn't want to take the chance.

Drifting off to sleep, she heard a noise. Something ran along the veranda outside. She got up and checked the door was securely locked, just in case. She heard a dog bark once, twice, further away from the house. Then silence. She slept.

6

—————

Judith didn't sleep well. Images of the young mother and child kept her awake. In her gut, she knew they needed help, and she was cross with herself for not trying harder while still on the train. Or at the station.

Lying in bed, she heard Kristen leave early for work. Judith wandered out to the kitchen and turned on the kettle but, after a moment, turned it off. She'd walk to the café and have breakfast there. She needed to stretch her legs. A quick shower and she was dressed and ready to go.

Her knee ached until she reached the end of the street, and then it seemed to settle as she warmed up. Ten minutes was all it took to reach the café, and she was pleased to see the door open and Millie bustling around near the counter. Kristen and Hannelore would be in the kitchen.

'Morning Judith.' Millie smiled warmly. 'You're early today. How was your trip to see Bernadette?'

'Good morning, Millie.' Judith walked to the counter. 'We had a lovely couple of days. We ate too much but walked a lot too. Bernie had me up doing yoga in the park both mornings.' Judith shook her head with a half grimace. 'This old body is not used to that.'

'Stop it! Yoga is good for you. But at this time of year, early morning, brr!' Millie smiled at someone behind Judith. 'Morning Steve. Your usual? Take a seat, and I'll bring it out.' Focussing back on Judith, Millie asked what she'd like to order.

'Large cappuccino on skim milk, please, Millie. And scrambled eggs on ciabatta. The small version.' Judith tapped her card. 'I know we don't usually open the bookshop on Monday, but I'm keen to rearrange a couple of shelves to make room for stock arriving on Wednesday.'

'Stock? Something new?'

Judith laughed. She loved Millie's enthusiasm for the little bookshop. It had been open for three months and was proving popular with locals and tourists.

'Lots of new ones. I'll fill you in at book club tonight.' Judith stepped aside for another customer and contemplated where she should sit. She walked across to a small table near Mayor Steve, who was reading the paper.

Steve looked up as she sat down, then folded his paper. 'Judith. Hello. Would you like to join me?'

'Thank you, Steve. Um, if you're sure.' Judith hesitated. She knew Steve had very little time to himself in his role as Mayor.

'Of course. You'll be doing me a favour.' Steve grinned and pulled out a chair for her.

Pleased, Judith picked up her tote bag and moved to the

chair he offered. Millie arrived at the same moment with their drinks.

Steve leaned towards Judith. His eyes were twinkling. 'I do sometimes hide behind the paper. But not from you, Judith.'

Judith laughed. 'Oh, thank you, Steve. And yes, I did wonder.'

'You've been away for a couple of days? Did I hear you say Maitland?' Steve stirred a spoon of sugar into his coffee.

'Yes, to see my younger sister.' Judith toyed with her spoon. 'I took the train this time. Bernadette lives right in the city, and it's always a struggle to park. I came home on the evening train last night.'

'How was it? The train trip? I've not travelled by train in a long time. Many on board?' Steve sipped his drink, but his attention was fully on Judith.

'Love the train. It's easy to relax. But no, not many. Only five got off in Barrington.' Judith wondered if she should mention the young mother to Steve.

Millie delivered their breakfast, and Judith sprinkled salt and pepper on her eggs. Steve seemed thoughtful, so she passed him the condiments but didn't speak, instead taking a small bite.

Steve sighed. 'The train. There's a move to reduce the services on weekdays. One suggestion is to use buses on the route after Maitland. It wouldn't be good for Barrington. Locals and tourists are using it. Just not enough.'

'Interesting. I personally won't drive to the city if the train is available. For me, it's stressful. The traffic and parking. The train is more cost-effective.' Judith thought again about the young woman from last night.

'The broader tourism body doesn't seem engaged. They're all about the coast, largely.' Steve chewed for a moment. 'But perhaps we should meet with local tourism operators and Meggie and Harriet. I wonder if they could provide some options for packaging a train journey into local stays.'

Judith nodded. Steve seemed to have more to say. 'The problem is transport once they get here if they want to go further afield. There are limited car hire options and only three taxis.'

'Weekdays is the issue, you said Steve?' Judith had an idea forming.

'Yes. Passenger numbers are low, Monday to Thursday.' Steve took a bite of his toast. 'Mmm. Love this ciabatta toast.'

'Me too.' Judith nodded. 'The bookshop is getting some interest mid-week. We don't open on Monday, but we could. The volunteer roster is strong. What if we organised some day trips? Arrive by train and get one of the school coaches to ferry people from the station. Visit the bookstore, meet the author-in-residence, have lunch at the café and return to the train. Day trips.' She paused. 'It doesn't do anything for accommodation houses, though.'

'That's a really interesting option, Judith. I knew it was a good idea to have breakfast with you.' Steve grinned. 'The train travellers to this area are, generally, slightly older and often women. I'm guessing they might also be your mid-week book-shop customers?'

'Yes. You're right.' Judith could see he hadn't fleshed out his thoughts completely.

'We could package two-day, one-night options. In-town accommodation, like The Lofts and the motels, with dinner at the RSL or pub. They could walk everywhere once we've brought them across from the station. Bookstore one day, and maybe a hosted heritage walking tour the next?' Steve finished his coffee and looked at Judith, his face alight with interest. 'I'll talk to my fellow Councillors and our tourism officer. If they're keen to explore, we'll talk further with the chamber and business community. I hope you'll be involved in the discussions. I value your input.' He glanced at his watch and pushed his chair back from the table. 'Take your time, Judith – I have a meeting in ten minutes. Thank you again for keeping me company.'

Judith chuckled as Steve left, striding quickly through the door after waving a cheery goodbye to Millie. She finished her breakfast and glanced at her watch. It wasn't quite eight, but she'd pop into work and re-organise the shelves as planned.

As she was about to leave, Millie came to clear the table, smiling, as always. 'You and Steve seemed deep in conversation, Judith. He almost bounced through the door when he left.'

'Yes. We were talking about the train service to Barrington.' Judith's face clouded over. She'd forgotten for a moment about the woman from the night before.

'What is it, Judith? You look worried.' Millie sat in the seat Steve had vacated.

'Oh. Not about the conversation with Steve. But something happened on the train last night.' Judith shook her head, still unsure why she was so concerned.

Millie looked across to the front counter. Hannelore was chatting to a customer. 'Want another coffee, Judith? I could use a short break.'

'Alright. Yes. But small this time.' Judith patted her tummy. 'Good breakfast. Steve was just saying how much he likes the toast you're using.'

'The bakery makes it for us. Hannelore could do it, but she spoke to them, and since they've been making it for us, their sales in the bakery for it have grown. Win-win.' Millie grinned. 'One minute, I'll ask Hanna to make our coffee.'

Ten minutes later, Judith relayed her story about the young mother and child on the train to Millie. 'I'm not sure why it's still bugging me. We drove around not fifteen minutes later, but there was no sign of her. Kristen is convinced she was picked up by a friend or relative.'

'But you don't think so?' Millie frowned slightly.

'No. But I have no idea where she went in such a short time.' Judith shivered. 'I hope she's safe and spent the night in a warm bed.'

Millie touched Judith's arm. 'You're a kind woman, Judith. We're lucky to have you here.'

7

———

Jamie woke in the night. He thought he heard Warwick cry out, but when he checked, his son was fast asleep with one leg on top of the covers. He tucked him in and padded quietly back to his own room. *Their room. His and Debbie's.*

He drank from the water glass beside the bed and rolled into the centre, laying on his back. It was quiet outside; dawn was hours away. Sometimes, if he woke, like tonight, he'd think about his life with Debbie before she was taken from him. Debbie and Scarlett. And some nights, he'd cry quietly in the dark.

Tonight, he didn't think about Debbie. His mind was on Samantha. And her little girl. The fear in her eyes had shifted something in him. He had no idea what she was running from. Or who. And no idea what she had suffered. But he didn't need to know. That she had suffered and was fleeing something. Someone. Was enough.

Jamie wasn't sure if he could help her at all, but he'd call Nik in the morning and ask.

AFTER DROPPING Warwick to his Mum, Jill, who would take him to Kindy on her way to Council, Jamie moved a small group of weaners into a larger paddock, before fixing the hinge of the gate to the main hayshed. A young bull had knocked it the day before, and it was hard to close.

Just after nine, his morning chores completed, Jamie returned to the house to make a cup of tea. While the jug boiled, he called Nicole.

'Good morning Jamie.' Nicole always sounded friendly and cheerful.

'Hi Nik.' Jamie cleared his throat. 'I'm just calling to check on Samantha and Evie.' He paused and tapped a teaspoon on the kitchen counter. 'I'm not sure what happens in these situations. But is there anything I can do for them? Or for you, Nik?'

'That's very kind, Jamie, and what you did last night was brilliant.' Nicole paused, and Jamie put his phone on speaker while he poured hot water over the teabag. 'To be honest, I don't know anything myself yet. It's quiet downstairs, and they were exhausted last night, so they're probably still asleep. I'll know more once I've spoken to Samantha today.'

'Okay. Good. Thanks, Nik. I couldn't get the image of them out of my head last night. The fear in Samantha's face. How timid Evie was.' He drew in a breath. 'I can't imagine what they've been through.'

'Of course you can't, Jamie. You're a good man. The treatment I suspect Samantha has received would be alien to you. You've already helped more than you know. You showed Samantha last night how a good and decent man behaves.'

Slightly embarrassed, he coughed quietly. 'Well, if there's anything you need.' Jamie had no idea what help he could offer, but he felt better for saying it.

'Thank you.' Nicole stopped, and Jamie picked up the phone, wondering for a moment if she'd hung up. 'But Jamie, they may only be here for a few days. And I will let you know if there's anything you can help with. Thank you again.'

Jamie ran a hand through his thick, brown hair. He felt slightly dissatisfied by the phone call. He'd hoped for more information. But thinking it through, even if Nicole did know about Samantha's personal situation, she may not want to tell him. If she was running from an abusive partner, the fewer people who knew about her, the better. *He got it.*

Jamie pulled the tea bag from his cup with too much force, and it sent a small spray of tea over his shirt. He couldn't explain why he was invested. But little Evie's shy giggle when Woz ran his toy car over her legs, echoed in his mind.

8

With Robbie at work and Lucy on the bus to school, Nicole took a fresh cup of tea downstairs to her office. She worked with the door open so her guests would see her if they stepped out of the apartment. She heard a gurgle in the water pipes, indicating a tap had been turned on, and assumed they were up.

Not wanting Samantha to feel pressured or hurried, Nicole listened quietly to music as she answered emails and confirmed bookings for The Stables accommodation. After her quiet conversation with Jamie, she heard Evie laugh out loud in the apartment. That was a good sign.

Just after nine-thirty, the apartment door clicked open. Evie appeared first. Her hair was damp, and she wore an oversized sweater and bright pink leggings. Nicole had an assortment of women's and children's clothes in a trunk in the main bedroom, and she'd told Samantha the night before to take anything she might need.

Samantha appeared behind Evie, wearing a colourful long skirt and a bulky jumper with the sleeves rolled back over her wrists. They wore socks but no shoes.

'Good morning, Samantha.' Nicole walked around her desk to greet them. 'Hello Evie. I love the pants you've chosen for today. Pink is one of my favourite colours.'

Evie stood close to her mother, hiding her face in Samantha's skirt. 'Good morning, Nicole.' Samantha spoke quietly. Nicole knew from experience that she'd be unsure of her surroundings and would have a lot of questions.

'Did you sleep okay?' Nicole smiled again at Evie.

Samantha nodded. 'Yes. Thank you.' Her eyes slid away from Nicole's and she worried her bottom lip with her teeth.

'Good.' Nicole spoke brightly. 'Would you like to come upstairs to my kitchen for a cup of tea? Have you had anything to eat?'

Samantha nodded and took Evie by the hand. 'We had some toast. Thank you. And orange juice.'

Nicole grinned. 'Excellent. Come upstairs for a warm drink.' She leaned down and spoke directly to Evie. 'Would you like a hot chocolate, Evie?' The little girl peeked out from behind her mother's skirt and nodded before hiding her face again.

Nicole moved to the door leading upstairs. More quietly, she said, 'It's just me this morning. My husband has gone to work, and my daughter Lucy is at school.'

'Okay.' Samantha picked Evie up and followed Nicole upstairs. She gazed around the large country kitchen, and Nicole gestured to the high chairs at the kitchen counter as she walked around it to turn on the kettle.

'There's a wooden box over there, Evie.' Nicole pointed to a chest in one corner of the room. 'It has books and toys in it, if you'd like to have a look.'

Samantha set her daughter on the floor, and Nicole was happy to see Evie run over to the box. She lifted out a doll and a book and then looked back at her mother. Samantha nodded, and Nicole saw her smile for the first time. 'Go on, Evie, Nicole said you can play with the toys there.' Evie plonked down on her bottom and began pulling more toys out.

Samantha looked like she might stop her, but Nicole said quietly. 'Let her play. We can talk.'

Nicole prepared a pot of tea and placed milk and sugar on the counter. She made a hot chocolate for Evie but murmured to Samantha, 'I'll let this cool a bit.'

With a quick look to ensure Evie was happily playing, Nicole poured two cups of tea and sat beside Samantha. 'Firstly, please call me Nik.' She poured a small amount of milk into her teacup and pushed the little jug closer to Samantha.

'Sam. I used to … I like to be called Sam.' Samantha added a dash of milk to her own cup.

'I'm sure you have questions, Sam. And you can ask me anything. But before you do, I want to tell you that you and Evie are welcome to stay here as long as you need to. There is no pressure for you to move on.' Nicole spoke gently. 'And you don't have to tell me anything at all, or you can tell me everything. The choice is yours.'

Samantha seemed to relax slightly when Nicole said she could stay, but she straightened her back and shook her head. 'I can't pay you, Nik. I can't even get government help. Not right now, anyway.'

'That's alright. You don't have to pay me. You have accommodation and food. If there is anything you need that I haven't provided, just let me know.' Nicole sipped her tea and grinned at Sam as Evie rushed over, holding a toy car, her little face bright with delight.

'Vroom, vroom.' Evie ran the car across her mother's thighs, then scampered back to the toy chest.

'Um. The little boy.' Samantha met Nicole's eyes for the first time. 'Last night. The man, Jamie. And his little boy.' She looked down at her hands. 'He was kind. His little boy had a toy car, and, um, Evie laughed.'

'Jamie. And little Warwick, although everyone calls him Woz.' Nicole chuckled. 'He is a good man.' She was going to add that he had called that morning, but instinct told her that would disturb Samantha, so she said nothing.

Evie wandered back, and Samantha held her on her lap, letting her sip the hot chocolate slowly. Nicole took the lid off an old-fashioned biscuit tin and slid it within reach. 'Anzac biscuits, if you'd like one. Freshly baked yesterday.'

Samantha took one and broke it in half, offering it to Evie, saying, 'What do you say?'

'Thank you, Mummy.'

'Good girl.' Samantha gave the biscuit to Evie and took a

bite of her own. She chewed for a moment, and Nicole took a biscuit for herself, not wanting to pressure Samantha to speak, if she wasn't ready.

'Thank you, Nik. We'd love to stay.' She hesitated. 'As long as it's safe.' She set Evie down and watched her trot back to the toys. She had almost everything out of the box.

'Do you think you're not safe?' Nicole's heart hammered in her chest for a moment, remembering her own journey years before. 'Could there be someone following you?'

Samantha shook her head. 'Not following. Not yet anyway. But he will try to find us.' Her eyes were filled with tears, yet her expression remained determined. 'I left a false trail. He will be looking for me elsewhere.'

'Alright. So you're safe, for now.' Nicole thought for a moment. 'Do you need legal help Sam?'

'Maybe. One day.' Samantha finished her cup of tea, then turned, looking directly at Nicole. 'If he finds me now. Finds us. He'll take Evie. And our lives will be over.'

Nicole's heart began hammering again, but she kept her demeanour cool. 'Alright. We will need to know more when you're ready, Sam. But if you say you're safe for now, then we'll work with that.' *Oh gosh. Poor Sam. And Evie. What on earth have they been through?*

'There's something else.' Samantha had the determined expression Nicole was beginning to recognise.

'Yes?'

'I have a wound. I think it's infected.' Samantha breathed in sharply. 'Do you have any antibiotics, Nik? Or antibiotic cream?'

'Um. Let me get the first aid kit.' Nicole walked quickly from the kitchen to the bathroom. The first aid kit was well stocked but wouldn't have antibiotic tablets. She rummaged around, finding paracetamol and a topical cream, band-aids and bandages.

Returning to the kitchen, Samantha was at the sink, their cups washed and dried and the counter wiped down. 'Thank you, Sam.' Nicole placed the first aid items in a plastic dish. 'Do you need help with this? I'd be happy to take a look.' Nicole hesitated. 'We have a lovely hospital here. If you need more attention than this,' she indicated the medications, 'we can go to outpatients.'

Samantha picked up the container, peeking in. 'This should help. Thank you.' She walked across to Evie and helped her pack away the toys. Evie kept the little toy car in her hand.

Samantha gave Nicole a questioning look. 'Take it downstairs with you, Evie. There's a toy box down there, too.'

Samantha's face brightened, and Nicole chuckled when she said, 'Oh, she's already found *that* toy box.'

Nicole walked them downstairs. 'Is there anything else you need, Sam? Today?'

Samantha began to shake her head, then paused.

'What is it, Sam?'

Samantha blushed. 'Underwear. A couple of pairs. And a bra. If that's possible.'

'Of course.' Nicole gave Samantha a quick look up and down. 'Size ten? C cup?'

'Yes.' Samantha grinned.

'I'll be ten minutes.' Nicole waited until they closed the

door to the apartment and then shot upstairs to Lucy's room. There, on the desk beside her bed, was a Kmart bag. She'd bought new underwear for Lucy two days ago. She opened the bag. One bra and three pairs of knickers, all with the tags still on. And the right size. The bra was white, and the undies pink, yellow and pale blue. Perfect. She could buy more for Lucy this week.

Making sure she took the receipt out of the bag, she carried it downstairs and knocked on the apartment door. She heard some scuffling noises, then Sam opened the door but concealed herself behind it.

Nicole thrust the bag at her. 'These are new and should fit.'

Samantha's mouth dropped open, but she took the bag. Nicole smiled gently. 'I'll be in my office, where you found me this morning. When you're ready, come and have a look around the gardens and other buildings. There's no one else here until Lucy gets home from school. And I can explain our set-up a bit more.' Nicole hesitated. 'But no pressure. Stay in and rest if you'd rather.'

Not twenty minutes later, Samantha and Evie appeared at Nicole's office. Samantha looked down at herself and whispered to Nicole. 'Perfect fit, thank you.'

'Good.' Nicole walked to the front door. 'Would you like the guided tour?'

Evie skipped through the door while Samantha held back. 'I have no way of thanking you, Nik. Not now. But I will one day, I promise.' The words were spoken with a fierceness Nicole was beginning to recognise in Samantha. Some women who had come through Nicole's doors in the last few years had seemed sad and defeated, but not Samantha. She was ready to fight for herself and Evie. For their freedom, their safety, and, God willing, their happiness.

Nicole touched Samantha lightly on the shoulder. 'You're already doing that, Sam. You found your way to me.'

9

Barrington Book Club & Reader Festival Update (six months to Festival)
Attendance: Judith, Millie, Hanna, Rose, Rachael, Meggie, Harriet & Nicole
Apologies: Laura, Melanie, Kristen
Book: *The Bad Bridesmaid* by Rachael Johns

'Hi Millie!' Rose breezed through the door with Harriet and Meggie right behind her. 'The nights are getting cooler.' She removed her coat and unwrapped the long olive-green scarf from around her neck, throwing them on a chair set to one side for that exact purpose.

'They are, Rose.' Millie chuckled. 'I turned the heat on an hour ago, and I have warm snacks tonight.'

'Thank you, darling Millie. You are too good to us.' Rose

hugged Millie quickly and carried her tote bag to their table at the back of the café.

Rose settled in her usual chair, facing the counter and front door. Judith and Rachael arrived together, and she noted that Rachael handed two bottles of wine to Millie. *Good. Millie is far too generous.* Rose had a giant box of chocolates in her bag to put on the table later. They always seemed to enjoy something sweet at the end of the evening.

They were just beginning to settle around the table when Nicole arrived. She called out a cheery hello as she removed her coat.

Millie locked the café door. 'Coffee Nicole? Or a glass of red wine?'

'Oh, red wine please.' Nicole took two of the glasses Millie held and followed her to the table just as Hannelore appeared from the kitchen, carrying a platter of warm pastries. Mini quiche, tiny pies, spring rolls and something that smelled suspiciously like garlic bread.

Judith clapped her hands. 'This is perfect Millie! Warm savouries and red wine.'

Rose waited, feeling slightly on edge, until the group had found their chairs and had a drink in front of them. She cleared her throat, and they all turned towards her. 'There's no easy way to say this. We have a problem.'

Judith was first to respond. 'Is it the grant application Rose? For the Reader Festival?' She paled when Rose nodded.

'Yes. We thought it was a sure thing. That we'd get it through the special meeting.' Rose shook her head. 'But the saleyards project is over budget, and in the end, that's where the small surplus was allocated.'

Rose looked across at Rachael. 'It didn't help that Steve and I had to recuse ourselves from voting. We just didn't have the numbers.'

Rachael nodded. 'It was never a sure thing. And we still have sponsors lined up.' She nibbled her bottom lip.

'What about the other grant, Rose? The federal one for bringing the arts to the regions?' Meggie looked up from her iPad as she spoke. 'I'm just checking the timing of notification for that one now.'

Rose nodded. 'We made three funding applications to support the first Barrington Reader Festival. Council has turned down the cash request, but they have offered some in-kind support, including media and publicity support, use of the library and town hall at no charge and technical staff to manage lighting and audio visuals.'

'As they should.' Judith was sitting up straight with her arms folded across her chest.

'The end of this week!' Meggie looked up from her iPad. 'The federal grant approvals will be made public this week, and that was the larger request. I think we still have a chance there.'

'I don't know Meggs. When we look at past successful applicants, they are all more art-related. Like, fine arts, silo painting, art trails and so on. There's very little that is literary based.' Rose slumped back in her chair. They had been so sure one of the grants would come through that they'd pushed on, and now the festival was just six months away. 'We have to call it this week. If the federal grant isn't approved, I think we have to postpone until next year.'

'No!' Hannelore turned to Rose. 'What was the third application? What do we know about it?'

Rachael answered. 'It was with the State tourism body. It's a relatively small ask, for assistance with a new annual festival. Judith and I met with them in Sydney, and they liked our idea. But since then, we've heard nothing. I've called a couple of times, and they tell me the same thing.' Using her fingers to make quotation marks, she added, 'it's a very competitive process.'

Rose shook her head. 'I think they are waiting to see if we get support from one of the other funding bodies first.'

'What do you think, ladies? If the arts grant isn't successful, should we postpone?' Rose really didn't want to; she had a fabulous lineup of authors interested and didn't want to let them down.

'No.' Judith spoke firmly. 'We may have to rethink a few elements and work out what we can do with the support we have.'

'No to postponing.' Hannelore was firm and Rose almost smiled at her seriousness.

'No.'

'No.'

'We can do this, Rose.' Harriet was tapping her own screen now. 'We may be able to get a few more sponsors and more in-kind help from service and sporting clubs. We can do this.' Looking up for a moment, she grinned, 'and maybe the arts grant will come through.'

Rose nodded, feeling heartened. It was a lot of work for volunteers to take on, but if locals, authors and festival-goers matched the enthusiasm in the room, they'd be alright. 'Thank you. We'll push on then. Some of the funding was to pay author travel and accommodation expenses. Perhaps we can find some savings there. Or lower the number of authors?'

'They're the main drawcard, Rose. And they deserve to be paid for their travel and accommodation. And if the arts grant comes good, appearance fees too.' Judith was firm. 'I'd rather find savings elsewhere if we have to.'

Rose nodded, relieved. The authors she was speaking to were excited, and most would do it at cost, but Judith was right. They deserved to be recompensed for their time too. And she hoped lots of books would be sold.

'Now. This month's book. *The Bad Bridesmaid.* Who loved it?' Nicole chuckled as she asked, then leaned in. 'Who else has been to Norfolk Island? Robbie and I spent a week there last year, and there was so much in the book that made me giggle. Author *Rachael Johns* had Norfolk down pat – it's a really unique place. And people.'

'Oh gosh. I laughed so much.' Judith shook her head. I went over there the year Colleen McCullough died, with three of my sisters. We had an absolute ball.' She giggled, with a hand to her mouth. 'I think we met some of the locals in the book. Seriously. So funny!'

'I loved it too. I told Harry I want to go over there for a holiday, but I got this look.' Hannelore made a serious face, then raised her eyebrows so high they almost disappeared into her hairline. Everyone laughed.

'The story was lovely. Fred's mother with so many marriages.' Rachael grinned. 'And blended families can be hard, even when they're all adults.'

Rachael looked at Nicole, who laughed. 'I think Lucy and Harry could get up to some of those tricks.'

'Nah, Nik. Harry adores you.' Hannelore flicked her fringe back from her face. 'I especially loved the banter in this one. I laughed out loud quite a few times. And a good ending.'

'Oh yes. I'm all for a happy ending.' Judith closed her copy of the book, then looked surprised as they all laughed loudly. 'What?'

'Happy ending, Auntie!' Kristen snort-laughed, then sipped her wine.

'Really, Judith?' Even Rachael was chuckling now.

Rose sat back; her anxiety about the festival lessened. It will be okay.

10

Samantha allowed herself to rest for a couple of days, quietly spending time with Evie in their rooms, or outside in the garden once Nicole's husband and daughter had left for the day. Evie loved throwing balls for the two dogs, and Samantha was happy to lie on the grass beneath a large shady tree and just watch.

The trunk filled with clothes had offered up more options for both of them, and Samantha loved seeing Evie running around in denim overalls. Unencumbered by her usual long skirts, she had taken to climbing the large tree in the front yard and even the timber fence of the horse paddock, happily watching the horses when they came in to eat the hay Nicole's husband threw to them in the morning.

Samantha peered again at the sore on her breast. It was no longer inflamed and beginning to heal. Her other wounds were healing too, and she was grateful. Peering at herself in the bathroom mirror, she ran her fingers through her hair. Barely reaching her shoulders now, she liked tucking it behind her ears. Samantha knew it made her look younger. When she saw herself like this, she imagined she *was* younger. As she was *before him*. Before she lost herself. Shaking her head, Samantha allowed herself a small smile. But without him, there'd be no Evie. She raised her chin then and spoke directly to her reflection. 'I'd go through it all again, to have Evie.'

'Who are you talking to Mama?' Evie poked her head around the bathroom door, her eyes wide.

Samantha knelt and held her arms out to Evie, who flew into them and snuggled against her chest. 'I was talking to myself, Evie. Sometimes I like to say things out loud.'

'Sometimes I talk to Scout and Minnie.' Evie nodded her understanding. She didn't ask questions very often, and Samantha loved her daughter's absolute faith in her. Evie had really taken to Nicole's dogs.

Hearing footsteps on the stairs outside their door, Samantha took a deep breath. She needed to speak to Nicole. 'That sounds like Nik. Shall we go and say hello?'

Evie nodded and unwound her arms from Samantha's neck. 'And the dogs. Can I play with the dogs?'

'Of course. Come on then.' Taking Evie's hand, Samantha strolled from their apartment to Nicole's office. Nicole was finishing a phone call when they appeared and gestured for them to come in.

Standing, Nicole welcomed them brightly. 'Hi Sam, hello Evie.' Picking up a coat from the back of her chair, she shrugged it on. 'It's cold outside today, but I was about to check the water trough in the horse paddock. Would you like to walk over with me?'

Samantha had their coats across one arm. She'd thought she might chat with Nicole while Evie played with the dogs. Turning, she held the smaller coat out for Evie 'Put your arms in, Evie, and I'll roll the sleeves up for you.' The coat Evie liked best was a pale blue wool, lined with a matching blue gingham check pattern. Samantha could see it was good quality, but it was several sizes too big. Evie didn't seem to mind and stood still while she folded the sleeves back.

Nicole opened the front door, and Evie began to jog towards the horse paddock while Samantha put her own old coat on. 'She loves that blue coat. I've tried to get her into a smaller one, but she refuses.'

She felt, rather than saw, Nicole glance at her. 'It was Lucy's. Her favourite, too, for a couple of years. It's very cute on Evie. She'll grow into it.'

Samantha thought about Nicole's words as they strolled towards Evie, now standing on the bottom rail of the horse-paddock fence.

'We may not be here long enough. For Evie to grow into it, Nik.' Samantha didn't want to sound ungrateful, but she was already in Nicole's debt.

'I understand. I hope you can stay a while. But if you need to go, Evie may have the coat.' Nicole climbed through the fence and walked across to the water trough. 'I'll turn the tap on. It's a bit low.' She called back.

Samantha stood on the bottom rail, with her arms on either side of Evie, now perched on the top rail. Nicole walked back to them. 'Evie, would you like to pat the horses while we wait for the trough to fill up?' She gave Samantha a questioning look but held her arms out to Evie, who allowed herself to be scooped onto Nicole's hip with no hesitation.

Samantha watched, anxiously at first, as Evie leaned out to stroke one horse, then another, while Nicole quietly introduced them. 'This one is Diana, and that's Honey. The big black one is Jack, and we won't pat Lawson because he's not quite as friendly.' Evie murmured a quiet hello to each horse and seemed fearless as she reached out, touching a mane here and a shoulder there. She giggled when the horse called Honey turned and nuzzled Evie's tummy.

Still carrying Evie, Nicole strode to the trough and turned off the tap, then meandered back to Samantha and the safety of the fence. Evie was wriggling with excitement but clambered down from the fence when she saw the dogs standing beside Samantha. Picking up a twig, she threw it and waited until Minnie brought it back in her mouth. Laughing loudly, she ran to the grassy area under the big old tree in the front yard, the two dogs scampering with her.

'Thank you, Nik.' Samantha swallowed a sob, keeping her voice as steady as she could. She couldn't look at Nicole. 'That was just beautiful.' Samantha paused and drew in a breath. Tears filled her eyes, but she didn't want them to fall. She glanced across at Evie, rolling in the grass with Minnie, while Scout lay nearby, watching indulgently.

'Evie's a lovely little girl, Sam.' Nicole moved close enough that their shoulders touched. 'And she's a credit to you.'

Samantha nodded, then chanced a look at Nicole. Her

lovely face was filled with compassion and her smile was encouraging.

'What do you want for Evie, Sam? What are your dreams for her?' Leaning back on the fence, Nicole watched Evie cavorting with the dogs as she spoke.

'Right now, for us to be safe. That *he* won't find us.' Samantha gave Nicole a quick look, then turned to watch Evie play. 'But you're asking more than that, aren't you Nik?'

'Yes, Sam. I understand the immediacy, the urgency, to be safe. Lucy and I went through something, too, but that's a story for another day. But I understand. And I know it's hard. Really hard.' Nicole's face changed for a moment, as if remembering, and Samantha understood then why Nicole was helping her. Why she helped others too.

'Honestly, Nik. I'd like her to grow up somewhere like this.' Samantha waved an arm around. 'In the country. On a farm, even. And go to a country school.' She chewed on the inside of her cheek. It was a bad habit; she had an ulcer there. So she stopped.

'Really? Country life isn't for everyone.' Nicole smiled. 'Let's walk over to the house. It must be morning tea time.' She continued as they walked slowly across to the courthouse. 'We've had a few women and children come through here. A small number have stayed around, but many return to the city and some have moved further away. But it warms my heart to know you already have an affinity with this area.'

'Actually.' They were at the front door now, and Samantha stopped, then looked directly at Nicole. 'I grew up in the country. On a farm. Further south.' She turned and looked at Evie, then called out. 'Evie! Come in for morning tea with Nik.' Evie ignored her, and Samantha was surprised. She always came when she was called. 'Evie!' Her tone was louder, sharper, and Evie looked up, waved, then trotted over. The dogs were right behind her.

'You must come when I call you, Evie!' Samantha took her hand firmly, trying to tamp down her fear. *Not coming straight away may be life or death one day.*

'Mama!' Evie wailed loudly and tried to pull her hand free. Samantha felt wretched then and knelt down, taking Evie in her arms.

'It's alright Evie. It's alright.' She looked up at Nicole, but all she saw was kindness and empathy.

'Let's make some morning tea, shall we?' Nicole's voice was bright. 'Would you like a hot chocolate Evie?'

Evie stopped crying, nodded, then took Nicole's hand, eagerly walking upstairs. Samantha followed more slowly, trying to ignore the pang of jealousy she felt at Nicole's easy manner with her daughter.

———

LATER, while Evie played with a puzzle from Nicole's toybox, Nicole rephrased her question. 'And you Sam? What do you want for yourself? Imagine you're safe. No longer running. What would that look like for you?'

Samantha shook her head, then gazed through the window. She could see one of the horses cantering around the paddock. Lawson, she thought. Focusing back on Nicole, she spoke quietly. 'I can picture that. Being safe. It's what has kept me going. Kept me strong.' She drew in a breath. 'I see a little house. Not grand like this.' She waved an arm around the beautiful room they were in. 'Just small. Like a miner's cottage or a farmhouse. With a garden, where I can grow some of our food, and maybe chickens.' She grinned then. 'And now I see a dog in that picture. Evie has taken to yours.'

'That's a lovely image. I can see that for you and Evie. I really can.' Nicole's words warmed Samantha's heart. 'You said you come from the country, Sam? From a farm?'

'Yes. My parents were share-farmers in Gippsland. On a dairy. But they had sheep, too. And I had a horse. I used to ride all the time and help bring the cows in after school. I was happy then, and that's why I dream of something like that for Evie.' Samantha sipped her tea.

'Are your parents still there, Sam? On that farm?' Nicole spoke softly.

Samantha shook her head. 'Dad died when I was in high school. Cancer. It was very sudden. We barely had the diagnosis, and he was gone. But I think he knew, for a long time, and ignored the signs. Mum couldn't stay on the farm. She had trouble getting work, and we fought all the time.' She shook her head. 'I missed Dad so much, and when Mum took up with someone else, I was furious. I didn't think she liked him that much, but I realise now, it was probably to keep a roof over our heads.' She swiped a tear from her cheek. 'He was alright, good to Mum and even me. I just couldn't see it. Then.'

'And your mum now? Do you think she would help you? Could you go to her?' Nicole pushed the plate of chocolate chip cookies closer. Samantha could tell they were homemade. Evie had already had two.

'No. She's dead too. More than a year ago.' Samantha couldn't stop the tears now, and Nicole handed her a tissue. 'I didn't go to her funeral. It was over by the time I found out.'

'I'm sorry, Sam.' Nicole placed an arm around Samantha's shoulders, and she leaned into her, crying silently. She didn't want Evie to see her like this.

'But that's the false trail I've laid. I bought train tickets to Melbourne and then Gippsland. It was almost all the money I had. But I wanted him to think I'd gone to my step-father. I made a point of asking about the train connections and where to change in Melbourne. He'll send someone to find me down there, but I imagine they'll stop in a few days or a week.' Samantha sat up, wiped her eyes again and tucked the tissue into her sleeve. 'Then he'll broaden his search.'

11

———

Nicole's heart hammered so loudly that she thought Samantha would hear it, but she managed to keep her voice quiet. And kind. 'How did you get my name, Sam? Who sent you to me?'

'It was serendipitous Nik.' Samantha smiled, and Nicole almost drew in a breath. She was a truly lovely young woman; her features lit up when she smiled. 'I, um, wasn't out of the house much.' Breathing in through her nose, she shook her head and glanced quickly at Evie. 'I was never, um, able to go out. But someone needed a doctor quite urgently. The paramedics came. There were two, a man and a woman. *He* watched them the whole time and made sure I wasn't alone with either of them. But right at the end, as they left, the lady paramedic handed me some medication and said it should be refrigerated straight away. She gave me such an intense look when she said it that I knew *that she knew* my situation. I took the medication and went straight to the kitchen and found a piece of paper folded up between two sheets of tablets.' Samantha's eyes were wide with amazement as she spoke. 'She took such a risk, giving it to me. I tucked it quickly into my bra because he was right there, behind me, as I opened the fridge door. For a moment, I was angry at her. If he had discovered it, he would have beaten me ... but I am grateful now. So grateful. It was hours later before I was able to read it in safety.'

'Oh, Sam.' Nicole shook her head. 'You've been through more than most, and you've stayed strong.' She shuddered slightly. 'So once you had my details, you left. And came here on the train?'

Samantha gave a brittle laugh and looked away for a moment. 'Not exactly. I was given that piece of paper almost eight months ago, Nik. It took that long to.' She wiped her eyes, and Nicole felt her own filling with tears for this brave young woman. 'To create an opportunity to escape. If I planned it badly.' She stopped, and Nicole automatically leaned closer. Samantha whispered her next words, and Nicole barely heard them over the rushing of blood in her own ears. 'He would have stopped me taking Evie. And that would have killed me.'

Nicole placed her hand over Samantha's and squeezed. 'Brave girl. Thank you for taking that risk. Thank you for finding your way here.'

Samantha squeezed her hand back, but her expression was of astonishment. 'You're thanking me? Why Nik? I thank you, in my mind, every minute that we're here.'

'You were meant to find me. And we will keep you safe, Sam. You and Evie. I promise.' As she said the words, Nicole prayed she could keep that promise. She needed to tell Robbie tonight what she knew of Samantha's story.

'When you're ready Sam, can you tell me a little bit more? About who *he* is. How he kept you imprisoned. Why we can't seek help from the police.' Nicole decided as she spoke. 'I want you to stay here, Sam. You and Evie. Don't run again. We will find a way to keep you safe and free you from this constant fear of discovery.'

Samantha's face crumpled, and she began to cry silently. Nicole slid from her chair and took Samantha's thin body in her arms, using her own body to shield Evie from the vision of her mother's distress.

12

Judith placed her phone on the kitchen table
and raised an eyebrow to Kristen. 'That was Mayor Steve. He
has local tourism operators meeting with him on Thursday at
Council, to discuss how we can create mid-week itineraries for
train passengers from Sydney and Newcastle. He said it's
important I'm there.'

'You do have great ideas Auntie.' Kristen pivoted as the
doorbell rang. 'That will be Hanna and Harry. Callum is
meeting us at the pub. Are you sure you don't want to join us?'

'No. You go on.' Judith waved Kristen away with her hand.
'I'm going to do some research for this meeting. I want to be
prepared, it's only two days away.'

'Okay.' Kristen hesitated. 'Um. Exactly what are you
researching?'

'Well. Older women, many of them now single, often join
groups. You know, gardening clubs and the like. I thought we

might be able to offer our mid-week come-by-train packages to groups. Easier to get thirty at once, than selling it to thirty individuals.'

'That's clever.' Kristen waved as she left the room. 'I'll be back around nine. We can talk more then, if you like.'

'Yes, enjoy your night.' Judith heard the door close as she spoke and chuckled. Kristen's romance with Callum was progressing nicely and she couldn't be happier for her niece.

After heating up leftover lasagne, Judith ate with one hand while scrolling groups and jotting down marketing ideas on her iPad with the other. She would have liked to run her ideas past her sisters, but Kathy and Diane were on a cruise and Bernadette had mentioned going to a movie tonight.

By eight she had cleaned the kitchen and was snuggled under a blanket on the sofa by the fire, reading, when Kristen come home. Judith heard voices in the kitchen and at first thought Callum was with her, but then realised it was Hannelore.

'Oh, you're still up. Good.' Kristen poked her head into the lounge. 'Hanna's here, we're making hot chocolate. Want some?'

Laughing, Judith nodded. 'Yes, of course. Bring it in here, it's much warmer.'

'And that's not all Auntie. We have ideas.' Kristen withdrew from the room before Judith could question that. She made room on the coffee table for their drinks and set her book aside.

'Hi Judith.' Hanna's voice was bubbly as she walked in, two steaming mugs in her hands. 'This one is for you. Extra marshmallows.' Her eyes twinkled and Judith grinned back. *These young women are keeping me young.*

Kristen stepped into the room, closing the door behind her. She set her mug down and a small bowl of chocolates. 'We're home early because we were chatting at dinner ...'

'... and we have ideas for getting groups here on trains.' Hannelore finished Kristen's sentence and Judith sat up a little straighter, trying not to laugh at their earnestness.

'And your young men? What have you done with them?' Judith sipped her hot chocolate, allowing the creamy-chocolatey goodness to linger in her mouth for a second before swallowing.

Hanna waved her hand with a grin. 'Oh they had some ideas too, but once we finished the pizzas they suggested we come back here and help you.'

'They said they'd go through to the other room and play a game of snooker.' Kristen nodded seriously.

'Snooker. Of course.' Judith lowered her gaze as she set her mug on the side table. She didn't want them to know she was laughing and she really did want to hear their ideas.

'You mentioned marketing to groups would be easier than marketing to individuals.' Kristen began, her tone serious.

'That's right.' Judith waited.

'And you said gardening groups and the like.' Kristen added, before glancing at Hanna.

'And gardening groups would enjoy coming here, for sure.' Hanna added. 'But what about book groups?'

'Book groups?' Judith frowned.

'Most small towns, and suburbs, have book clubs these

days. What if we could tap into those.' Hanna had moved to the edge of her seat.

'And of course, some book club members will still be working. You know, younger women like us.' Kristen added.

'But many would be retired or semi-retired.' Hanna's face was alive with excitement, and ideas.

Judith felt like she was watching a tennis match, her head swivelling from one girl to the other as they spoke.

'Book clubs are a great idea. But where do we find them?' Judith had searched book clubs on her iPad, but they were mostly online groups on social media, or private.

'Auntie!' Kristen looked surprised. 'Libraries, Auntie. You worked in the system, surely libraries in the areas we are targeting for the train travel, would have lists of book clubs both formal and informal?'

'Well they do. But there are privacy laws and so on. We can't ask them for their customer lists.' Judith was still frowning.

'You don't have to get their lists. We could market through the libraries. Via their newsletters or websites or even with flyers on their noticeboards.' Hannelore grinned. 'What do you think Judith?'

Sitting back, Judith ran the idea around in her mind for just a moment. 'Make the train packages specifically for the book shop here, and market through various libraries? Would there be enough interest to get groups here?'

'We think so. There isn't another Indie book shop in a regional area north of Sydney. And we have the author-in-residence program. We could package it up with a heritage walk, time at the book shop, and perhaps an afternoon author talk or book signing. Just one per week, for say six weeks, to see how it goes. And of course, pub dinners and overnight accommodation.' Hanna stopped, took a breath, and gazed at Judith, her eyes bright with excitement.

'I like it. Well done girls. I'll make some notes and get a list of libraries in suburbs close to the train stations. I'll take this to the meeting on Thursday.' Judith paused. 'Would you like to come with me? I'm sure Steve wouldn't mind.'

'I would Judith, if that's okay.' Hanna raised an eyebrow to Kristen.

'Not me. I'll cover for you at work. I'm happy to help, just not in the up-front-salesy stuff.' Kristen seemed flustered as she picked up a chocolate. 'But I think you should speak to Rose beforehand. She might have something to add.'

'Brilliant. I'll speak to Rose and see if we can have a meeting-before-the-meeting at the café tomorrow. If it's in the afternoon, perhaps you can join us?' Judith's gaze took in both girls. If she made the meeting with Rose around four, young Lucy would be in the café with Millie.

'Yes.' Hanna glanced at Kristen. 'As long as Mum doesn't need us. But if we have the meeting at the café, we can always help her if it gets busy.'

'And Lucy will be in after school.' Kristen glanced at her watch. 'It's almost nine Hanna, you told Harry you'd pick him up.'

'Oh! Already!' Hanna jumped up, reaching across to pick up their empty mugs.

Judith stood too, grinning. 'Just go Hanna, We've got this. Don't keep Hot Harry Stewart waiting.'

Hanna giggled. 'I don't think he knows that's what you call him Judith, but he'll find out one day.' She wagged her finger at Judith before hugging her quickly. 'Tomorrow afternoon. See you then.'

Judith cleared the coffee table and was washing up their cups when Kristen returned from seeing Hanna out. She passed her niece a tea towel. 'You girls were great tonight. Your ideas are spot-on and I love your enthusiasm.'

'Thanks Auntie.' Kristen seemed to concentrate on the mug she was drying, but Judith sensed she wanted to say more, so she waited. 'For a while I stayed in Barrington to help Mum after Dad died. Keep her company.' She sighed. 'And I've always been a bit shy. Happy to help in the background. But I wondered if I was missing other opportunities. If I should try somewhere else.' Kristen leaned against the kitchen counter and gazed at Judith. 'But now I know this is where I am meant to be. There are lots of opportunities here and I love working with Hanna and Millie. And my own little accounting practice on the side. And since you came Auntie, I just feel like everything has fallen into place for me.'

Judith was moved beyond words. Kristen didn't often share her inner thoughts, but she'd articulated exactly what Judith had been thinking herself. She hugged her niece quickly, then stepped back. With a twinkle in her eye, she added, 'And Callum. Callum's another good reason to stay in Barrington.'

Kristen laughed loudly, then tried to flick Judith with the damp tea towel. 'But don't tell Callum that, Auntie. He needs to work that out himself.'

13

***

Jamie pulled up at the Barrington Store to get fuel before he picked Woz up from kindergarten. Robbie Stewart drove in beside him.

'Hi Robbie.' Jamie opened the fuel cap and picked up the hose.

'Jamie. Cold enough for you?' Robbie wore an overcoat with the collar turned up. The wind was from the south. 'I think we'll get snow in the Tops this month.'

Jamie shivered involuntarily. The mention of snow always got him. 'You're right. It has that feel to it.' He finished pumping fuel and replaced the fuel cap, but leaned on the side of his vehicle while he waited for Robbie.

'How are things at your place?' Jamie really wanted to ask how Samantha was, and little Evie. It was two weeks since he'd found them that night. He wasn't sure they were still at Nik and Robbie's, but he was keen to find out.

Robbie looked at him for a moment, but said nothing as he finished filling up. Then he turned back to Jamie, speaking quietly. 'Samantha and Evie are still with us. They haven't been off the property.' He glanced down at his feet, then looked back at Jamie. 'To be honest mate, I haven't met them.'

At Jamie's shocked look, he continued. 'Oh, I've seen them, from a distance, but I haven't spoken to them.' He shrugged. 'I don't know the details, but Nik says Samantha believes her ex will take Evie if he finds them. And that she'll never see her child again if he does.' Robbie grimaced. 'But mate, I do know he physically hurt Samantha, and was controlling her to the point of imprisonment. It took her eight months to find an opportunity to leave after she was secretly given Nicole's name and address.' Robbie looked anguished now. He whispered the words again. 'Eight months, Jamie.'

'Hell.' Jamie kept his voice low too. 'I knew it was bad, that she was running from something bad. Imprisoned, you say?' Jamie felt a glow of anger in his gut at the thought.

'Yes. Nicole has Samantha's trust now, and that her ex hasn't found her here is a good sign.' He shook his head again. 'But at some point she will need help to legally gain her freedom and custody of Evie. Samantha's not ready to make that step yet. And Nik doesn't want to scare her. We're pretty sure she has nowhere to go. No other family.' Robbie's face was grim.

'Bloody hell. It's so hard to believe, in these times, that this can happen.' Jamie was trying to reconcile what he has just heard.

'Actually mate, you might meet her before I do.' Robbie chuckled. 'Meet her again, I mean.'

'What do yo mean?' Jamie's ears had pricked up. He was even more curious about Samantha and her daughter now.

'She told Nik she wants to thank you for helping her that night. And I think Evie has asked about Woz a couple of times. Something about a little car.' Robbie patted Jamie on the shoulder. 'I think Nik will invite you and Woz over, once she double checks it's what Samantha wants.'

A warm glow replaced the anger in Jamie's gut. Good. He'd like to see her again. 'Tell Nik, anytime.' He walked into the store with Robbie then, to pay for their fuel. Jamie bought a Freddo Frog for Woz, his favourite.

14

———————

They had a routine now. Samantha and Evie would join Nicole for coffee once Robbie left for work and Lucy went to school. Even though the days had cooled, they often sat on the veranda while Evie frolicked with the dogs.

'How are you feeling Sam? It's been more than two weeks and I'm hoping the injuries you arrived with have healed?' Nicole felt awkward asking, and personally thought Samantha looked much better than when she arrived. She had colour in her cheeks and made eye contact when she spoke. Evie had blossomed too. So quiet at first, now she ran around with the dogs, laughing loudly and calling out.

'Injuries?' Samantha paused, then continued quietly. 'Yes, thank you Nik. All healed.' She grimaced slightly. 'But I'll have the scars for life.'

'Oh Sam.' Nik blinked away a sudden rush of emotion. She carried her own scar, on the side of her face, mostly hidden by her hair. She touched it with a shaky hand, the fear of that day would never completely leave her. Samantha covered Nik's hand with her own.

'I'm sorry Nik. That you went through something too. You and Lucy. I know it's selfish of me, to feel sorry for myself. I'm not the only one and many have been through much worse.' Samantha blinked away a tear.

Nicole nudged Samantha's shoulder with her own, chuckling. 'Now we're both feeling sorry for ourselves. Aren't we a pair?' She was relieved to hear Samantha's echoing chuckle.

'I'm feeling stronger, Nik, in a lot of ways. Not just physically, but mentally and emotionally too. I need to think about the future. Evie should start school next year.' Samantha drew in her breath sharply. 'I have two options Nik.'

Nicole nodded. 'Go on.' she spoke quietly. This was the first time Samantha had talked about her plans for the future.

Samantha gazed over at the horses in the paddock, away from Nicole. 'One option is run again. To keep running until Evie is eighteen. Move frequently. Interstate. Change our names. Our look.' She fingered her hair.

'I've wondered about your hair, Sam.' Nik wasn't sure if she could ask, but went on when Samantha nodded. 'When you came it was obvious you had put a dark dye through it. Hiding what I thought was your natural blonde colour. But it has faded, from washing I expect, since you've been here, and yes, the hair underneath is blonde. But the roots coming through are dark, like the dye.' Nik wrinkled her nose in confusion.

'I can see it too. I wondered how obvious it was. I've been dying it blonde since I was seventeen.' Samantha glanced at Evie and a tear trickled down her face. 'I had to. And Evie too, when she turns five.'

Surprised, Nicole looked at Evie. Her hair was a dark honey colour, and would possibly darken further as she got older.

'So the dark hair that's coming through? That's your natural colour?' Nicole was still confused.

'It's a cult Nik.' Samantha gazed across the lawn, her eyes following Evie as she played a game of catch with Minnie. 'I've been living in a cult since I was seventeen. We're all blonde. The women, and girls, don't cut our hair. We wear long skirts. We're subservient to the men. There's a hierarchy, an order. My husband.' She stopped, her voice choking on the word husband. 'My husband was near the top. He controls the finances for the group.'

Nicole frowned. 'Would I know it? There was one, in the seventies or eighties with a woman and a lot of blonde children. I think they dyed their hair.'

'It's more secretive than that. And bigger. Hiding in plain sight. It's like a compound, and we were in the inner circle with very tight security.' Samantha stopped, her voice wavering with emotion.

Nicole moved closer and put an arm around Samantha's shoulders. 'You don't have to tell me Sam. I can see how hard it is for you.'

'But I do.' Samantha turned then, looking into Nicole's eyes as she spoke the words quickly. 'At first I felt safe and protected. I didn't mind dying my hair. He told me I looked beautiful. And the clothes were for modesty, he said.' Her whole body shivered. Nicole just nodded and held Samantha's hand. 'Then one day he caught me trying to phone my mum. I just wanted to let her know I was safe. I was happy. That was the first time he punished me.'

Samantha stopped speaking and breathed hard through her mouth. Nicole wanted to hear the rest, but she knew the revelations would shock her. She squeezed Samantha's hand. 'He invited over the three leaders. Two of them were older than my father. I had to serve their drinks. They touched me. When I cried, one of them slapped me and *he* laughed. *My husband laughed.* Later, when they left, he was rough with me. And afterwards he burnt me with a cigarette for the first time.'

'I learnt to do as he asked. If I did he didn't use me as roughly. I kept my head down and planned to escape. There was someone there, a woman, married to a very low-ranking man. She worked in the laundry and the other women treated her badly. One day we were alone in the laundry and she told me to leave. To escape. She used to be married to one of the high-ranking men, but she refused his demands.' Samantha sobbed. 'She had a child, a daughter, and they took her away and she was being raised by one of the others. I was shocked, but I believed her. I could see it all around me. All the women were just trying to survive and keep their children.'

Nicole whispered, 'stop now if you need to Sam.'

'No. I may never say these words again. I had an escape plan, but the week I was leaving I became ill. Really ill.' Samantha looked up. 'I was pregnant with Evie. I was sick from the first couple of weeks. And somehow, things got better for a while. He made no demands, and treated me well. Even more so when I delivered a girl. For a little while, I thought I was happy, that as long as I did what he wanted, life there could be okay. We were safe, I thought. He even let me write to my mum and tell her about Evie. But she wasn't allowed to visit.'

Nicole rubbed Samantha's back, as she leant forward in the chair, the telling of her story taking an emotional toll. Nicole could barely believe her ears and knew she'd need time to process all she'd heard, later.

'But when Evie turned three he started to talk about her future. Which one of them she would marry. How she would grow up there, never knowing anything else, and become another servant to their demands, like me. I couldn't let that happen. Then a year ago, he told me he was taking another wife and that I was being transferred to a different husband. His new wife would keep Evie and raise her.' Shaking her head, the tears falling freely, Samantha whispered, 'his new wife had been chosen, but she was only fifteen. He would marry her when she turned sixteen. She had no choice. I knew the girl and she was terrified. That's how it would be for Evie too, when she was old enough.' Samantha gazed at Nicole, the tears falling soundlessly. 'He told me my mother had died, that same week.'

It was like a plot from a movie, yet Nicole believed every word. 'My friend, the older woman from the laundry, tried to help me leave. She created a diversion, became very unwell when the men were all in a meeting and I called the ambulance.' Samantha looked up at Nicole. 'That's when I got your number.'

'And how did you escape? In the end, how did you get away?' Nicole was fully invested now.

Samantha cried, shaking her head and Nicole said no more.

'I'm going inside. If Evie asks, I'm in the bathroom.' Samantha stood, gazed at Nicole for a brief moment, then walked inside.

Nicole strolled over to Evie and the dogs, helping Evie throw tennis balls for the dogs to collect. Even Scout ran after one or two. Samantha's words rang loudly in her ears.

Samantha returned with a jug of juice and three glasses, and they sat together quietly while Evie chatted about the dogs and their game. Nicole tried to relax, with her eyes closed and the sun on her face, enjoying the sheltered position on the front verandah.

'The night before his wedding, he attacked me.' Nicole's eyes flew open. 'He forced me, laughing the whole time. And then he said he'd brand me, so I'd always remember him.' She faltered, then continued. 'He burnt me with cigarettes. Here.' Samantha touched her breast and Nicole drew a hand to her mouth in horror. 'And here.' Samantha gestured between her legs and Nicole cried.

'Oh Sam. Oh Sam. I'm so sorry.'

'He married her, that young girl, the next morning and I was too sore to attend the wedding. He didn't want me there anyway and left me in the house with Evie, convinced he'd broken me. Everyone was distracted and I managed to get us over the wall at the rear of the compound, and we walked though bushland until it got dark. We slept in a park, in a pergola, that night. I don't think he realised we'd gone until the next morning. He would have been too busy. That was lucky for me.' Samantha raised anguished eyes to Nicole who could only shake her head. 'But not for her.'

'I'd stolen money, over the years. Mostly small change from

his pockets, sometimes notes. Enough for a taxi to Central Station, the fake tickets to Gippsland, and the train tickets here.' Shaking her head, but smiling now, she spoke quietly. 'And that's when Jamie found us on the road, and he called you.' Samantha breathed out in a long, shuddering breath. 'So now you know my story, Nik. I'm sorry. It shocks me to say the words and hearing them would be hard.'

'Oh no, darling Sam. I'm amazed at your strength. You saved yourself and you saved Evie. Bless you for that.' Nicole hugged Samantha fiercely, taking comfort in her tight return hug. But when Evie barrelled into them yelling, 'me too, hug me too!' They pulled apart and laughed.

'Inside with you Evie. Wash your hands, it's lunchtime.' Samantha waited until her daughter ran inside, then turned to Nicole. 'Please don't look at me differently, now that you know everything.'

'I may look at you with more admiration Sam, but I'll try and keep a lid on it.' Nicole made the joke, but her head was reeling. *Her ex should be in jail.*

'But Sam, you said you had two options. One was to keep running. What is your other option?' Nicole almost held her breath while she waited for Samantha to answer.

'To stay here. To fight for custody of my daughter. To raise her here, in Barrington.' Samantha's eyes glistened, but her tone was steely.

'Then that's what you'll do Sam. You'll stay and fight for your freedom. And we will help you.' Linking her arm through Samantha's they walked into the house.

15

'I'VE STARTED MAKING A PLAN, NIK.' SAMANTHA SET down the basket of sheets she'd retrieved from the clothesline and leaned against the laundry door. 'And I need to earn some money.'

'A plan? Good.' Nicole pushed the start button on the washing machine and straightened, flicking a strand of hair from her forehead. 'I really appreciate you helping me with housekeeping here for my B and B rooms and I'm happy to make it more permanent, and pay you.'

'I'm not taking money from you Nik. You've fed and clothed us and kept a roof over our heads for almost three weeks already. Helping you change over the rooms and do laundry is the least I can do.' Samantha frowned for a moment. There was more to say to Nik.

'I'd like to meet Robbie and Lucy, properly. I've kept my head down long enough. And I want to see Jamie again, and thank him for that very first night. He was kind.' She chuckled. 'And every time Evie picks up that little toy car, she talks about Woz. She needs company too. More than me. And you. And the dogs. I have to believe we can start over, and meeting people is important.' She drew in a deep breath as she heard her own words. 'I have to stop running. I need to make a stand.' One of the dogs barked and she turned, watching Evie run by on the grass wearing the too-big blue coat and gumboots, the younger dog, Minnie gambolling beside her.

'I agree.' Nicole smiled. She was so lovely. Like a big sister, Samantha thought. 'What else?'

Samantha pulled the page from her pocket with the notes she'd written last night. She was wearing jeans for the first time since her teens, and she loved the feel of them on her legs. It made her remember her younger years, when her Dad was alive and they were on the farm. *When everything in her world was good.*

Unfolding the paper, she read her list to Nicole. 'Number One. Meet Robbie and Lucy. Number two. Thank Jamie. Ask if Evie can play with Woz sometimes. Number Three. Get paid work. Number Four. See a lawyer.' She looked up, unsure of Nicole's reaction, but she was smiling and nodding.

'That's a good list Sam. Let's start at number one. Would you and Evie like to come upstairs for dinner tonight? I have a roast in the slow-cooker, so there's plenty.' Nicole was beaming.

Samantha hesitated. Yes, of course she wanted to. But what would they think of her? She'd been downstairs all this time and never spoken to them. She opened her mouth, but Nicole continued. 'Actually, Robbie's son Harry, my step-son, will be home for dinner too.' Nicole giggled. 'He's not home much, but you have probably seen him. He spends a lot of time with his girlfriend, Hanna.'

Samantha started to shake her head. That was too much. Too many new people. Evie ran by again and waved. 'Hello Mummy, hello Nik!'

They waved back and Samantha drew her shoulders back. 'Yes. We will come upstairs for dinner. Thank you.' *Maybe they'll be so noisy and busy eating that they won't focus on us much.*

'Settled. Come up around half five, we eat early at this time of year.' Nicole's phone tinged and she pulled it from her pocket, hitting the green button. Samantha heard an excited voice as Nicole put the phone to her ear, gesturing *I have to take this* as she walked back toward her office. Nicole laughed a couple of times and at one point said quite loudly, and with much excitement, 'that's great news Rose!'

Samantha pulled a sheet from the basket and began to fold it. *One day I'll have friends who call me with good news too.*

———

SAMANTHA KEPT Evie inside after lunch, watching a movie on the sofa. As she hoped, Evie fell asleep. She didn't nap much these days, but going upstairs for dinner would be exciting for Evie and Samantha didn't want her to be tired from the outset.

While Evie slept Samantha showered and washed her hair. Afterwards, she studied her reflection in the mirror. The home-dye job was patchy and she looked scruffy. Fingering the hair away from her scalp, she looked at the small amount of re-growth. Her natural hair, what there was, was a rich auburn and looked shiny and healthy. Pulling the hair back in a tight pony-tail, Samantha turned her head from side to side. She was still thin, but her skin glowed with good health. Good food, enough sleep and less fear in her life had done that. She had good bones. She remembered her mum telling her that when she was still at school. *You have good bone structure and high cheekbones, love.* And a delicate square-shaped face with a wide, generous mouth. Samantha turned her face from side to side again. *I wonder.* She peeked into the living area, but Evie was still asleep, the televi-sion providing a quiet background hum.

Samantha reached into the bathroom drawer, pulling out a pair of small scissors. Before she could second guess herself, she hacked through the ponytail, tight against her head. Then she picked up the hanks around her face, section by section, and cut them as close to her head, to her natural hair, as she could. She did the same at the sides and back, then picked up the hair form the basin and sink and put it all in the bin. With Evie still sleep-ing, Samantha undressed and jumped under the shower again, just to make sure she'd washed all the little pieces of hair completely out.

Finally dry and dressed, Samantha finger-combed her shorn locks, allowing little bits to sit up a bit on top. It was a pixie-cut, she thought. And when she could afford it, she'd get it done again by a hairdresser. Stepping back from the mirror, she raised her eyebrows, made a face at herself, then smiled broadly. *I look different. I no longer look like Sarah. I am truly Samantha Scott again.*

Evie stirred, then called out for her. 'Mummy! I fell asleep! Is it time to go to Nik's place now?' She stepped into the bathroom, rubbing her eyes and wrapped her arms around Samantha's waist. Then she looked up and her little mouth widened in shock. 'Mummy!'

Samantha perched on the edge of the bathtub, so she was eye height with Evie. 'I cut my hair Evie. I cut all the old hair off.' She ran her fingers through the top of it. 'Do I look like a boy now?'

Evie shook her head slowly. 'Nooo. Not a boy. A girl.' Evie touched Samantha's hair, then giggled. 'It's a bit spiky on top!' Her fingers explored further, then she turned Samantha's head each way with her small hands. 'I like it. It's just your real hair now.' Evie peered at Samantha's face, touching her jaw, then her cheekbones and eyebrows. 'Will you grow it long again Mummy?'

'I don't know Evie. One day perhaps. But I think I like it like this.' She laughed. 'But I might need to knit myself a beanie. It's cold here.'

Evie clapped her hands, then picked up the scissors still lying beside the basin, holding then out to Samantha. 'Cut mine too Mummy, please.'

Samantha frowned. Evie's hair was almost to her waist. It had never been cut. A trim wouldn't hurt. 'What if I cut it a bit shorter Evie, but not as short as mine?'

Evie nodded. 'Shorter. Like yours.'

'Stand nice and still for me.' Samantha brushed Evie's hair, then took the scissors and cut it straight across at the back, about level with her shoulder blades. 'Turn around.' She held the big hank of hair she'd cut off and Evie's eyes widened. 'Now close your eyes, I'm going to cut you a fringe at the front, so I have to brush the hair over your face first.'

Evie didn't move a muscle as Samantha cut her long hair into a fringe, just level with her eyebrows. 'Open your eyes.' Samantha threw the hair into the bin and brushed any last little bits out. 'Okay. I'm going to lift you up so you can see yourself in the mirror.'

Samantha lifted Evie into her arms, their cheeks touching. She turned around slowly and Evie looked at her reflection and giggled. 'It's not as short as yours Mummy, but I like it.'

'I like it too. It suits you.' Samantha walked into the bedroom they shared. 'Now what shall we wear tonight to go to Nik's with our new haircuts? Shall we wear skirts, like we used to, or pants?'

'Pants. I want to wear these pants.' Evie held up denim jeans with butterflies appliqued on the legs, and a pale pink jumper.

'I think that's perfect for tonight. Now what shall I wear?' Samantha opened the bottom drawer of the chest of drawers. She had gone through the box of clothes Nicole supplied and moved a few pieces in her size to the drawers. She pulled out a pair of dark denim jeans that seemed hardly worn at all.

'You have a pink shirt too, Mummy, let's be twins.' Evie pointed to a slightly faded pink denim shirt with long sleeves.

Samantha laughed. She didn't know if it was her haircut, or wearing jeans, but her happiness was reflected in Evie's face. 'Okay, I'll wear a tee-shirt underneath and we'll definitely be twins.' She leaned down until her forehead was touching Evie's. 'What if they can't tell us apart?'

'Mummy!' Evie laughed so much she fell on to her bottom, and Samantha had to sit on the bed. She hadn't felt so carefree in years.

———

At exactly five-thirty, Samantha took Evie's hand, opened the door to the main house and walked up the stairs. They could hear voices and laughter and Samantha almost stopped and turned back, but Evie felt no hesitation and maintained her pace until they were almost at the top, where Nicole appeared.

'Sam, Evie, so lovely you can join us.' Samantha saw Nicole's eyebrows raise at their haircuts, but she quickly replaced it with a warm, welcoming smile. Nicole hugged her, whispering in Samantha's ear, 'you look amazing! Gorgeous!' Then to Evie, she said, 'Have you changed something Evie? I can't quite work it out?'

Evie laughed loudly and turned around in a complete circle, her hair flying around her shoulders. 'I've had my hair cut, Nik! First time ever!' She almost sang the words and Samantha's heart swelled, seeing her daughter's joyful expression.

They followed Nicole into the kitchen area. Robbie stepped forward first, saying quietly, 'it's really lovely to have you here, Sam. And you too Evie.' Somehow his gently-spoken words encompassed more than just the dinner and she felt immediately included. Lucy was next. She said a shy 'hello' to Samantha, but knelt down and chatted to Evie, who took to her straight away. Within moments they were over at the toy chest, searching for a particular game.

Harry stood up from his spot at the kitchen counter, his hand out-stretched. 'Hi Sam. Is it okay if I call you Sam? I'm Harry.' He gave her a lop-sided grin, looking so much like a younger version of Robbie that she almost laughed.

'Hello Harry. Yes, please call me Sam. All of you.' She looked at Robbie for a moment. 'Thank you for having us for dinner. And for having us here.' She waved her arm around, hoping they understood she was thanking them for *everything*. And how sincerely she meant it.

'You're very welcome Sam.' Nicole nudged her shoulder with her own, then turned back to Harry. 'Can you finish setting the table please Harry, Lucy seems to be occupied.' She turned to Robbie, 'and a bottle of the Tyrrells red, if you will Robbie.' Almost as an afterthought Nicole looked at Samantha. 'Do you drink Sam? Wine? Or would you prefer a juice or something hot?'

'Oh.' Samantha wasn't sure. She'd had alcohol a few times in her teen years, but not wine. And nothing since. She blushed. 'I'd like to try the wine. Just a small glass please.'

'Good.' Nicole glanced across at Lucy and Evie. They were setting up a complicated looking game on the rug near the fire. 'The girls are busy, would you help me serve up please Sam? I think we'll put the meat and vegetables on platters and we can all just help ourselves.'

'Yes. Of course.' Samantha was happy to have something to do and by six they were sitting around the table. Evie had asked to sit next to Lucy, so Samantha was beside Harry with Nicole and Robbie at each end of the table.

Robbie poured the wine, the men's glasses fuller than hers and Nicole's. Lucy helped Evie serve herself, and with dinner on their plates Nicole lifted her glass. Robbie and Harry did too, so Samantha picked hers up. 'To Sam and Evie, our newest friends. Welcome to Barrington.' Nicole took a sip, so Samantha brought the glass to her lips. The aroma reached her before she took her first sip, it smelt of warm berries she thought. She allowed a small taste into her mouth, and let it sit on her tongue for a moment. Nothing like the drinks she'd had when young. That had been spirits. Bourbon if she remembered correctly. She swallowed and took another sip. This was smooth and tasty. Not sweet, but not bitter either. She liked it. She looked up. Robbie had started his meal, and Lucy was cutting Evie's meat up for her. Nicole was pouring gravy over hers.

Only Harry was watching her. Samantha looked at him curiously, then blinked. He leaned closer, his voice quiet. 'If that was your first time with wine, you did well.' He grinned.

Samantha couldn't resist his cheekiness and nodded, smiling too. 'I like it.'

She thought she'd spoken quietly, but Robbie pointed at the open bottle on the table in front of him. 'Of course Sam likes it Harry. It's a Tyrrells red. Only the best, mate. Only the best.'

Samantha caught Harry's eye, the teasing expression on his face, and she laughed out loud, then covered her mouth with her hand, looking at Robbie. 'Sorry!' It came out as a squeak.

'Robbie's got a thing about certain wines. It's a good thing you like it.' Nicole laughed too, and Sam relaxed. This was how a family should be. Loud. Teasing. Happy. And then the conversation flowed.

Nicole told them about her friend Rose calling earlier in the day. A grant for a festival they were running had come through. They were all excited and after Samantha asked a couple of questions, Nicole told her how the bookshop had opened near a cafe in town on Valentine's Day. That her friend Rose was really *Rose Gordon*, a local author. That they had a book club and they were planning a reader festival in a few months' time and had been worried about funding. Samantha's head was swimming with information, and more questions.

The men cleared the plates and Lucy served what she called a 'simple dessert' but it was a home-made apple crumble with fresh cream and ice cream. It tasted divine. Lucy said she works at the café after school for someone called Millie. Then Harry said he was dating Millie's daughter Hanna and she was a pasty chef. Samantha had finished her wine and declined a second one. She really enjoyed it, but already she felt like her head was spinning. Whether it was the wine, the company, or the excitement of the whole evening, but she couldn't remember having a better night. She decided she might have to get Nicole to tell her who was who, again tomorrow.

She had also found out that Robbie and Harry were long time locals, but that Nicole and Lucy had only been in Barrington a few years. Samantha had known Robbie was Nicole's second husband, but somehow during dinner, with all the friendships and projects and people's names it had seemed like she had grown up here too.

The funniest thing had been saying good night. Robbie had waved from the kitchen and Nicole walked to the top of the stairs. Lucy picked Evie up, she had been falling asleep on the sofa, and carried her downstairs in front of Samantha. As she made to follow Lucy, Harry appeared at the top of the stairs.

'Goodnight Sam. I can't wait for you to meet Hanna.' He grinned and Samantha smiled back. 'And by the way, your hair.' He touched his own hair as he spoke. 'It's cute. Very Audrey Hepburn. Suits you.'

Samantha blushed and mouthed 'thank you', then turned and ran lightly down the stairs. She felt lighter, younger and almost carefree. She wanted to meet Hanna, and some of the others they'd mentioned. She felt sure she'd like them, and if the Stewart family was any indication, they'd like her too.

Later, after Evie was asleep, Samantha lay in bed going over the events of the evening. It had been fun. But she'd learned something too. That this place was a community, a bit like the small town where she'd grown up. The last seven years, where she'd lived, was supposed to be a community but for her it had become a prison. Not just for her, but for all the women and girls. And no one really helped anyone else. Not because they didn't like them or want to. But because they feared the consequences.

Before turning the bedside lamp out, she reached for her list again. She placed a huge tick beside number one. She'd organise number two tomorrow. Thank Jamie, ask if Woz can play with Evie. *Thank Jamie.*

16

Jamie couldn't help smiling as he waited for the kettle to boil. Nicole had just called to invite him over tomorrow afternoon, once he'd picked Warwick up from Kindy. Samantha had *asked* Nicole to invite them, saying she wanted to thank him. Jamie switched the kettle off and made his tea. Sure, he wanted to see her and little Evie. But only to check they were okay. She didn't have to thank him for anything. Anyone in Barrington would have stopped for her.

But Nicole said Sam had insisted and she also said that young Evie still talked about Woz and his little car. He was pleased. Seeing her would put his mind at rest. Just knowing she was still at Nicole's was reassuring. Perhaps she would stay in the area, once she was on her feet again. He wondered too, if she was safe from her ex now. She had certainly been panicked, and running, when he met her that night.

Jamie told his mum, Jill, the next morning that he would

pick Warwick up and they were going to Nicole's. He asked her if she knew about Samantha and Evie, but Jill shook her head. 'Even if I'd seen Nicole recently, and I haven't, she never mentions the women she helps.' Jill had looked at him, a bit too closely he thought. 'Tell me how you know them?'

After relaying the story, about finding Samantha walking by the roadside that night, three weeks ago now, Jill wrapped her arms around him. 'You're a good man Jamie. Like your Dad. You've always been a good man.' She stepped back, still studying his face. 'It's likely they're traumatised and may take a long time to recover. Women don't flee with just the clothes on their backs for no reason.'

Chuckling, Jamie gave his mum a quick hug. 'I know that Mum. But Nik says Sam's asked to see me and that Evie talks about meeting Woz that night. I get the sense that it's part of her recovery, an effort to move forward with her life.' He shrugged then. 'I only did what anyone in this town would do, but I admit I'm keen to see them again.' He caught the look that briefly crossed Jill's face and laughed. 'I'm curious Mum. It was an unusual situation.' He added more quietly, 'The fear on her face when I first stopped, which she overcame so I could call Nik.' He shook his head, just thinking about the terror she must have felt. 'She's brave, Mum. I've no idea what she's been through. But I know she's brave and a good mother.'

———

It wasn't what his mother said that echoed in his mind as he went about his chores. It was what she didn't say. It was over a year since he'd lost Debbie, and after that first milestone he wondered if people would start pushing him towards romance again. But they didn't. Not so far. His parents and close friends knew Debbie was irreplaceable. And that he still grieved her. He suspected he would continue to grieve for her until the end of time.

So he put on a brave face, mostly for Warwick, and in truth, his son provided untold pleasure and happiness. In those moments Jamie's laughter and smiles came easily. But at night, while his son slept, Jamie felt the pain most. Not just the loss of Debbie and their baby daughter, but the loss of the happy life they could have had. *Would have had.* Sometimes, when he was at his lowest, he thought he was living a half-life. That he was only half-present. But more and more, faking the smiles came easier, until some days he wasn't faking at all.

And then he thought about Nicole and the help she provided to women and their children. He had never personally witnessed it, but Debbie had told him some of the stories. And she had said there were many more that were never mentioned. Some came and went in just a day or two, but they were helped along the way by Nicole. Food, clothes, shelter and sometimes funds and connections to legal services. He admired Nicole enormously for that. He knew she'd been through something too, when she came to the area with Lucy. Robbie and Harry had been part of *their* healing. Jamie hoped his gesture of assistance to Samantha and Evie would help their recovery, in some very small part.

17

———

'Jamie and Warwick will come tomorrow after Kindy, for afternoon tea.' Nicole dumped the dirty sheets and towels into the large basket in the laundry and grimaced at Samantha. 'Laundry. It never stops, does it?'

Samantha laughed. 'No, but I do love sleeping in clean sheets.' She pushed some towels into the washing machine, then giggled. 'Did you know I didn't use your pillows until the other night, when I cut my hair?'

Her surprise must have shown. 'Why ever not?' Nicole stopped what she was doing and gazed at Samantha, who laughed loudly.

'I can tell you now. My hair. The cheap dye I used. I bought it from a supermarket and put it through in the basin of a public toilet the first night, when we slept in the park. I was worried it would stain your white pillowcase, so I used my old coat to start with, and the clothes I arrived in after that.'

Samantha touched her hair with her hand. Nicole thought the short pixie-cut suited her. 'And I was right too. Every time I washed my hair, some of the colour came out.'

Nicole grinned. That Samantha could laugh about it warmed her heart. 'Well, I'm happy you're using my pillow cases now. I'm impressed you would even think to do that, Sam, with everything you'd been through. It was obvious you were exhausted when Jamie found you.'

'And speaking of Jamie. Do you know what they'd like for afternoon tea tomorrow? Should I bake something? Muffins?' Samantha's eyes were large as she asked the question.

'Honestly, they're easy to please. Anything chocolate. I was going to ask Lucy to bake something tonight.' Nicole waved her hand away, but when she saw the look on Samantha's face, she stopped. 'But if you want to make something yourself, of course you should. We have all the fixings for chocolate muffins. You can cook in your kitchen, or pop up to mine and we can chat while you do it. After lunch perhaps?'

'Thank you Nik. I'd like to make something myself. I have no other way of thanking him.' Samantha paused, then raised her eyebrows. 'Will his wife come too, or does she work? I'd be very happy to meet her, of course.'

Nicole paused then. *Samantha didn't know about Debbie.* How could she know? 'Sam, Jamie's wife Debbie died last year, in a car accident.' Nicole gulped, the words bringing her own grief for Debbie's loss to the surface. 'It was a shock to us all. He lost his new baby daughter too. So it's just him and Warwick, but his house is on the family farm, not far from his parents, and he has support from them and Debbie's parents too.'

Nicole watched as Samantha processed this. 'Oh.' She looked across to the big tree, where Evie was swinging. Robbie had set the swing up a few days ago and it seemed she was either swinging or running around with the dogs. Turning back to Nicole, her eyes were shiny with unshed tears. 'That's sad. He's so young.' She gazed at Nicole for a full minute in silence, before saying, 'I thought maybe his wife was a nurse. You know, he was with his son by himself that night, and for some reason I thought she must be a nurse, working night shift.' Samantha shook her head slowly. 'It never occurred to me that he had lost her.' A tear slid down her cheek and she wiped it away. 'And his baby girl too?'

Nicole nodded. 'Saddest day for the whole town. Debbie wasn't a nurse. She owned the café in town, the one that Millie now runs. Everyone loved her.'

Samantha picked up the empty laundry basket. 'I'll see if the sheets on the line are dry, shall I?' Nicole followed her outside and they worked together in companionable silence, each lost in their own thoughts.

———

SAMANTHA WORE the same jeans and shirt she'd worn to dinner and Evie was cute in stretchy pink leggings and a bright yellow shirt. Nicole suggested they have afternoon tea on the veranda, so Evie and Warwick could play on the swing, or the lawn. Evie had found every car, tractor and truck in both toyboxes and brought them outside. She had them lined up on the first step to the veranda, and despite Samantha asking her to move them to one side, she refused. 'Woz likes cars.' She said it with such finality that they gave in.

Jamie drove in slowly and parked to one side. Nicole noted he was in his usual farm uniform of jeans, boots and a chambray shirt, although they looked freshly laundered. He raised a hand in greeting, then opened the back door of his four-wheel drive. Warwick scrambled down and ran across to them, he'd already unstrapped himself from his car seat. Jamie strode behind his son, grinning sheepishly.

'Hello.' He blinked when he saw Samantha. Nicole realised he wouldn't have been expecting her short hair.

'Hello Jamie.' Samantha stepped forward and shook his hand. She looked tiny beside him, but her smile was friendly. Nicole knew she'd been nervous beforehand, but she was holding her own. Samantha gently drew Evie forward. The little girl had been excited all day about seeing 'Woz' but now appeared tongue-tied. 'Say hello to Jamie. And Woz.' Samantha prompted her.

Warwick was fidgeting from side to side, his eyes firmly on the line up of vehicles on the step. 'Wanna play farms?' His voice was loud as he bent down, placing his hand on a large green and yellow tractor, not waiting for Evie to answer.

'Yes.' Evie picked up a truck and a motorbike and ran them further along the timber veranda boards. Warwick followed and within moments they were playing some sort of game, coming back for more vehicles from time to time.

'Have a seat Jamie. I'll just bring out the teapot.' Nicole walked inside as Jamie sat on a chair beside Samantha.

18

―――

'While Nik's inside, I just want to tell you. That is, I want to thank you, for stopping that night.' Samantha tried to keep her eyes on his. In her old life, she wasn't supposed to look men in the eye, but she remembered her father telling her when she was young that it was the right thing to do.

'Honestly Sam, anyone from around here would have stopped for you. I just happened to be the first one to see you.' Jamie had taken his hat off, and she noticed he ran his fingers along the edge of the brim as he spoke. He smiled then, a big happy grin and she couldn't help but smile in return. 'But I'm so pleased you have stayed on here with Nik. And Robbie. They're good people.'

Nicole appeared at that moment, and Samantha looked up at her as she placed the tray of tea things on the table. 'Jamie was just telling me that anyone local would have stopped for me that night. But I'm not sure it's true.'

Laughing, Nicole took the lid off the container of chocolate chip muffins Samantha had baked. 'Well if that's true Jamie, perhaps you don't deserve one of the muffins Sam made for you.' She waved the container under Jamie's nose.

'Oh well. If muffins are involved I'll change my story.' He picked one up in his enormous hand, his smile a bit lopsided. He took a bite and closed his eyes while he chewed. 'Yep. Just me, Sam. Only person who would stop for you.' He waved the half-eaten muffin around and Samantha laughed so much, she leaked tears.

'Good one, Jamie Tait.' Nicole nudged him, then called the children over. She had hot chocolates for them, and cut a muffin in half. They gulped down their afternoon tea in record time, then ran back to their game.

'They're happy.' Jamie gazed at his son and Samantha saw his face cloud over, but just for a moment. 'Being an only child can have its down side.' He turned to her. 'Are they the same age, Sam? Woz will be five at the end of November.'

'Oh, yes. Almost. Actually Evie will be five in January.' Samantha watched the children at their game. They were chatting and sharing vehicles, each one directing part of the play. Evie hadn't played with children her own age much, but Samantha played with her often, teaching her to share and be creative. She thought Evie had a very active imagination and often made her own games up.

'I've um, brought something for Evie.' Jamie reached down for the small bag he'd placed beside his chair. Samantha hadn't noticed it earlier. 'It was Warwick's suggestion, when I asked him. Um, only if it's okay with you, of course.' He placed the brown paper bag on the table in front of her, and Samantha looked at him for a moment, before opening it and peeking in. 'Oh! Oh gosh. She will love these!' She passed the bag across to Nicole, who looked inside.

'Farm animals. That's perfect for her. Well done Jamie. And Woz.' Nicole handed the bag back to Samantha.

'Thank you!' She wasn't sure whether to show Evie now, or later, but Warwick had appeared at the table and saw the bag on her lap.

'Evie! Evie! Farm toys!' He grabbed the bag before Samantha could stop him and raced back to Evie, still driving a farm truck. 'Evie, look!' He tipped the bag up and out fell plastic animals of all sorts, plus some plastic fencing and tiny haybales.

Evie pushed the truck away. 'Oooh!' She began setting the animals on their feet, putting cows together, and pigs and sheep in separate little herds. She was laying on her tummy now and Warwick wriggled down beside her, his little tongue sticking out as he turned the plastic fencing into a yard.

Samantha raised her hands to her cheeks. They were burning with pleasure and she was trying hard to keep her emotions in check. Even Nicole was gazing at the kids, bright eyed. She chanced a quick look at Jamie, who met her gaze steadily. 'Our children are friends, Sam.'

His words broke the ice and she laughed. 'Yes, I think they are, Jamie.'

Shortly after, Robbie returned home and joined them. Samantha leaned back for a moment, happy to be a part of the easy conversation and warmth around the table. The children had moved over to the swing, where Evie became quite bossy and made Warwick push her. He did for a while, then wandered back to his father. This seemed to be the cue for Jamie to leave, and he stood, thanking Samantha for the muffins and Nicole for the tea.

Samantha called Evie over to say goodbye, but she refused to get off the swing. Warwick waved to her cheerily and Samantha shook her head. She'd talk to Evie about it later. She wondered if Jamie thought Evie was rude, but he scruffed Warwick's hair and said, 'girls, Woz. They don't always do what you think they will.' He winked at Samantha then, and she relaxed.

'Help me bring the tea things up please Robbie.' Nicole had the muffin tin in her hand. 'See you Jamie, Woz. Thank you for visiting.' Nicole's tone was cheery, but she followed Robbie inside after he shook Jamie's hand. Samantha retrieved Evie from the swing and walked over to the car, Evie on her hip, while Jamie fastened Warwick's safety belt.

Jamie closed the door and looked down at her. 'I'm happy to see you looking so well Sam. I don't always notice such things, but your haircut suits you.' He touched Evie on the shoulder lightly. 'I like your haircut too, young lady.'

Tears welled in Samantha's eyes. 'Thank you Jamie. For everything.' She turned, and hurried back to the house.

Evie waved over Samantha's shoulder as the car backed around. 'Bye Woz!'

19

———

Barrington Book Club & Reader Festival Update (Five
months to Festival)
Attendance: Judith, Millie, Hanna, Kristen, Rose, Rachael,
Meggie, Harriet & Nicole
Apologies: Laura, Melanie
Book: *A Snowy River Summer* by Stella Quinn

'Laura and Ben are still away, and Melanie
messaged that Tiffany has a cough, so she doesn't want to join
us tonight in case it's something.' Rose used her fingers to indicate quotation marks when she said *something*, then she hugged
Rachael and Judith before they settled at their table.

'It's that time of the year. I've had to juggle volunteer rosters
in the bookshop for the last two weeks. There's a cough going
around.' Judith opened a bottle of red wine and poured for the
others. Millie closed and locked the café door after Meggie,

Harriet and Nicole arrived. Rose could hear Hanna and Kristen chatting in the kitchen, no doubt preparing a platter of something lovely for their meeting.

'Hi girls.' Meggie was always cheerful, her very presence seemed to brighten the room, and Rose grinned in response. *Darling Meggs.* And Harriet too. They were as thick as thieves and Rose adored them.

Harriet reached for the nearest glass of wine, just as Hanna, Kristen and Millie placed platters of hot savouries and a grazing board down. 'I know we're here for book club, and I couldn't love this story more. Who knew tractors could be sexy, huh?' She took a sip of wine. 'But with only five months until the festival, I vote we deal with that first, then chat books.'

Rose let out the breath she didn't realise she was holding and opened her laptop. 'Thank you Harri, great idea. We have a bit to get through.' Looking at the faces around the table, her friends, she almost sang the next words. 'And the federal arts grant has been approved, for the full amount we requested!' She'd phoned or messaged them all yesterday, but she was totally pumped and wanted to relive the excitement in that moment, with all of them.

'I know!' Hanna looked at Kristen, then Rose. 'We couldn't believe we got the full amount. And with the in-kind help from Council, we'll be okay, won't we? We won't need to trim the program at all.'

'No, we won't.' Rose held up her glass again. She was feeling particularly smug about her next announcement. 'Um, I know we're talking festival and not book club.' All eyes were on her now, so she twirled her glass, nearly spilling the wine. 'But, um, who liked it? The Stella Quinn book?' With twinkling eyes she added, 'asking for a friend.'

'Rose!' Hanna sat up straight and Rose could see she knew where this was going. 'You haven't? Have you?'

Rose tried to look nonchalant, but suspected her cheesy smile was giving it away.

'You've got Stella Quinn! Really? She's coming?' Hanna was almost bouncing in her seat and the others were leaning in, their faces expectant.

'I do.' Rose paused, drawing out the moment. 'For both days of the festival. She'll do the panel with me and Fiona MacArthur, the book signings on both days and she's arriving the day before. She said she wants to help.'

'Oh gosh. Stella Quinn.' Nicole looked amazed. 'Is she as funny in person? Her books always give me a few laugh-out-loud moments. I'm really excited to meet her.'

Rose nodded. She knew the answer to this. 'I met her at a conference last year. Actually, we participated in a debate.' Rose could see the group had more questions, but she didn't want to derail the festival meeting. 'She was so funny. We won the debate on pure wit, I think. But that's a story for another day.'

'I'll email it to all of you, but the program is looking quite full. We have Fiona MacArthur staying upstairs, Stella is going to stay with me, and Cathryn Hein, Michelle Montebello, Phillipa Clark and Heather Reyburn will be at The Lofts. But I also have Elle Watson, Editor with Tyrrell Publishing coming, just for the Saturday night. Have you got room Nik, for her at yours?'

'I should have room, I'll check, but I have taken some bookings for The Stables already.' Nik picked up her phone, then glanced up. 'Is she driving? Elle? Or is she coming by train?'

'Oh. Hang on.' Rose opened the email app on her laptop. 'Actually, she is coming by train. Yes, probably better to have her in town at The Lofts.' Rose frowned. She wanted readers to be able to get accommodation too. 'Cathryn and Michelle are coming together, by car. Perhaps we can swap them to your cottage Harri, if that's still available?'

'Perfect. Two bedrooms, two bathrooms. I'll block it out for them and we can book Elle Watson in at The Lofts.' Harriet made a note on her phone. Rose was pleased. That left five of the eight lofts available, plus all the other bed and breakfasts and motel rooms in town, for readers. Not to mention the caravan parks and farm stay properties out of town. 'I'll confirm with Wendy at the tourism office tomorrow.'

They spent another half hour running through the program before Millie and Hanna talked through the catering options. It was all in hand, and Rose was liaising with volunteers from the service clubs while Rachael had taken on the communication with Council.

'Now that the program is full, I'll open the website up for bookings, both for ticketed and free events, tomorrow.' Meggie glanced at Harriet. 'And we'll start the social media marketing. The Facebook page is ready to go live.'

'I'll send press releases out to local media, and some in Newcastle and Sydney, but we won't hit that hard until a few weeks before.' Harriet put her phone down and reached for a mini quiche.

Kristen raised her hand and Rose laughingly said, 'you don't have to ask permission to speak here, Kristen.'

'Ha, ha, Rose.' Kristen wrinkled her nose at Rose, then passed a printed page across the table. 'Our insurance is in place. We had to have it ready for the federal grant, so when that came through I arranged the cover note. We will have to pay the bill once the first grant payment is received.'

'Oh gosh Kristen, thank you.' Rose raised a hand to her forehead. 'And this is why we have you on the team. Keeping the paperwork on track.'

'More wine?' Millie passed another bottle around the table. Rose relaxed as they packed away their festival notes and chatted through their thoughts on Stella Quinn's latest rural romance. Most of them had read Stella's earlier books, and were total fans.

They were beginning to clear the table and Rose glanced at her watch. Almost eight. They'd achieved a lot in two hours. Most of the work was done via email and their private messenger group, but meeting like this had really helped moved the event forward. And she'd been excited to confirm their funding and the authors attending.

'Can I take a moment, if you don't have to rush?' Nicole spoke quietly, yet instantly had their attention. Hanna had been standing, but she returned to her seat.

'You all know I, um, accommodate women from time to time. And their children.' Nicole fiddled with the stem of her empty wine glass.

'We do Nik. But you rarely speak of them. And to be honest, I'm never sure when you have someone there.' Rose was surprised, Nicole liked to keep the assistance she provided *under the radar.*

'That's true. Sometimes I only have them for a night. Sometimes longer. And you all know a few that have stayed on in the area, like Avery up at the Bee Sanctuary.' Nicole paused. 'I have someone now. A young mother and her small daughter, they've been with me for more than three weeks. Without telling you too much, she's been in a situation of, er, coercive control and some personal trauma. Her name is Samantha and her daughter is Evie.'

Rose could see Nicole was invested in Samantha, and feeling protective. 'What do you need Nik? What do *they* need?' Rose knew Nicole was telling them for a reason.

'Samantha wants to stay here. In Barrington. But she may need to take a stand. There could be a custody case.' Nicole shook her head. 'I'm still learning the details and it has taken Samantha. Sam. A while to recover and begin to share her story.'

Judith was leaning forward and Rose saw her exchange a look with Kristen. 'I don't mean to interrupt, but did they arrive on the evening train? Three weeks ago last Sunday? I think I travelled with them from Maitland.'

'Oh, yes they did. She said there was a lady in the carriage who spoke kindly to her, but Sam was too terrified to respond, that first night.' Nicole beamed. 'So that was you, Judith? Oh, Sam will want to meet you.'

'How did she get to your place Nik? It's just that, after Kristen picked me up and we went home, um, the way she left the train station, on foot and carrying her little one, played on my mind. We drove back, and then around town for an hour hoping to find them. I suspected she had nowhere to go. I was going to book her into a motel, but I should have known it was you meeting them.' Judith nodded across to Kirsten, as if to confirm her words.

'That's so thoughtful Judith. Not many people would do that.' All eyes were on Nicole. 'But no. I had no idea she was coming, she just had my name and address on a scrap of paper.' A couple of people murmured their surprise, but stopped so Nicole could continue. 'Actually, Jamie Tait, and little Woz, found her walking along the side of the road, just over the bridge, and he stopped. She was scared at first, but once he got Woz out of the car and she saw he was a father, she relaxed. Enough to show him the paper with my name on it. Jamie could see she was terrified and realised straight away that she was on the run from a bad situation, so he called me. He waited with her until I arrived.'

'Oh gosh. Good for Jamie. Not everyone would have stopped. And she was still a long way from your place, Nik.' Rose felt a rush of affection for Jamie. *Of course he would stop.*

'You're right. He's one of the good ones. But the reason I'm telling you this, is I want to begin to quietly integrate Sam and Evie into the community. She wants to find work, and she wants to move out of my accommodation when she can afford it, so that someone else in need may stay.' Nicole shook her head. 'She's very young.' She looked at Hanna and Kristen. 'Probably only your age, girls.' Nicole frowned then. 'She had dinner with us a few nights ago and met Harry and Robbie for the first time.' At their amazed looks, she added, 'She's been keeping a low profile. She's very fearful of her ex finding her. But Hanna, did Harry not mention her?'

Hanna shook her head. 'Not a word.'

'He understands that the fewer people who know, the better.' Nicole chuckled. 'But I must tell him that doesn't include you.'

'I don't mind.' Hanna flushed. 'I think I just fell in love with him a tiny bit more.'

Judith patted Hanna on the hand. 'Me too Hanna, me too. Hot Harry Stewart has principles.'

At Judith's words, and expression, the table descended into laughter and chatter for a moment, but Rose held her hand up. 'What else Nik? What else can we do?'

'Thank you Rose.' Nicole looked around. 'I'd like to get her a phone. Do any of you have an old one that we can set up for her? One you're not using?'

'I do.' Harriet chuckled. 'I bought the latest smart phone because, you know, it does so much more. But there's really nothing wrong with the old one, I'm just keeping it as a spare.'

'In case you drop one in the bath, Harri?' Meggie nudged Harriet with her elbow.

'One time. I dropped my phone in the bath that one time!' But Harriet was laughing too. 'I can bring it to you, with a charger, tomorrow Nik. I'll pick up a pre-paid SIM for it.'

'Thank you.' Nicole clapped her hands. 'Also, Sam knows how to drive, but she doesn't have her licence. She hasn't driven since she was seventeen. I think I'll ask Jamie to give her a couple of driving lessons. I want her to feel independent. I'm not sure what we'll do about a vehicle, but getting her licence needs to come first.'

'Jamie?' Rose wasn't sure about that and she shared a look with Rachael. 'Why Jamie?'

'He came to see her a couple of days ago, at her request. She wanted to thank him. He had called me once, and spoken to Robbie, to check on her welfare. And Evie and Woz are the same age and seemed to hit it off.' Nicole looked into Rose's eyes and she felt slightly uncomfortable. 'Don't read too much into this Rose. It's about showing Samantha there are good men in the world. In this community. Robbie and Harry of course, and over time, your own menfolk. It will be part of her healing.'

'Of course.' Rose murmured, feeling chastened.

'And I think it's been good for Jamie too. He spends too much time on his own.' Nicole's tone was warm, but firm.

'And a job Nik? What sort of a job?' Rachael asked.

'She has no formal qualifications, but she grew up on a farm. Cattle and sheep, I think. And she's been keeping house, growing food and she's a really good mum. To be honest, I'm not sure and it's why I wanted to share with all of you. The hive mind, to think outside the square.' Nicole looked around the table. 'So thank you. Let me know if you have any thoughts. I'm going to start introducing her to you, but slowly.'

'Would she do some shifts here Nik? At the café?' Millie waved an arm towards the kitchen.

'I think serving at the counter would be too people-ey for her just yet. And I wondered about evenings with Hanna sometimes, because she is quite a good cook. But I'm not sure she'd leave Evie, even with me, at the moment.'

'Okay Nik. Let's put some thought into it.' Judith stood. 'Are we walking together Rachael, or is too cold?'

'Give me five minutes Auntie, and I'll drive us home. You too Rachael.' Kristen bustled out to the kitchen with a tray of empty plates.

'You go Kristen. Hanna and I will finish up.' Millie walked to the front door and unlocked it, handing the others their coats and scarves as they left.

Rose was the last to leave. 'Brilliant again Millie. Thank you Hanna.' She raised an eyebrow. 'You never know everything that happens, even in a small town, do you?'

Rose embraced Millie and Hanna and walked to her car. As she drove home, over *that* bridge, she pictured a young woman walking by the side of the road, carrying a child. She shook her head sadly. Then she thought about Jamie, her childhood friend, which made her think of Debbie and suddenly she was softly crying. Outside the homestead she sat for a moment in the car, until the front door opened and she saw Angus silhouetted in the doorway. Scrambling out, Rose strode up the steps and into his arms.

20

———

Driving up to Nicole's house, Judith marvelled
at how faithfully it had been preserved and maintained. Nicole
walked out to greet her, but they didn't linger outside, the day
was cold with a strong southerly wind.

They stepped into the foyer and Nicole closed the front
door. 'Gosh, it hasn't stopped blowing all day. Robbie says we
might get rain if the wind drops.'

'I don't know Nik, but I wouldn't like to be driving after
dark, there are sure to be branches across some of the roads.'
Judith shrugged off her overcoat and scarf, handing them to
Nicole who hung them on a coat hook in the hallway.

'Come upstairs. Samantha and Evie are waiting for you.'
They began walking slowly up the stairs, Judith taking her time
while silently cursing her dodgy knee. 'She wanted to greet you,
but her scones were almost ready to take out of the oven.'

'Scones.' Judith chuckled. 'Who told her I love scones?'

'Doesn't everyone?' Nicole raised her eyebrows, but her tone was teasing.

Pausing at the top of the stairs, Judith looked past Nicole to see Samantha walking towards her. Except she looked quite different to the young woman Judith recalled from the night on the train.

'Hello Judith. Again.' Samantha's greeting seemed tentative, and Judith wanted to put her at ease.

'Hello Samantha. Or may I call you Sam?' Judith shuffled closer, ignored Samantha's outstretched hand and enveloped her in a warm, tight hug. At first the younger woman seemed tense, but after a short moment her arms crept around Judith's back and she relaxed into the embrace. Judith held her gently, and after about thirty seconds – she'd read somewhere that hugs should last at least thirty seconds to be therapeutic – she loosened her grip and leaned back, looking into Samantha's face.

'I'm sorry Judith.' Samantha took a half step back, her words almost running together in her haste to say them. Judith began to speak, to wave away the apology, but the younger woman shook her head. 'I need to say it, please.' Judith smiled her encouragement then, and waited. 'I was rude to you that night on the train. Abrupt. You were being kind, to me and to Evie. I'm sorry.' Samantha shook her head sadly, shot a glance at Nicole then raised her eyes to Judith. 'And Nicole told me that you and your niece drove around looking for me that night, that you wondered if we were in trouble.' She shook her head and a tear slid down her cheek. 'If only I had spoken to you...'

As Samantha's words trailed off Judith reached out and

rubbed her shoulder gently. 'You didn't know me, Sam and you were protecting yourself and your child. It's me who should apologise. I wondered if you needed help. I should have just asked. We would have driven you here, in a heartbeat.' She correct herself. 'Should have driven you here.'

'Mummy! Can we have scones now please?' Evie appeared beside Samantha and grinned impishly up at Judith. 'Hello.' Then she skipped back to the kitchen and climbed on to a chair at the counter.

Judith laughed out loud. Samantha joined her and Nicole hustled them into the kitchen. 'It is time for scones, Evie.'

In the end they sat at the dining table, it was easier for Judith. She bit into a scone, slathered with jam and cream and closed her eyes for briefly, before looking across the table. 'Good scones, Sam. Hmmm.'

Samantha smiled shyly. 'I've been practicing. Cooking quite a lot since I came here.' She grinned. 'Robbie and Harry always have room for baked goods.'

'If you don't mind me commenting, I think you and Evie look healthy, and happy. I love your short hair, it suits you. You look very different to that first night, and I'm pleased to be able to say that.' Judith didn't want to embarrass the girl, but the haunted, frightened look was gone, replaced with a quiet confidence.

Samantha leaned towards Nicole, but directed her reply to Judith. 'It's Nik. She's given us shelter and safety, food and clothes.' She tilted her chin up slightly. 'But even more than that. She's given me the confidence to stop running, and fight for my rights. As a woman and a mother.'

'Oh, stop it Sam!' Nik nudged the younger woman. 'I'll get a big head.' Reaching for another scone she added, 'I think it's Barrington magic, not me at all.'

'That too. Barrington magic.' Sam passed the cream to Nicole.

'It worked it's magic on me too.' Judith chuckled and looked across the room, where Evie was playing with a set of plastic farmyard animals, on the rug, having devoured two scones. 'Evie is very busy over there.'

'She loves those toys. Jamie and Woz gave them to her a few days ago. She's hardly played with anything else.' Samantha's face was full of love and Judith felt a shiver run down her back. She didn't know the details of Samanthas's past. Did not need to know. But it was obvious Samantha would do anything to keep Evie safe and happy.

Changing the subject, Nicole turned to Judith. 'How are you going with the bookshop roster Judith. You said the other night that you'd had to juggle, because some volunteers had been sick?'

'Still juggling, and working a bit more myself.' Judith took the opportunity to ask Samantha a question. She'd been thinking about it since the book club meeting. 'Sam, do you like books? I think you were reading one on the train that night?'

'I was.' She made a face. 'I'd read it before, dozens of times. I didn't have access to many books. Before. Or a library, so the ones I had were well-read. Reading, to me, is like dreaming in the daytime. Imagining a better place, different people.'

'Oh good. I wonder if you would be able to help out at the bookshop from time to time? It runs mostly on volunteers.'

Judith didn't want to be pushy, but hoped Samantha might be interested.

'Um. What would I have to do? Can I bring Evie?'

Samantha sounded keen, so Judith elaborated. 'To begin with, just placing new stock on the shelves and tidying up a bit. We have an upstairs mezzanine area that has been set up for children which I think Evie would love. Some afternoons we have volunteers read to the smaller children while their parents shop. Would that be something you'd like to do?'

Samantha nodded. 'Yes, if Evie can be with me. I love children's books and I've always read aloud to Evie, although those books were limited too.' She looked at Nicole, as if seeking approval. Judith frowned for a moment, but Samantha continued. 'If Nicole can drive me there.'

'Well that's settled. Is tomorrow too soon? Perhaps Nik can drop you in the afternoon for an hour or so. Come and have a look and I'll show you around.' Judith could see Samantha was still unsure. 'This first visit will be very informal. If you're not keen to do more, that's alright too.'

'I hope I can help Judith. As a volunteer.' Samantha sounded more confident. 'But I do hope to find paid work too. But if it's possible, I'll do both.'

'Good. I'll see you tomorrow.' Judith leaned on the table to steady herself as she stood. Her knee twinged, be she ignored it, focussing on Samantha. 'If you choose to volunteer on a regular basis, while you're looking for other work of course, I can also give you some training on the point-of-sale system and general computer skills and could then provide a reference, if that helps.'

Seeing the way Samantha's face lit up was worth the effort it took to walk up the stairs to Nicole's kitchen.

'Oh yes. That would be wonderful, thank you Judith. I'm not sure what work I can get, you know, because of Evie.' They all glanced at Evie, who was playing happily on the rug with her farm animals. 'At least until she starts school next year, but I know I need to learn those skills.'

Judith drove home feeling quite pleased with herself. She'd see Samantha the next afternoon and if it worked out, she'd roster her on with herself. Samantha could run up and down those mezzanine stairs and help with the little ones in the afternoon story-time group.

21

It was Sunday again, four weeks since the night Jamie had stopped for Samantha and Evie on the road, after dinner with Debbie's parents. He'd dropped Warwick to them after breakfast and was now heading there for an early dinner, with a bottle of his father-in-law's favourite red wine and some roses from his garden for Rachael.

'Jamie!' Rachael hugged him at the front door. 'We've just bathed Woz.' She grinned. 'There was an incident, in the compost.' She wriggled her eyebrows and Jamie laughed. His son was always up to something.

'Dare I ask?' Jamie followed her inside to the lounge area. Warwick was in his pyjamas, his hair damp, laying on his tummy studiously drawing on a large piece of paper. Steve was sitting beside him, leaning against the lounge with his legs stretched out, also drawing what looked like a large bird at the top of the page.

'Hello Woz! Steve.' Jamie tried to keep his laughter in check. 'What are you, er, designing there Steve?'

Warwick frowned at his father and pointed to his grandpa's handiwork. 'It's a dragon Daddy!'

Jamie sat down with them and nudged Steve. 'Of course it is. But from over there it looked like a camel with wings.'

'It's a dragon.' Warwick was adamant and Jamie shared a look of delight with Steve.

Rachael returned to the room, handing the men a beer. 'Just one Jamie, then we'll have dinner.' To her husband she added, 'Jamie brought a bottle of that red you like. It will go nicely with the roast lamb.'

They chatted quietly, Steve finishing his contribution to the picture and Jamie colouring in a tree trunk, at his son's request. A short time later Rachael declared dinner was ready and they moved to the dining room. Jamie picked up his son and galloped him there while he squealed with delight.

Over dinner Steve told Jamie how Warwick had helped him shovel a pile of compost into a new garden bed. At some point his grandson had decided that it needed 'flattening' and he'd jumped into the middle of it without his boots, and promptly fallen over. Jamie loved how Steve and Rachael were never phased by Warwick's antics and had simply brought him inside for his bath a bit earlier than usual.

After dinner Rachael put a children's show on the television for Warwick, when Jamie said he wanted to have a chat.

Jamie sipped the tea Rachael had made. One beer and one glass of red was all he'd allow himself when driving, especially with his son in the car. 'You've heard about Samantha and Evie?

Staying out at Nicole's?' When they nodded, he continued. 'It's four weeks since they arrived that night. When I, er, and Woz, found them by the road.'

They had their listening faces on, and Jamie wished he knew what they were thinking. 'Sam, that is, Samantha, wants to stay in Barrington. And fight for custody of Evie, if she has to.'

Rachael frowned briefly, then asked quietly. 'So her ex-husband doesn't know where she is?'

'It seems unlikely at this stage. Samantha is sure he'd come for Evie if he knew they were here.' Jamie fiddled with the teaspoon on the saucer. 'There are things she needs. I want to help her.'

'Go on.' Steve nodded encouragement.

'She wants to find work, or to get some skills to help get a job.' He lowered his voice then. 'I think she's been largely, um, housebound since she was about seventeen. She has domestic skills of course.'

'And you can help her, how Jamie?' Rachael's tone was measured, but there was a hint of tension in the room. Jamie wondered if it was just his imagination.

'Her driver's licence lapsed years ago and she wants to reapply, but she needs a few lessons beforehand, just to refresh her. Nicole suggested I give her the lessons in my car.' Jamie looked from Steve to Rachael to gauge their reaction.

Steven leaned toward Jamie. 'You don't need our permission, Jamie, to do that. But I do have a question. Why you and not Nicole herself, or Robbie?'

Jamie relaxed. 'I asked Nik the same question, Steve. It's

helping Samantha's recovery, and introduction into this community. Nik says Sam needs to know that there are good men around, and she needs to learn to be comfortable in their presence. Or not terrified at least. She's getting to know Robbie and Harry and my involvement that first night puts me in line to help too.' He raised his shoulders in a how-can-I-say-no shrug. 'She recently met Judith again. She was on the train with her when she arrived, but Sam kept Judith, and her kindness, at bay. Judith is going to help her get some skills that might help with work, by having her help at the bookshop sometimes. The big thing for her, for Sam, is she's too afraid to leave Evie, even with Nicole, in case her Ex finds her and takes her.'

Rachael reached for Steve's hand. 'The poor girl.' She shook her head sadly. 'I can't imagine what she's been through, but her mother-instinct is to protect her child at all costs. Good for her, I say.'

'I agree.' Steve poured the last of the wine into his glass. 'It's good you can help, Jamie. Is there anything we can do?'

'Not straight away. I'm giving her a lesson tomorrow. If she's comfortable, she can drive into town for her shift at the book shop. I'll put Evie in Warwick's seat, but I was hoping you could pick him up from Kindy, Rachael, as I think the timing will crossover. Then I'll come here to get him and let you know how it went.'

'Of course Jamie, happy to do that.' Rachael's face was filled with warmth, her love for her grandson a given. But when Jamie met her frank gaze, he felt the affection she held in her heart for him too, and was grateful.

Jamie peered into the lounge. Warwick was asleep on the

couch. 'I'd better take the lad home.' Jamie stood up and pushed his chair in. 'Oh, Nicole will pick them up from the book shop, so it's only the drive in.'

As he drove over the bridge on the way home, Jamie didn't immediately think of Debbie, and the accident. Instead he thought about the night he found Sam and Evie. Doing something for her, even if it was just a couple of driving lessons, felt good. It would help Samantha move forward. Perhaps he could begin to move forward too.

22

———

'You'll be fine, Sam.' Nicole placed one hand on Samantha's shoulder and waved to Jamie as he parked the car.

'It's been years. I just hope I haven't forgotten it all.' Samanth picked Evie up and walked across to the car.

'Hello Sam, Nik. And hello to you Evie.' Jamie smiled broadly at them, before opening the back door for Samantha to put Evie in the car seat. His voice softened when he spoke to Evie, instantly making Samantha less nervous.

He walked her around to the driver's side and opened the door. 'It's automatic, and everything is fairly standard. If you'd like to get in, I'll show you how to adjust the seat to find your best driving position.'

Samantha slid onto the seat. It was a white SUV, but not large like the Landcruiser Ute that Robbie drove. More like a regular car, but a bit higher off the ground. She listened attentively as Jamie showed her the seat adjustment, and it only took her a moment to find the right position. She placed both hands on the steering wheel, then glanced at the dash. It all looked different to the old Falcon sedan she'd learned to drive in, with manual gears.

Jamie settled into the passenger seat and Nicole stepped back to the house veranda, waving and calling out, 'Enjoy your drive!'

'Are you driving, Mummy?' Evie giggled in the back seat. 'Do you know how?'

Adjusting the rear-view mirror to make eye contact with her daughter, Samantha smiled confidently. 'Of course. I used to drive a lot, before you were born.'

'The handbrake is on and the car is in neutral.' Jamie spoke quietly. 'Just put your foot on the brake and push this button, here, to start the engine.'

Samantha did exactly as he said and the car hummed to life. She took a breath. This was exciting. Another small step towards independence.

'And you can now shift into gear, here, and release the brake.' Jamie pointed as he spoke, but she had already worked it out in her head. 'I thought we might drive to my farm and then turn around, before driving into town. If that suits you?'

'Yes. I'm a bit nervous about town. And parking.' Samantha nibbled her bottom lip.

'Alright. Let's head out towards the road, but you will need to turn left to go to my place.'

Samantha moved cautiously down the driveway, the car rolling along the gravel track quite smoothly. At the end of the driveway she braked and turned the left indicator on. She found it before Jamie told her and felt quite pleased with herself.

'Good. If there's no traffic coming from town, just move out onto the road and speed up. My driveway is only two kilometres this way.' Jamie seemed relaxed in his seat and Samantha's confidence increased. She kept an eye on the speedometer on the dash, but barely reached the speed limit when it was time to slow down.

'Okay, there are two farm gates. This first one takes you into the homestead, where my parents live, and the one beside it takes you to my house. Just for today, let's take the first one, there's plenty of room to turn around at the homestead.' While Jamie spoke Samantha slowed the car. It jerked at first when she touched the brake too hard, but she quickly used less pressure and slowed, then turned.

'A cattle grid.' She said it to herself quietly, but slowed right down to go over the bumpy grid, then increased her speed only slightly to ease down the driveway. She could see trees and a chimney up ahead, and as they drove closer the homestead came into view. 'What a lovely home. Is it very old?' Without waiting for an answer she pulled in beside another vehicle in front of the house, braked, and shifted into neutral.

'Well done. You don't need lessons at all Sam.' Jamie grinned, then jerked his head towards the house. 'It's not as old as some, but it was built in the nineteen twenties.'

Samantha laughed. 'Not as old as some? That makes it more than one hundred, Jamie.'

'What's a hundred Mummy?' Evie wriggled in her car seat.

'Is Woz here? Can I play with Woz?' She began to unclip her seatbelt.

Samantha spoke sharply. 'No Evie! Don't undo that.' She gripped the steering wheel for a moment, then turned in her seat to look at Evie. 'Warwick isn't here Evie, he's at Kindy today.'

'I want to go to Kindy with Woz.' Samantha heard the tremor in Evie's voice, heralding tears, and quickly replied. 'Not today, but we're going to the special book shop today, to see Judith and read some books.'

'Oh! Books!' Evie bounced happily in her seat. *Crisis averted.*

'Do you think you can back out of this spot, then do a three-point turn to head out to the road again?' Jamie had waited patiently while she spoke to Evie, and Sam was grateful.

'Yes. I can do that.' Sam shifted into reverse and looked in the rear mirror.

'Before you release the brake, look here.' Jamie pointed to the screen in the middle part of the dash. 'It has rear cameras to help you back around. Good for seeing dogs, or bikes.'

'Oh. That's so much easier, isn't it?' Samantha released the brake and backed carefully around, then executed a three-point turn. She chuckled. 'This car almost drives itself.'

Jamie laughed quietly and they shared a look of amusement. 'Almost. But not quite.' He chuckled again and Samantha moved the car back along the driveway, slowing almost to a stop to drive over the cattle grid again. She indicated to turn right and increased her speed and turned smoothly onto the road to Barrington.

'Are you a farm girl, Sam?' Jamie's question surprised her and she shot him a super quick look. 'I mean, did you grow up on a farm? You know about cattle grids.' He trailed off. 'I just wondered.'

Watching the road ahead she replied, but didn't look at him. 'I grew up on a farm. Dairy, beef and a few sheep.' She chanced a quick look in the rear mirror, but Evie was gazing out of the car window. 'Um, but we left the farm after my father.' She stopped. She'd never truly gotten over her father's death. Sucking in a breath through her nose, she added, 'after we lost Dad when I was still at school.'

'I'm sorry Sam. About your Dad.' Jamie's tone was sincere. A moment later he leaned forward. 'The bridge is coming up and we need to slow to the town speed limit.'

Samantha checked her speed and slowed down. Jamie's voice had changed, there was a slight edge to it. She checked her speed again, and although it was right, she slowed a bit more.

Once they were over the bridge he released a breath. 'Okay, turn right around this roundabout and we're on the main street. We'll drive all the way down, then I'll show you the car park behind the main street shops.'

Nerves fluttered in her stomach as she encountered other cars, and she had to wait for a dusty old Fairlane to pull out of a parking spot in front of the newsagency. But she followed Jamie's instructions and they found an easy park behind the shops. She braked, shifted into neutral, pulled on the handbrake and turned the vehicle off.

'How did that feel for you, Sam?' She heard a lighter tone in Jamie's voice now and looked at him face on. 'Honestly, I think you're fine. You've remembered everything, and even driving a strange vehicle didn't phase you.' He seemed delighted, and proud of her. That was unfamiliar.

Samantha considered her response for a few seconds. 'Honestly Jamie?' She couldn't help smiling. 'That was the best. Not just the driving, but what it will mean for me.' She shook her head, very aware she was still grinning madly. 'Thank you sooo much for doing this.' She waved her arm around the car.

'Books please Mummy!' Evie had her hand on the clasp of her seat belt.

'Yes, you can undo it.' Samantha stepped out of the car and walked around to Evie's side. Jamie already had the back door open and put his arms in to lift Evie out. Samantha was going to step forward to get her as she wasn't sure if she'd go to Jamie. But Evie held her arms out and he swung her out of the car, setting her down beside Samantha.

'What do you say Evie? Is Mummy a good driver?' Jamie looked down at Evie and Samantha saw her nod her head vigorously. 'I do too.' He closed the door and locked the car. 'I'll walk you to the book shop Sam, it's just down the main street, next to the café.'

'Thank you Jamie.' Taking Evie's hand, she walked with Jamie down a laneway to the shops, then along to the book shop.

Jamie stopped at the door. 'I won't come in, I need to pick Woz up. And while I think your driving is fine Sam, let's do it again later in the week. After that, you can apply for your licence.'

'Alright. Thank you. If you have time?' Samantha could see Judith in the shop, waiting for them.

'I have time. I'll make an arrangement then, with Nik.' Jamie's expression was kind.

'Oh wait.' Samantha dug the beautiful new-to-her phone out of her pocket. It had a bright pink cover, which she loved. 'I have a phone now. From Harriet.' She tried to keep the excitement from her voice, but failed, as she shoved it into his hand. 'If you put your number in, I'll text you later, and you can arrange the driving directly with me.' She was very proud of the phone, another symbol of her growing independence.

STEPPING INTO THE BOOK SHOP, Samantha picked Evie up in her arms in an effort to shield her own nerves. But after Judith greeted her warmly and showed her around, pointing out the little desk where visiting authors signed books, she was too fascinated to be nervous.

There were a few people in the shop, browsing. Within minutes of her arrival a young woman rushed through the door, calling out, 'I'm late Judith, are there many up there?'

'Slow down Hanna.' Judith held her hand up and the girl, about her own age Samantha thought, skidded to stop. 'There are three up there, and Samantha might join you, with little Evie.' Judith moved slightly, so that Samantha was face to face with the young woman.

'Oh! Hello!' The friendliness of her tone threw Samantha for a moment. 'You're Sam!' She grinned at Evie. 'And Evie!'

Her eyes swivelled back to Samantha. 'I'm Harry's girlfriend, Hanna.' She held her hand out to shake. 'I'm so pleased to meet you.'

Samantha juggled Evie to her other hip and shook Hanna's hand. The woman was gorgeous and filled with life and light. Samantha felt a bit dull by comparison, but smiled warmly. She really liked Harry, and Nicole had told her that his relationship with Hanna was serious, so she wanted to try to be friendly too. 'It's nice to meet you, Hanna.'

'I'm a volunteer.' Hanna looked across to the spiral stair-case. Following her gaze, Samantha could see coloured beanbags in the mezzanine area. 'It's my turn to do story-time, but I'm a bit late. Bring Evie up, if you have time.'

'Yes. I was hoping you and Evie could sit in on story-time today.' Judith gave her a tiny push towards the stairs and Samantha followed Hanna. She set Evie down, and held her hand as they walked up the stairs.

Evie whispered, 'Princess stairs,' and Hanna looked down at her, whispering back, 'I think so too.'

Evie chose a bright pink bean bag right next to Hanna's purple one, and patted the side. 'Mummy, you can sit with me.' Samantha sat on it carefully, but once settled Evie climbed into her lap. There was an older woman there with three children younger than Evie. She said hello and sat in a rocking chair with the smallest one on her lap. The other two, twin boys, shared a light blue bean bag and jostled each other until Hanna opened the first book, the original Peter Rabbit story. Hanna read beautifully, using her voice to bring the characters to life and Samantha found herself immersed in the story as much as Evie.

She wondered if she'd have the confidence to read aloud like this, herself.

The time flew by and when the last book was closed, the older woman took her children downstairs. Samantha helped stack the bean bags up while Hanna tidied away the books they'd read. Evie loved helping and chatted to Hanna without any reticence. Samantha felt a bit shy, so she asked Hanna about her work. She became very animated talking about her wedding cake business and how she shared the café kitchen with her mother, Millie. After Hanna left to return to the café, Samantha sat with Judith for a short while, for a run-through of how the computer system worked.

Nicole arrived soon after, and they left in a flurry of thank yous and goodbyes.

Samantha didn't speak until Nicole had driven over the bridge. 'The driving lesson went well, I think.'

'Oh good. Even in town?' Nicole turned the headlights on.

'Yes. I was a bit nervous, but it all came back to me. And the car was automatic and really easy to drive, not like Dad's old Falcon.' Samantha glanced into the back and saw that Evie had fallen asleep. It had been an exciting afternoon for her. 'Jamie said we should have another drive this week, but he thinks I will be able to get my licence then.'

'How do you feel about it all Sam? You don't need to rush, just go at your own pace with these things.'

Nicole's words gave Samantha confidence to speak again. 'I adore the book shop. And Judith is lovely.' She turned then, laughing. 'I met Hanna. Harry's Hanna. She's beautiful. She came in to do story-time.'

'Hanna is fabulous. And she's perfect for Harry.' Nicole gave Samantha a quick look. 'But?'

'I don't know about volunteering there. I'm not sure I have the confidence. Although I'd love to take Evie to hear the stories again.' Samantha shook her head. 'I love books and all. I'm just not sure it's for me. Especially if there were a lot of people, you know, coming in and out.' She sighed. She wanted to add that Hanna was about the same age and she had a career, skills and had already started a business. Even if she hadn't lived the life she had, Samantha wasn't sure she'd have been able to do any of that. Like Hanna.

'And that's okay Sam. You're just beginning to get on your feet and exploring options is part of that. You might feel differently one day, or you may always shy away from that type of work, but at the moment it's about understanding you have options.'

'Thank you Nik. I'm not sure what to say to Judith. I think she'll be disappointed.'

'And that will only be because she likes you.' Nik grinned, as she slowed down. The courthouse entrance was just ahead. 'And maybe she'd pictured you running up and down the spiral staircase for her.'

Nicole spoke lightly and Samantha shared a giggle. But she wondered if she'd ever find something she would be good at.

23

Robbie wrapped his arms around Nicole from behind. 'It's been cold out there today and dinner smells delicious.'

Turning, Nicole took his face in both hands and loudly kissed his mouth. 'Even your face is cold, Robbie.' Reaching back to the stove, she lifted the lid of the large pot and dipped a wooden spoon in, offering him a taste. 'Beef Burgundy. Full of root vegetables and I have damper in the oven to serve with it.'

Robbie took the spoon. 'So tasty Nik. Just what we need after a day in the paddock.' He placed the empty spoon in the sink. 'Harry's having a quick shower. I might too, if there's time?'

'Take all the time you need. This can wait.' Nicole turned the heat down. 'How was work today? Have you finished the fence?'

'Harry is going back to Rawdon Vale tomorrow to tidy up

the last of it, but yes, we've finished.' Robbie kissed her quickly and grinned. 'I'll be quick.'

Thirty minutes later Nicole, with Harry's help, had served dinner. Lucy rushed in from her room. 'Sorry Mum, I just had to finish an essay for school.'

'All good Lucy. Oh, just get the butter please, for the damper.' Nicole pushed the still-warm bread towards Robbie. 'Can you cut that up?'

'How did Sam go with Jamie today? For the driving lesson?' Harry tasted the stew, closing his eyes in appreciation for a second.

'Really good. She said she felt confident and Jamie told her he'd take her again this week, then she should be able to apply for her licence.' Nicole smiled at Harry. 'She met Hanna this afternoon at the book shop. She described her as beautiful and friendly and seemed impressed by all she's achieved at such a young age.'

'Hanna is all that and more!' Harry chuckled and Lucy poked him the ribs. 'Actually, Hanna messaged that she met Sam and Evie, that they went to story-time. She said they're lovely and Evie is super cute!'

Nicole concentrated on her meal for a moment. 'Sam lacks confidence, and although she'd like to volunteer at the book shop, she's not keen to work in such a busy environment. She's not sure what work she will be able to get around here and I know she wants to start earning.'

'Can't she get any government assistance? You know, as a single mum?' Lucy crinkled her brow, looking confused.

'In theory. But in reality, it may alert her ex to her location, and she's not ready for that. But I will talk to her about it.' Nicole smiled at her daughter. 'You're on the right track, Lucy.'

———

NEXT MORNING, after everyone had left the house, Nicole found Samantha in the laundry. 'We always seem to catch up in here.'

'We do. Can I help you with anything Nik?' Samantha turned the dryer on. It was full with a load of towels, they'd take ages to dry on the line on such a cold day.

'To get your driver's licence you'll need some identification. I should have thought of it before, but we'll need your birth certificate.' Nicole walked through to her office, with Samantha beside her. The door to the downstairs apartment was open.

Samantha glanced inside. 'Evie is watching a video, it's a bit cold to play outside. But yes, can you help me apply for my birth certificate?'

'Sure. We can do it now.' Nicole touched her screen and it came to life as Samantha drew her chair closer. 'Um, I've never asked, but is Samantha your real name? Your birth name?'

Samantha's mouth formed an O of surprise, then she brought her hand to her face. 'It is Nik! Samantha Scott is my birth name. But oh, I forgot that I've never told you this! He changed my name. When we got married. For the last seven years I've been Sarah Graham.'

'Really?' Nicole's hands were poised over the keyboard. 'All this time I wondered if Samantha was a name you'd taken.' She raised her eyebrows. 'It's a bit like your hair, isn't it? You dyed your hair dark to escape, but that's really your natural colour.' The page to order a birth certificate came up.

'I did.' Samantha watched as Nicole entered the details she'd written down, into the system.

'Okay, we have a problem.' Nicole read through the information on the screen. 'To order a copy of your birth certificate we need two forms of identification.' Seeing Samantha shake her head in dismay, Nicole sighed.

'I don't have anything, Nik. Nothing that says I'm Samantha Scott and nothing that say I was Sarah Graham.' Samantha voice rose, she was close to tears. 'Thank you Nik. For trying. But I'll never be free of him. I'll never be able to get my licence, a job, a Medicare card or government help. I'm stuck, in no-man's-land, forever!'

'Wait!' Nicole grabbed Samantha's arm as she was walking from the room. 'Stop Sam. Don't upset Evie. Let's talk this through.'

Samantha turned and Nicole led her back to the desk, handing her a box of tissues and waited while she blew her nose. Nicole turned her chair, so their knees were touching, facing each other. 'I wonder.' Her mind was running ahead with a whole new scenario.

Tossing the wadded-up tissue in the bin by Nicole's desk, Samantha brightened. 'Have you thought of something Nik?'

'Sort of. Two things, actually.' Nicole reached for her notepad. 'Do you think your name was legally changed to Sarah before you married?'

'No. I didn't sign anything.' Samantha shook her head.

'And you were married. To.' Nicole laughed. 'I don't know what his name is. Your Ex?'

'Adam. Adam Graham.' Samantha twisted the edge of her jumper with her fingers. 'You won't contact him, will you?'

'Of course not.' Nicole put her hand over Samantha's, speaking firmly. 'I'd never do anything that might put you and Evie in his path again. But I am wondering, if he was in this cult, as you call it, if you were really married? Legally married?'

'Oh.' Samantha screwed her face up in concentration. 'I don't know for sure. I signed a certificate on our wedding day. I always thought it was legal. There was a ceremony.'

'Yes, but if he can take another wife without legally divorcing you, then the second marriage may not be legal.' Nicole was still trying to work through what this could mean for Samantha. If it would help.

'Third.' Smantha stared hard at Nicole.

'Third what?'

'Marriage. He had a wife before me. And other children, older children. She was still alive. I thought they were divorced, but now. I don't know.' Nicole could see that Smantha was trying hard to keep her emotions in check. 'He was planning to give me to another man, Nik. Force me to be his wife. But there was no talk of a divorce, or a wedding, for that.' Samantha shook her head. 'They make up their own rules.'

'This could be a breakthrough for you Sam! But I think we need some legal help.' Nicole smiled. She could see that Samantha was heartened, but Nicole was reluctant to get her hopes up too soon. 'There might be a way to go with this Sam, and I know someone. A family lawyer. He's retired, but I think he will help us. Help you.'

'You said you were thinking about two things?' Samantha nudged her, but it was more light-hearted now. Her face was suffused with hope.

'Yes. The first, that you may not be legally married to you-know-who.' Nicole giggled. 'I don't want to say his name out loud, I already despise him.'

Samantha brought a hand to cover her mouth, as she giggled. 'Nik! Stop it! And the other thing?' Samantha was almost holding her breath.

'Your original documents, like your birth certificate. Did you take them with you when you left your mother?' Nicole watched Samantha's face cloud over.

'No. No I didn't. What teenager thinks they'll need that? I had my Driver's Licence, but that's all. Oh, and a debit card, but he-who-we-won't-name cut that up in front of me.' Her smile faltered.

Sucking in a deep breath, Nicole took hold of Samantha's hand again. 'I'm sorry you lost your Mum last year, and didn't get to say goodbye or attend her funeral. But I need to ask, do you think your stepfather would still have your documents?'

'I don't know. I've never thought about it.' Samantha shook her head. 'I was horrible to him.'

'You were a teenager. You'd lost your Dad, moved off your farm and your Mum had someone new. I'd be surprised if you weren't horrible to him. But you did tell me once he wasn't that bad, that he put a roof over your heads and treated your Mum well.'

Slowly Samantha nodded. 'He did. He did all that. He even said he was going to get me an old car, when I finished school.' She began crying again. 'Why didn't I stay there? I ruined my own life!'

'Sam. Sam, listen to me.' Nicole had moved, now gently rubbing Samantha's back as she tried to contain her sobs. 'Your life might have been different, and easier. But Sam, you wouldn't have Evie. You've gone through hell to keep Evie safe. Focus on her now.'

Samantha nodded. 'It's almost lunch time. I'd better check on her and make our lunch.'

'No rush Sam, but if you can remember how to contact your step-father, we could try that. His name, telephone number, even his address. There's a chance he has kept your paperwork.'

'Okay. I'll write down what I remember. I'll find you after lunch.' They moved towards the hallway together. Samantha threw her arms around Nicole and hugged her tightly. 'Thank you Nik, for everything. Thank you.' Then rushed into her apartment, calling out to Evie, 'it's lunch time!'

24

<hr>

'Thanks for picking him up Mum.' Jamie was in the homestead kitchen. His mum, Jill, lifted a tray of chocolate chip cookies out of the oven. He reached over, attempting to slide one off the tray, but was rewarded by a slap on his hand.

'You're worse than Woz!' She laughed then, and nudged him. 'Go on, take one. Watch you don't burn your tongue.'

'Speaking of my offspring, where is he?' Jamie peered into the next room where the fire was roaring, but there was no sign of Warwick.

'Where do you think he is?' Jill shook her head, chuckling, as she slid the cookies onto a plate. 'He's outside with your father. Tying the dogs up and locking the chickens away for the night.' She checked her watch. 'Generally a ten-minute job, but with the two of them it could be thirty.' Jamie grinned at his mother. His parents were fabulous with Warwick, just like Debbie's were.

'He's a lucky little boy. Four doting grandparents and a whole farm to run around.' Jamie had grown up here. So had his father and his father before him. 'But I hope you didn't have to leave an important meeting at Council to pick him up. I couldn't reach Rachael and I had to finish shoeing the horses, we need them for the muster this week. Took longer than I expected.'

Jill shrugged. 'There was only one item left on the agenda and Steve and Rose were all over it. Nothing controversial, so I slipped out just before the vote.'

'Well thanks, Mum. I would have been rushing and,' he pulled the shirt away from his chest and sniffed, 'I smell like horse.'

Leaning closer, Jill screwed up her nose. 'And dog and diesel.' She strode to the kitchen window and peered out. 'But I'm used to it. And here come the lads now.' Handing him a plate with only four cookies, she pushed him toward the kitchen table. 'Put this on the table and I'll bring the tea over. Unless you'd rather have coffee?'

'Tea is perfect.' He did as she asked, then strode from the kitchen to meet his dad, Ross and little Warwick at the back door. He heard Warwick's childish voice first. 'So if Molly doesn't start laying again, we'll eat her?' Shaking his head, he sighed. Farm kids learned about life and death very early.

'No Woz, we'll let her have a little rest first. Maybe we can set her on a clutch of eggs to hatch.' Jamie laughed to himself. He wondered if Warwick could really tell the chickens apart. He couldn't.

'Daddy! We fed the chickens and locked them in and tied

the dogs up. I fed them too.' Jamie loved the way his son liked to relay any farm-related chores he'd done.

'Good work son.' Jamie helped him out of his coat. 'Run inside and wash your hands. Granny made chocolate chip biscuits for afternoon tea.'

'Goody!' And he was off.

Jamie turned to his father, noticing for the first time how grey he was getting. 'Thanks Dad.'

Ross just smiled. 'No thanks needed. He's gonna be a farmer, that one, just like you.'

'I think you're right.'

———

'I'M TAKING Samantha for a driving lesson again tomorrow afternoon Mum. May I bring her here? And Evie? I'd like you to meet her.' Jamie broke a biscuit in two, passing one half to his son.

'Of course. I'll have Warwick here, it's only a half day at Kindy.' Jamie saw a quick look pass between his parents.

Sighing, he added. 'It's not like that, Mum.'

'Like what?'

'Like anything. Samantha needs another drive, but she also needs to meet people. Crowds aren't good, so bringing her here informally is better for her. Less nerve-racking. And Evie and Woz play well together.'

Jill nodded. 'Steve said something only yesterday. That Samantha is re-learning some of her skills, like driving. That she's been in a terrible, um, domestic situation.'

'And I honestly don't know much about that. But she's a nice girl, a good mum and Evie is a sweetie.' Jamie drained the last of the tea in his cup in one big gulp.

'It's good you stopped for her that night son.' Ross wasn't one for big speeches, but his words were warm and sincere. 'Heaven knows the condition they'd have been in if they'd spent the night by the side of the road.'

Jamie shivered. 'Doesn't bear thinking about.' Returning to the driving lesson, he asked Jill if half past two would be okay.

Arrangements in hand, he stood up, scooping Warwick into his arms. 'We'll go through the back Mum, and get his boots and coat on.'

———

SAMANTHA DROVE IN CAREFULLY, parking beside his father's old farm Ute. She gave Jamie a worried look. 'I should have brought something.'

'It's not a big deal Sam. We'll look in on Mum and Woz, then do a bit more driving, up a couple of steep roads.' Jamie hadn't wanted to make her nervous, so he'd only mentioned dropping in to the homestead once they were on their way.

By the time Samantha walked around the car, Jamie had Evie out of the car seat, holding her in his arms for a moment. But then the front door banged open and Warwick raced out, followed by a half-grown Kelpie pup. 'Daddy! Evie! Hello Evie!' He ran once around the car, then back to stand in front of his father. 'Can we play out here with BlueDog? Can we?'

Jill had walked out during the ruckus and firmly said no.

'We talked about this Warwick Tait. It's too cold. You and Evie can play in the lounge with your farm Lego.' Warwick grabbed Evie's hand, tugged it, then ran back to the house. Evie followed, her little legs flying to catch him.

'Hello Samantha, I'm Jill. Jamie's mum. And Granny to that monster.' She smiled easily and Jamie was pleased to see Samantha relax, her shoulders dropping a little. 'Come in, I've got a pot of tea brewing.'

Samantha fell into step beside his mother. 'Your home is beautiful, Jill.' Jamie trailed behind them.

'The house is lovely, it probably needs some updating, but it suits us. I'm not as much of a gardener as some, I always liked helping on the farm, with the cattle and so on. You'll get to see Barrington Homestead at some point, where Rose Gordon, er Hamilton, lives. An older, larger homestead with beautifully laid out English-style rose gardens in the front and an orchard behind. Now that's something worth seeing.' Jill had ushered them in through the front door as they spoke and they removed their boots and coats.

The children were playing a game with farm animals and equipment on a rug in the large farmhouse style kitchen. That was clever of his mum, to have them play where Samantha could see them.

They sipped their tea and Jamie polished off two biscuits. Samantha had put one on her plate but had barely nibbled it. He'd never seen her so animated, talking with his mum about the farm, and what it was like when her boys were young.

'You're so lucky Jamie, to have grown up here. And now

Warwick is too.' Samantha bit into her biscuit. 'And you're on Council, Jill? Was that a bit of a change for you?'

'Not so much, really. I was involved with the Country Women's Association for years. Local President, then District. I'm used to meetings and agendas and how things are done.' Her eyes twinkled. Jamie could see she was enjoying Samantha's questions.

Nudging Samantha, Jamie added. 'Mum's a big fan of the meeting-before-the-meeting.' He chuckled.

'Stop it Jamie.' Jill gave him a look.

'What's the-meeting-before-the-meeting?' Samantha was genuinely curious.

'When you want something to go through, at a committee level, you meet with people beforehand who you think will support your motion. Then it's smooth sailing on the day.' *His mum giggled. Actually giggled!*

She nudged Samantha and said in a quieter voice. 'I've always thought women are quite good at it. Strategic, you know?'

Samantha laughed. 'It's a skill I've needed Jill. One I might have learned if I'd stayed at home a bit longer.'

'Never too late Sam, never too late.'

Jamie looked at his watch. 'We probably should go for that drive, Sam.'

'Yes. Of course. Thank you.' Samantha stood up, gathered their cups and saucers and carried them to the sink. 'Jamie, may we change our plan? Just a bit?'

Surprised, Jamie hesitated. 'Sure. Is there somewhere else you'd like to go?'

Nibbling her lip, Samantha looked from Jill to Jamie. She blushed. 'Oh, no. It doesn't matter. I'm ready. We can go now.'

Jamie held his hand up, but spoke lightly. 'Not so fast Sam. You can't half-ask something. Finish your thought. If it's not possible, I'll tell you.'

'It's just.' Samantha looked at her feet for a moment. 'Your farm. Talking about your farm. I just wondered. That is. I'd love to see it. Just a bit. But only if that's okay?'

Jill laughed. 'A girl after my own heart. Of course you should.' To Jamie she added, 'take your Dad's Ute.'

'We can't mum. There's no seat for Evie.' Jamie grimaced. He'd love to show Samantha around the farm, if that's what she wanted.

'Pfft.' Jill gestured to the children, playing together on the floor. They'd built a whole farmyard. 'Evie can stay here with me and Woz, she'll be fine.'

'I don't know.' Samantha had lit up about seeing the farm, but looked uncertain now that she realised they couldn't take Evie in the farm vehicle. She knelt down beside Evie and asked her about the game. Evie happily guided her around their farmyard. 'Evie, I want to go for another drive with Jamie. Just for a little while. Would you like to stay here with Woz?'

'And Granny.' Jill added.

'Um, yes. And, er, Granny.' Samantha added, flashing Jill a quick grin.

'Okay.' Evie sat down near Woz and continued her game.

Jill nodded. 'Sorted. And Sam, I can call Jamie on his mobile if Evie gets unsettled, or asks for you.'

And that's how they ended up in his father's old car, Samantha at the wheel. She managed the manual gears with no hesitation and asked dozens of questions as they drove down the lane and through two paddocks. They stopped at a group of heifers, not ready to calve yet, but looking fat and healthy, before driving on.

'What's that building? Behind the shearing shed? Do you still have sheep?' Samantha drove slowly around the sheering shed, towards the stables. There was a hay shed on the other side of it.

'Yes, we still have some sheep. But more cattle these days. And this building is the stables and tack room. I had the horses in yesterday, getting ready for tomorrow's muster.' Jamie opened his door. 'Turn the car off, we can walk behind this building, I've kept the horses in if you'd like to see them.'

Samantha almost leaped from the vehicle, jogging to join him as they walked around the back of the building. There were four horses grazing in a small paddock. He'd thrown some hay to them earlier, too. She climbed on to the fence rail, just staring at them.

Jamie stood beside her and called to the horses. 'Hup. Come Misty, come Blaze.' They trotted over, letting Jamie and Samantha rub their cheeks.

'They're beautiful Jamie. Australian stock horses, right?'

'Yup. All of them.' Jamie was proud of his horses. Well-bred and well-trained, something he prided himself on.

'Which one is yours?' Samantha corrected herself. 'I know they're all yours, but which one do you ride the most?'

'Captain. The big bay here. He's powerful, has done a bit of camp drafting, and great on cattle work.' Jamie rubbed the gelding's nose. 'I'm tall, I need a bit of size under me.'

'Hello Captain.' Samantha crooned to the horse. 'You're very handsome, aren't you?'

'Do you ride, Sam?' Jamie was curious. Her love of the animals was obvious, and she wasn't scared of them.

'No.' She shook her head and climbed down from the fence. 'Well. I used to. But not in a long time. I was just a kid, self-taught. I used to bring the milkers up, after school, for Dad. My horse wasn't like these.' She waved an arm at the horses, her admiration clear.

As they drove slowly back to the homestead, Jamie had an idea.

25

———

Taking Evie's hand, Samantha led her through to the bathroom. Jill said she hadn't been to the toilet while they'd been out. Evie talked non-stop about playing with Woz, the farmyard they'd built and the milk and biscuits 'Granny' had given them. *How quickly she's forgotten the old rules. Be quiet, don't look at anyone's face, only speak when spoken to.* Samantha was thrilled of course, and hoped it was a sign that Evie would forget those early years altogether, in time. But *she* would never forget.

Returning to the large kitchen area, she noticed Jamie and Jill speaking quietly together. They stopped when she appeared and she blushed. They'd been talking about her. Samantha hoped she hadn't done anything wrong.

'Sam, I wonder if you'd be interested in helping us here tomorrow, with the muster?' Jamie's question caught her off guard.

'Of course. Anything.' She looked at Evie. 'I'm not sure how I can help.'

'I can pick you and Evie up in the morning, in Jamie's car.' Jill made it sound easy. 'And by the time we get back here, the lads will have brought the cattle down from the higher ground.'

'Harry Stewart is coming to help, he's bringing his own horse.' Jamie cut in. 'He'll be here early.'

'What do you need help with? I can make morning tea and lunch, here with Jill.' Samantha brightened. She'd be happy to help this lovely family in any way she could. They'd already given her and Evie so much support.

'That would be great, but I was wondering if you would help draft the cattle when we get them down to the home paddocks.' Jamie's eyes were warm and Samantha blushed. 'If you're keen to get back in the saddle, you can ride Misty, the smaller mare you met earlier. She's quiet, and knows what to do around cattle.'

Eyes shining, Samantha nodded. If she spoke, her voice would give away her emotion. She was so excited she could cry! But then she looked at Evie, and shook her head. 'Evie?' she said simply.

'If you're okay with it, as we're only on the farm, Evie can come with me and Woz.' Jill waved her arm towards the children. 'I can put booster seats into the Ute, I do it with Woz quite a lot but didn't want to suggest it earlier, because, you know, you couldn't drive into town like that.'

Samantha nodded. She'd grown up on a farm. She'd learned to drive the tractor by age twelve herself. And the farm motorbike.

'I basically just go ahead and open and close gates. Then I come back here to make sure morning tea is ready and drive that down to the yards. Evie and Woz can help me. Then I sit on that small platform at the yards and record the ear tags of the cattle we're selling, and which ones we're weaning, and so on.'

'It's just for the morning. Most of the work will be done by lunch time.' Jamie added. 'After lunch we drench the young ones, but Dad, Harry and I can manage that. Mum can run you home then.'

'I haven't ridden for a long time Jamie. I'm not sure how useful I'll be. But I'm keen to try.' Samantha looked from Jamie to Jill. She suspected they were trying to provide an experience for her that she'd enjoy. And they were right. 'Thank you. Both of you. Let's hope I don't draft the wrong animals together and we have to do it all again the next day!' She grinned, and was warmed by their laughter in return.

———

Evie fell asleep on the way home and cried when Samantha lifted her out of Jamie's car. She had wanted to thank him again, for the driving lesson, the afternoon at the farm and tell him once more how happy she was to help tomorrow. But Evie's wails brought a flush to her face, so she simply said, 'thank you' and dashed inside.

Jamie hadn't seemed to mind and waved as he climbed into the driver's seat, but Samantha was embarrassed. She bathed Evie, who continued to cry. She refused to eat any dinner and eventually fell asleep on Samantha's lap, her eyelashes damp against her little face, which seemed flushed.

After putting Evie to bed, Samantha wondered if she should cancel their plans for tomorrow. She nibbled the inside of her cheek, the mobile phone in her hand. While she thought the invitation was more for her sake, than theirs, what if it wasn't? What if they really did need an extra hand for the cattle work?

Samantha opened her contacts list. It was short. Nicole, Jamie and Judith. And Harriet's number had been there when she was given the phone. She should ask for Jill's number too. She messaged Jamie.

> Thank you again for today.

A few minutes later his reply popped through.

> No Problem. Did Evie settle? Woz was a bit overexcited, too.

> Really? She didn't eat dinner, fell asleep in my arms.

That made her feel better. She didn't want to tell him Evie had cried during her bath. She hoped she wasn't coming down with something.

> I think Mum gave them too many chocolate chip cookies. Woz ate dinner, but went straight to bed after.

That made Samantha laugh. Evie wasn't used to a lot of sugar. And it had been a big week with a lot more people-ing than they usually did.

> Over-stimulated, that explains it. I'll
> see Jill in the morning.

She was going to add, 'unless Evie isn't well', but didn't want Jamie to blame his mum if that happened.

> Goodnight Sam. Appreciate you
> coming to help tomorrow.

Putting the phone on the charger, Sam spent a half hour writing down what she could remember about Ian, her mother's partner. She didn't think they'd married and she thought his last name was Fairley or Farley. And she had the address in Korumburra, maybe he still lived there. He'd worked at the local dairy factory store, but could be retired now. The only phone number she knew by heart was her mother's mobile, and that wouldn't help. But she'd give it all to Nicole before she left in the morning.

Evie woke early, as cheerful as usual, and said she was hungry. Samantha prepared porridge with honey on top, Evie's current favourite. She finished and asked for more. Samantha happily offered a crumpet with butter, and a hot Milo.

While Evie finished breakfast Samantha dressed in jeans and a long-sleeve tee-short with a flannel shirt over the top. It was cold again today and she had a woollen scarf and coat to add, for the horse-riding and outdoor work. She dressed Evie in jeans, with layers too.

She heard car noise outside and peeked through the side window. Harry was loading his horse into the horse trailer hitched to the back of vehicle.

They were ready with a half hour to spare before Jill arrived, so Samantha went through to Nicole's office. The door was open.

'Hi Sam. I heard you were up. How did you go with your drive yesterday?' Nicole walked around her desk, leaning against it as she spoke.

'We had a slight change of plan.' Samantha felt heat infuse her face, which made her want to look away from Nicole's knowing eyes. But she didn't. 'I met Jill. She's lovely. She watched Evie and Warwick while Jamie let me drive around the farm in his father's Ute. Well, a bit of the farm. It's quite big.'

'Oh, that's great Sam. Was Evie okay without you there?' Nicole made a funny face. 'Jill is fabulous, but Evie doesn't know her.'

'She surprised me. Evie I mean. She was happy to stay. Even referred to Jill as 'Granny' because that's what Woz calls her.' Samantha rolled her eyes. 'But Evie was a nightmare last night. Over tired. Maybe over-stimulated. There were a lot of chocolate chip cookies. She cried for ages and went to bed without eating.'

'I thought I heard her when you first came home. I was going to knock, but if Evie was out of sorts, I knew you'd have your hands full.' Nicole folded her arms across her chest. 'We've all been there. But if she's okay this morning, I wouldn't be too concerned.'

Laughing, Samantha glanced back at the open door of the apartment. Evie was watching ABC Kids. 'I'm not. She ate a huge breakfast and is as bright as usual.' Reaching into her pocket she extracted the paper she'd written Ian's details on. She handed it to Nicole.

'All I know about my mother's partner, which isn't much. I don't think they ever got married. Not that they told me. That's his name, and where they lived the last time I got a letter from Mum.' Samantha shrugged. 'I don't know if he's still there, or if he sold it. I don't remember his number, I only ever called Mum. But he might still work at the dairy factory.'

'This is a good start.' Nicole placed the note on top of her keyboard. 'I've spoken briefly with that solicitor I told you about. He's retired now, caring for his wife, but he has capacity two days a week when she goes to respite. Is it alright if I ask him to act for you?'

'Um, I really need to find work first, Nik.' Samantha would love to say yes, but she was wary of running up expenses with a lawyer, even if he was retired.

'Pro Bono Sam. He's helped me out like this for others. He just wants to help you.' Nicole smiled gently and Samantha felt her throat constrict, a wave of emotion washing over her.

'Really?' Her words were a whisper. 'Oh Nik. I'm so grateful.' Without thinking she threw herself into Nicole's arms, hugging her tightly. 'You're my fairy godmother Nicole Stewart. You really are.'

Nicole squeezed her back, then placed her hands on her

shoulders and drew her gently away. 'I'd rather just be your friend. Or big sister.'

'All of that Nik. You're all of that.' Samantha beamed at her, although she knew she was crying at the same time. Nicole handed her a tissue and they shared a smile, although Samantha's was a bit watery.

'Douglas, that's his name. Douglas Barlow. He'll try to track down Ian, and see if he has any of your mother's paperwork. And he's going to look into the validity of your marriage, and also check into Evie's birth certificate. He wants to see which name was used for the mother, Sarah Graham or Samantha Scott. And the father.' Nicole opened her diary. 'It might take more than a few days, but Douglas would like to meet you, if that's alright. He can come here early next week.'

'Yes. Yes of course. Thank you.' Samanta took a deep breath. 'Should I dare to hope? That one day I will be free and independent?'

'There's always hope, Sam.'

Samantha waved towards her apartment. 'I need to get Evie ready.' She brought her hand to her mouth. 'Oh, I haven't told you! Jill is coming to pick us up, we're going to their place today. They asked me to help with the muster.'

Nicole's eyebrows shot up. 'That's great Sam. Harry took his horse out there a couple of hours ago, to help bring the cattle down from the hills.'

'Yes! Jamie has a horse for me to ride too, just for the drafting once the cattle are in the home paddock. And Jill is going to watch Evie with Woz, and make the morning tea.' She clapped her hands and spun in a circle, then stopped. 'I haven't ridden in more than seven years. I hope I remember what to do.'

'You'll remember.' Nicole nudged her with a cheeky grin. 'But you might need a hot bath yourself tonight. You'll use muscles you've forgotten you had.'

———

JILL DROVE in just as Samantha was tying the laces of the second-hand runners she'd found in the clothes box. She suspected they were an old pair of Lucy's, but she could tell that Lucy wore a size or two larger now, as did Nicole.

'Where's Woz?' Evie demanded as soon as Jill opened the back door of the car.

'He's with Grandpa Ross until we get back.' Jill patted Evie's hand. 'Here you go, all seat-belted in, and Mummy is going to drive us to my house.'

'Oh, it's alright Jill. You drive.' Samantha felt suddenly shy. She was comfortable with Jamie in the car, but wasn't sure if she would feel the same with Jill.

'No. You drive Sam. I'm under instructions from Jamie.' The way Jill rolled her eyes as she said it made Samantha snort-laugh, which set them all off, even Evie.

After a moment, Samantha relaxed. 'Sure. I'll drive. Thank you.'

She parked in the usual spot at the homestead and lifted Evie out of the car. Samantha could hear voices, and dogs barking, beyond the stables and shearing shed and wondered if she should walk over there. As she set Evie down on the stairs to the house, she heard a motorbike. It came into view, a farm bike making a tinny sound, a bit like the one her father used to have. Jamie was riding it, with little Warwick sitting in front of him, holding on to a little bar between the handlebars.

As Jamie came to a stop, Warwick waved to Evie. 'I've been chasing cows with Daddy,' Warwick called out. 'On the bikermote.'

Jamie lifted his son down. 'Motorbike, Woz.'

'Bikermote.' Warwick ran across to Evie. 'Now we have to help Granny cook stuff.' He took Evie's hand to lead her inside. 'She lets us lick the bowl.' Evie barely looked at Samantha as she followed Warwick inside.

'I think that's my cue. Woz will be getting eggs out of the fridge and showing Evie how to make cakes, if I'm not quick.' Jill hurried up the steps. 'See you in a couple of hours.' She disappeared from view, then popped her head back out. 'Don't worry about Evie, I'll call Jamie, or just bring them to you, if she's unsettled.' And she was gone, the door firmly closed.

'Gosh. It's a whirlwind around here today.' Samantha glanced at Jamie. 'I'll just follow you back over, shall I?'

Jamie stepped off the motorbike. 'I've, ah, got something for you. Come here for a minute.' He walked up the steps and picked up a pair of good quality riding boots, only slightly worn, from under a wicker chair. 'I think these might fit you. I didn't think you'd have a pair, um, with you.'

'Gosh, er, thanks.' Not sure what to say, Samantha sat on the top step and took one of the runners off. She slipped a foot into the riding boot. Maybe a half size too big, but very comfy. The leather was worn-in, and soft. The boots had been polished and looked after. Samantha put the other one on, set her runners together under the chair on the porch, and took a few steps. 'Perfect, thank you.'

Jamie strode back to the motorbike. 'Good. Thought they'd fit.' He started the engine and patted the seat behind him and grinned. 'Hop on, if you're game.' He must have seen her hesitation, and paused. 'Or you can walk over. I've got our horses ready.' He stopped. 'But I have to take the bike back, for Dad.'

'All good.' Samantha didn't want to fuss. She'd only hesitated because she realised, when he walked to the bike, that the boots must have belonged to his wife, Debbie. She felt privileged to wear them, yet sad for Jamie too. She swung onto the bike behind him. She didn't want to put her arms around him to hang on, it felt too intimate, so she held on to the rack behind her. 'I'm good.' She gave him a tap on the shoulder, to let him know she was ready.

He moved off slowly, possibly worried about her hanging on. Samantha leaned back, raising her face to the sky. It felt good to be on a motorbike on a farm. She stuck her tongue out and tasted the air. Freedom, The air tasted like freedom. Jamie may have seen her do that in his mirror, because he sped up a bit and she laughed out loud.

26

<hr>

Samantha was wearing Debbie's boots. Deb hadn't ridden much, but had loved wearing them, even to work in the café in winter. Jamie had looked at them the night before, in the bottom of the cupboard in the laundry. Most of Debbie's things had been packed up and put away, or given away. But he'd bought her the boots when she'd moved out to the farm, and he couldn't bear to part with them, then. But seeing them on Samantha, who had so little of her own, he thought Debbie would be happy for her to have them.

Her confidence on the back of the bike surprised him. He'd expected her to hold on to him. He'd thought about that last night too. How it would feel to have someone that wasn't Debbie, put her arms around his waist. Of course, he should have known that would be uncomfortable for Samantha. A tiny part of him was disappointed.

He handed the motorbike over to his father, and introduced

Samantha. His Dad didn't say much, just shook Samantha's hand and quietly thanked her for coming to help. Jamie loved the surprised look on her face, but she warmly murmured 'it was her pleasure and she hoped she was a help, not a hindrance.' A smile tugged at the corner of Ross's mouth, but then he whistled his dogs and strode to the yards.

'This is Misty. I think she'll suit you, Sam.' Jamie held the horse while Smantha swung into the saddle. She sat well and placed her feet in the stirrups. 'One more notch shorter, do you think?' He looked up at her.

'Yes please, they're a wee bit long.' She took her foot out for first one, then the other, while he made the adjustment.

'Try them now. Take the reins and just walk over to the stable and back and see how you feel.' Jamie stroked Captain's wither as he watched Samantha walk, trot, then walk Misty in a circle.

Stopping beside him she leaned down to pat Misty's neck. 'She's beautiful Jamie. I've never ridden such a lovely animal.' Her eyes were shining and Jamie felt a little surge of emotion at her happiness. But he didn't want to embarrass her, so he swung into his saddle quickly.

'Harry's brought them all down with me, but now we're sorting in the yards. I'll put you and Misty in the smaller paddock, to bring them through in groups of five or six. Want to try that?'

'Yes!' She tapped Misty with her heels and cantered after him.

They worked together for the next two hours, Ross in the yards and sometimes Jamie or Harry with him. Samantha stayed on Misty, moving the cattle in small groups to the yards as instructed. Jamie had just re-mounted Captain, to move some of the separated weaners to another paddock, when two slipped past him in a mad rush to rejoin their mothers.

He watched Samantha turn Misty and smartly canter after them, turning them back in time, while Jamie and Captain held the rest of the group together. 'Good work Sam. You're quite the stockman. Or should I say, stockwoman. You ride well.' She flushed when he said that, but just nodded and began to push the cows up to the gate Ross had opened, into a larger pen.

Ross whistled, and waved them all back to the yards. 'Jill and the little ones have set up in the lean-to beside the shearing shed, out of the wind. We'll stop for a cuppa now.'

Jamie brought Captain alongside Sam on Misty. 'We'll tie the horses up over here, and loosen their girths. They can drink from the trough and I'll give them some hay.' He called across to Harry. 'Harry, you can tie Lawson up with ours. There's room.'

'Righto Jamie.' Harry cantered ahead.

Jamie tied Captain up and loosened his girth, then went to help Samantha, but she'd already done it. He pointed across to where Jill was. Evie was standing on the table, waving. Jill had an arm around her. 'Would you like to give Evie a little ride, after morning tea? You can hold her while I lead, or put her up in front of you. Misty is quiet enough.'

'I think she'd like that. But only if we have time.' Samantha looked behind him. 'Ross wants us to move that mob that's going to market, around to the house paddock, he said.'

'Dad will be wanting at least two cups of tea, and I suspect there are scones too. We'll have time.' Jamie walked across with Samantha, and Harry caught up with them as they arrived.

'We have horses too, Sam, or haven't you noticed?' Harry grinned at Samantha and she lightly punched his arm.

'But you haven't had any work to use them for, Harry Stewart. I'm not here pleasure-riding you know. Misty and I, well, we're doing cattle work.' Jamie and Harry roared with laughter and Samantha looked chuffed. She held out her arms for Evie, who jumped into them, before they sat around the old picnic table.

Jamie saw his mum sit beside Samantha once they all had a mug of hot, sweet tea in front of them. 'Evie's had fun. She was just beginning to look for you when it was time to come down here.'

'Thank you Jill, for watching her.' Samantha bit into a scone, a little drop of cream was left on the tip of her nose and Jamie was about to lean over and remove it, when his mum handed a paper napkin to Samantha and gave him a look.

'I saw you bring those two young ones back to their mob. You may have undersold your skills, Sam.' Jill said the words, but Ross echoed them. 'Here, here. You've been a big help this morning, Sam.'

The wind had risen while they ate morning tea, and Jill took the children back to the house. 'I'll give Evie a ride another time, if there's an opportunity, on a warmer day.' Samantha touched her cheek with the back of her hand. 'Could it be snowing in Barrington Tops? It feels like snow in the air.'

Harry looked at the sky, then to the mountains in the west. 'I think you're right Sam. It's snowing up there.'

'Alright fellas. And Samantha.' Ross appeared beside them, the collar of his coat turned up and two dogs waiting patiently beside him. 'Let's get this done.' He rubbed his hands together. 'Then we can all get warm at the homestead. Jill's cooked a roast for us.'

27

Judith settled into the chair opposite Steve. 'So it's on? The tourism office is creating train travel packages?'

'Thanks to you and your list of libraries. Our communications team has made approaches to operators in the region, for accommodation and meal deals, and are including the bookshop and author-in-residence program and the town heritage walk.' Steve shifted in his seat, reaching for his coffee. 'And all those libraries are marketing the Reader Festival too. Sending links to the website in their newsletter and sharing social media posts. It's going to be big for Barrington, that's for sure.'

'That's great.' Judith was thrilled. 'When will the packages start?'

'From the start of July. State rail authorities have agreed to keep the mid-week services as they are for six months, then revisit the numbers.' He checked his watch, finished his coffee and pushed back his chair. 'I need to go, thanks again for your help.'

Judith stayed where she was. Millie had said she'd take a break once Steve left. 'Off to another meeting on behalf of the town Steve?'

'Sure. Let's say that.' He said loudly, before leaning closer and saying quietly. 'But nah. I'm going home to play with my grandson. Rachael's picking Woz up from Kindy.'

Laughing, Judith waved him away. 'That's way more important, Steve. Off with you.'

As Steve shot out through the front door, Millie arrived with more coffee and what looked like slices of orange and almond cake, Judith's favourite. 'I was waiting for my opportunity. The girls have the café under control, it quietens down at this time.'

Judith waved to Hanna, at the coffee machine. She knew Lucy was in the kitchen with Kristen. Looking around, she realised Millie was right. Most people had left while she'd been chatting with Steve. 'How is business Millie? For you and Hanna?'

'Busy. And having Hanna here when we get a rush on is fabulous. Her *Say Yes to the Cake* business is going well, she has wedding and birthday cake orders almost to Christmas. She works long hours though, often starting at dawn and working after we close at night.' Millie sighed, but Judith heard pride in her tone too.

'Is she working too hard, Millie? Are you worried?' Judith looked over at Hanna again, she was taking items out of the cake display.

'No. Not really. Harry has been a godsend, actually.'

'How?' Judith chuckled. 'Although he does look like manna from heaven to me.'

'Stop it.' Millie playfully slapped Judith's arm. 'No, he seems quite tuned in to her. To Hanna. And insists they have dinner together a couple of nights a week. It's become a bit predictable, so I stay out with Finn on those nights. And Harry schedules stuff on her days off. A horse-ride, picnic or a trip to the cinema. If he didn't, I think she'd work those hours. She's really passionate about her business. Harry gives her balance.'

Judith had to agree. 'He's the one for Hanna. It's been obvious from the start. They're young yet, but I get the sense they're already building a life together.'

'They are. Yup. Harry's one of the good ones.' Millie sighed. 'Moving to Barrington was a do-over for me. I didn't expect it to be permanent, but I can't imagine myself anywhere else now.'

'Well. There's Finn.' Judith tapped Millie's arm. 'He's one of the good ones too.'

'He really is.' Millie pushed the cake closer to Judith. 'It's a new recipe. Gluten free. Tell me what you think.'

'Divine. Not too sweet.' Judith wrangled a second bite onto the cake fork. 'But I shouldn't.' She patted her tummy. 'I need to lose weight. The doctor said it would take some pressure off my bad knee.'

'Maybe you'd like to walk with me some mornings.' Millie finished her slice of cake. 'That's how I justify tasting Hanna's new recipes.'

'I'd slow you down, Millie. I have been walking more, even

though it's cold. Walking from home to here is good for me. I've been leaving the car at home. Then get a ride with Kristen after work, if it's dark already.' Judith changed the subject. 'Have you met Samantha, and Evie, yet Millie?'

'No I haven't. Hanna met her in the book shop last week and said she's lovely, but a bit nervous.'

'She is, but that's totally understandable. She hasn't been back to the book shop, though. I spoke to Nik, and she said it might be a bit busy for Sam, you know, dealing with the public.' Judith sighed.

'I know she wants to find work, but if the book shop is too busy, the coffee shop will be worse.' Millie smiled at Lucy when she came to collect their plates. After Lucy returned to the kitchen, Millie continued. 'Nik said Lucy didn't speak to anyone when she first came here. After a while she warmed to Robbie and Harry, but it took time. I gather Samantha's been through a lot, perhaps just being at Nicole's with her little girl, and resting, is good for her.'

'I'm sure you're right.' Judith looked at her watch, she was going to walk home today. 'But I had the impression when she was with me, that she is keen to work.' She shook her head. 'Hopefully something will come up for her.'

28

———

Douglas Barlow arrived at exactly ten o'clock. Nicole took him up to her kitchen, where Samantha was waiting. Evie was playing on the other side of the room.

'Hello Samantha.' Douglas spoke warmly and shook her hand.

When Samantha began to speak, to thank Douglas for his help, he just patted her arm and said quietly, 'No thanks needed Samantha.'

They sat at the kitchen table. Nicole poured them each a tea as Douglas retrieved a folder of documents from his briefcase and put his glasses on. His words were measured and kindly. 'I do have some news, Samantha.'

'Please call me Sam.' She sounded young then, and nervous.

'Alright, Sam. Thank you.' Opening his folder he drew out some papers. 'Firstly. There is no record of your marriage. Either in your birth name or the name you took.'

Samantha nodded, and placed her hand on the table. Nicole covered it with hers, and gave it a squeeze. 'So Evie is, um, illegitimate?' She looked upset and Nicole squeezed her hand again.

'I don't really think that matters these days, Sam.' Douglas smiled warmly. 'In fact, it may be better, for our purposes.' Shuffling another page to the top of his pile, Douglas continued. 'I did find a legal marriage, however, for your er, Adam Graham. I'm reasonably sure it is him, and this marriage was almost ten years before yours.'

'Oh. So he was really married to his first wife?' Samantha seemed unsure if this was good news or bad news.

'And there is no record, that I could find, of his divorce.' Douglas put the papers down and reached for his teacup. Nicole could see he was giving Samantha time to digest what he'd said.

'Okaaay.' Samantha was unsure, but paying close attention to everything Douglas told her.

'In reality, he couldn't legally marry you if he wasn't divorced.' Douglas waited a moment until Samantha inclined her head in acknowledgement.

'This next piece of news may surprise you.' Douglas focussed on Samantha, and she nodded. 'I haven't found a record of Evie's birth. At all.'

Samantha's hand flew to her mouth and her eyes widened in shock. 'He said he did it. I always thought he did it!' Nicole was shocked too, and glued to every word Douglas uttered.

'It's alright. It might even be good, for your situation.'

Douglas spoke in a quiet, considered manner. *He really is a gentleman.*

'What do you remember Sam, from the day Evie was born?' Douglas sipped his tea again. speaking quietly. Taking his time was helping Samantha to process the news. Gosh, Nicole needed time to process it too!

'It was difficult. And long. I was young, not quite nineteen.' Samantha shook her head, remembering.

'Which hospital were you in, for Evie's birth?' As Douglas spoke, Samantha began to shake her head. Silent tears fell and Nicole quickly checked that Evie was happy and occupied with her game on the other side of the room, unaware of her mother's distress.

'No hospital.' Samantha whispered the words. 'It was a home birth.'

'Was there a midwife present?' Douglas was making notes now.

'No. No midwife. Or doctor. Just wives. The other wives. Helping me.' Samantha squeezed her eyes shut. 'Nothing for the pain. A lot of blood.' She opened her eyes. 'I thought I was going to die.'

'That's terrible, oh Sam.' Nicole couldn't stop the words and she edged her chair closer to Samantha's.

Samantha was quiet for a moment. She sipped her tea, looked right into Nicole's eyes, then at Douglas, inhaling deeply as she did. 'You said this might be good. How?'

'We can register her birth now. While it is supposed to be done within sixty days of birth, it can still be done later.' Duglas was making more notes. 'If you want to, we can register her with 'father unknown', but only if you're comfortable with that.'

'Father unknown.' Samantha said the words out loud, then stood, and walked across to Evie. She knelt beside her, on the rug where she was colouring in. Nicole and Douglas exchanged a look, but waited. Nicole took the teapot back to the stove, to top it up. Douglas made more notes in his notebook.

After what seemed like an hour, but was maybe only five minutes, Samantha returned to her seat. Nicole poured them all another cup of tea, without asking.

'What do we have to do, to register Evie now?' Samantha sounded stronger.

'It's not as easy, to do later. We need to prove her identity. Getting your identity proven may need to come first.' Douglas smiled warmly. 'I've made enquiries there too. But it's a lot to take in. So I can come back in a couple of days to talk further, if you want.'

'No. Please go on.' Samantha stopped, then blushed. 'But only if you have time. I realise I've taken up a lot of your time already, and not just today.' She waved her hand towards his folder and documents. 'You've already done so much.'

Douglas shook his head briefly. 'I have time. But not all my news is good.' At the look on Samantha's face, he held up his hand. 'It's not bad, just more complicated than we'd hoped.' He paused. 'Your mother's partner, Ian Farley, has passed way.'

'Oh.' Samantha seemed to think about it, and blinked back tears. 'I am sorry to hear that, truly. And not just because it means any documents mum had may be lost.' Her eyes met

Nicole's. 'I wanted to apologise to him. For the way I treated him, when I was young.' She shook her head. 'He really didn't deserve it.' To Douglas she asked, 'does this make it impossible to get my birth certificate? Are we stuck now?'

'No. Not impossible. There are other ways. You held a Driver's Licence, so I'm working on that. And I'll follow up with the bank regarding the debit card you had at one time.' Douglas drummed his fingers on the papers in front of him for a moment. 'But with your permission, I'd like to complete my line of enquiry regarding Ian Farley. His passing was only a few months ago and he has a grown-up family. It's possible your documents are with them, but they may not know it.'

Samantha shook her head. 'I don't mind if you try, but I expect it will be a wild goose chase. I didn't know his kids. We were supposed to have Christmas together, all of us, but I ran away just before it.' She bit her bottom lip. 'I don't want to put you to even more trouble, Douglas.'

'Humour an old man. I'd like to get to the bottom of this particular rabbit hole, while I'm working on other avenues.' Douglas reached over and patted Samantha's hand. 'But think about what it may mean to register Evie with no father on her birth record. For him to fight for custody, he'd have to prove he's her father. The onus is on him.'

'Prove? Like witnesses?' Samantha frowned.

'Well, DNA would be more effective.' Douglas narrowed his eyes. 'But that takes time. A few weeks at least.'

Sitting up straighter, Samantha brightened. 'He wouldn't!'

'Wouldn't what, Sam?'

'Take a DNA test. It's against his religion, or cult, or whatever. No medical intervention. It's why I had a home-birth.' She clapped her hands, and almost sniggered. 'It's against their rules.' She turned to Nicole and hugged her.

Douglas stood up and Samantha shot around the table and hugged him, too. He seemed a bit surprised, but patted her back gently with one hand. 'It's alright my girl. We're on our way.'

29

Barrington Book Club & Reader Festival Update (Four months to Festival)
Attendance: Judith, Millie, Hanna, Kristen, Rose, Rachael, Meggie, Melanie, Harriet & Nicole
Apologies: Laura
Book: *Cupid Country Chance* by Cathryn Hein

'THIS WAS SUCH A CLEVER AND ENGAGING STORY, THE one by Cathryn Hein, but I'm glad it was short. I don't have the bandwidth to read anything long at the moment.' Rose moved her laptop aside, to reach the savouries on the platter.

Hanna chuckled. 'I have a confession.' All eyes immediately turned to her. 'Not *that* kind of confession.' She giggled and rolled her eyes. 'Honestly. You girls!'

'We're all married, partnered, or single, Hanna. We're living vicariously though you and Kristen now.' Judith waggled her eyebrows and Kristen blushed. Rose chuckled inwardly. She couldn't love this group of women more.

'Stop it, Auntie.' Kristen nudged Judith then gave Hanna a pointed look. 'I want to hear this confession too. Does it involve Harry Stewart?'

Hanna's face flushed and she put a hand to her mouth. 'I *could* tell you all sorts of things about Harry.' She raised one eyebrow in Judith's direction. 'But I won't. No, thank you very much, ladies. I have a *book* confession. We are at *book club*.'

'Oh. Well go on then, young Hanna.' Rose sipped her wine, thoroughly enjoying the banter.

'This book, by Cathryn Hein. It's not alone.' Hanna paused. Rose sensed she was trying to create a bit of atmosphere. She certainly had everyone's attention.

'What do you mean, Hanna?' Millie looked at Judith, then Rose, then back at her daughter.

'There are three of them.' Hanna held up her phone. 'Three Cupid Country books. And my confession is, that I didn't stop at the first one. I read all three. They're fabulous. They're a bit like Barrington. You need to download them all.'

'Oh. Thank you! The first one was fun.' Nicole was already on her iPad, downloading the books. Several others murmured, 'yes' and 'I loved it too.'

Rose moved her laptop closer and opened it. 'Can we chat about the Festival now?' She tapped open the shared To Do List. 'I see that you've all been updating the spreadsheet, thank you, and most tasks are well under control.' Meggie had opened her iPad, so Rose threw to her. 'Meggie? How are you with marketing. And press?'

'Well, I'm glad you asked, Rose.' Meggie looked smug. Rose waited. 'Barrington Coast Television have confirmed they'll do the Weekend Morning Show, live, from here on the Sunday of the Festival!' Meggie clapped her hands and Rose caught her breath. 'This is really happening. Our Festival will be on TV!' She beamed at all the faces around the table, some surprised, others enthused. Hanna and Kristen hugged each other in excitement.

'But wait!' Meggie held her hand up. 'That's not all.' Rose leaned forward. What else has Meggie organised? 'The TV crew, with one host, are coming in two weeks' time to get some general footage for the show. The book shop and main street.' Meggie looked from Rose to Nicole. 'I mentioned this to Harriet on the way in, but they'd like to visit a few of the heritage buildings too, including a couple of homesteads. Harriet and Drum's Melrose Homestead, Barrington Homestead if that's alright with you Rose, and Nicole, they'd love to see what you've done with the Old Courthouse and Stables.' They'll run some promos in the lead up to the Festival.' Meggie raised her wine glass. 'And that's not even the best bit.'

'What else could there be Meggie?' Rose brought a hand to her chest.

'It's free. It's totally a get-your-event-on-television-for-free opportunity!' Meggie wriggled in her seat. 'Our first year, too! The concept has piqued the producer's interest.'

'Wow! That's brilliant Meggs. Only you and Harriet could pull this off!' Rose looked around. 'Heritage places, interesting architecture, repurposed buildings. Your place upstairs Rachael, as well as the book shop, I should think. And the café Millie.'

Rose was impressed, she hadn't realised how much *reach* their festival would have.

'You can't buy this sort of publicity, Rose. It's brilliant and we need to let the tourism operators know, Council's communications team and the Chamber of Commerce members.' Harriet waved a hand to Meggie. 'Do we have a date yet, Meggs? Are we providing the film crew with accommodation?'

'They're confirming the date in the next couple of days, and the number of people. We need to provide accommodation, so once I know numbers I'll sort that out. It will be mid-week, so that's good for us.' Meggie tapped away at her device for a moment and the others chatted among themselves. 'I've added a section to the To Do List Rose, and the spreadsheet. If everyone can check there, I'll put the details in.' Meggie's voice was serious for a moment, but when she looked up she laughed out loud. 'A toast ladies. To the Barrington Reader Festival!'

They raised their glasses and Rose felt a moment of anxiety. *What if they couldn't pull it off. Television. Yikes!*

Hanna brought a tray of petite sweets to the table. Rose picked up a tiny tartlet. 'Hmmm Hanna. You know we only let you come to book club because you make such delicious desserts.'

'Oh, sure Rose. And we only let *you* come because you know some famous authors.' Hanna giggled.

'Got me there.' Rose chuckled as she looked around the table. 'We're done with the Festival agenda. Any other news to tell?' She packed her laptop into its case and set it beside her chair.

Judith turned to Nicole. 'How's Samantha? And little Evie?

They haven't been back to the book shop, but I fully understand that it's a bit busy for her, at the moment.'

'Douglas Barlow is helping her, pro bono. They met last week.' Nicole smiled at Judith. 'And yes, I don't think retail is for her, as a job. Although she adores the book shop and I need to arrange for her to bring Evie in again.'

'Samantha hasn't got her licence yet, Nik?' Rachael frowned. 'I thought she had a couple of driving lessons with Jamie?'

'Her driving isn't the problem. She needs identity papers. Her old licence, her birth certificate. Douglas is following up some leads, but Sam's parents have passed away, so it's complicated.' Nicole picked up a piece of caramel slice, looked like she was going to take a bite, then put it back on her plate. 'She's been helping me with housekeeping for the other rooms. We've had guests in the stables and she's been great doing the room changeover, and laundry. I want to pay her for it, but she won't take payment while she's living at my place.'

'So she has a work ethic, and principles.' Rachael looked impressed. 'I'd like to meet her, when she's ready.'

'Actually Rachael, I'm not sure if Jamie has mentioned it, or Jill. But the thing that really lit Sam up, was the day she went out to Taits and helped with the muster.' Nicole shook her head, in wonder, Rose thought. 'Harry told me. Said she rode one of their horses and was very competent, despite not riding since her teens.'

'More than competent, I think Nik.' Hanna chimed in. 'Harry told me she was quite the horsewoman.'

'And Evie? Where was she while Samantha was doing stock

work?' Rachael seemed slightly on edge as she spoke. Rose felt a bit the same.

'With Jill. And Woz. Harry says the kids are as thick as thieves and Evie calls Jill 'Granny' because Woz does.' Hanna was oblivious to the slight tone Rose detected in Rachael's voice.

'Farm work. Perhaps that's her jam.' Judith raised her eyebrows. 'But she'll need her licence to make that work.'

As Rose drove home she thought about what Hanna had said. And Nicole. That farm work lit Samantha up. Rose decided she'd try to meet her soon. She wanted to form her own opinion of the young woman. And she wanted to see what she was like with Jamie. Images of Debbie and Jamie together flew though Rose's mind, and she caught her breath as she stopped the car. She felt protective of Jamie. He'd been her friend since childhood. And her best friend's husband.

30

School holidays had meant Nicole's regular accommodation had been busy for the last two weeks, not just weekends. Samantha kept out of the way of guests, but once they checked out she began stripping beds and cleaning. It was the least she could do for Nicole, and she enjoyed being busy. Evie was always by her side, and Samantha gave her little tasks to do, to give her a feeling of accomplishment.

Nicole hadn't mentioned Douglas Barlow and Samantha was reluctant to ask if she'd heard anything. He was helping her for free and she knew Nicole would tell her if he had been in touch. But she wondered. The more days that went by, the more she began to doubt that he could help.

Back in the laundry with the first load of towels in machine, she spun around in shock when Nicole spoke. Samantha hadn't seen her walk in. Her heart was racing. Even though two months had gone by, she didn't doubt for a minute that Adam was looking for her. He'd be *under-the-radar* as he used to call it. If he had an inkling where she was, he'd send someone else in first, to check out how secure she was. *If he could take Evie.*

'Sorry Sam. I didn't mean to startle you. It's a bit noisy in here with the machine on.' Nicole opened the door of the large linen press, sorting through stacks of neatly folded sheets.

'It's all good, Nik.' Samantha looked over Nicole's shoulder. 'Are you looking for a particular set of sheets?'

'We have the television people coming in three days. I've got the film crew in The Stables and the host and producer in The Carriage Shed.' Nicole grinned. 'I'm a bit nervous, actually. I just want them to have a great experience here, and in the region. It will be so good for the Festival.' She found the sets she was after, placing them on top of the table they used for folding and sorting. 'I feel lucky, but also a bit bad, that the whole team is staying here. Meggie wanted to spread them out across two or even three places in town, but they wanted to be in one location. Good for me, though.' Nicole nibbled her bottom lip.

'The other accommodation houses will understand, surely?' Samantha didn't like to see anything worry Nicole.

'They say they do, of course, it's great for the town. But I don't know. If someone else had the whole group, I'd possibly feel a bit miffed.' Nicole grimaced.

'They're staying here because you have the mix of accommodation they need. It's as simple as that.' Samantha fiddled with the corner of one sheet. 'I'll help while they're here, of course Nik, but I'll keep out of their way. You understand, don't you?'

'I do Sam. Helping me get their rooms ready is exactly what

I need. They've said they don't need housekeeping while they're here, it's only two nights, and you can help me after they check out, if you like.'

'Good.' Samantha really wanted to ask about Douglas, but busied herself moving towels from the washer to the dryer.

As if she could read her mind, Nicole paused, one hand hovering over a stack of pillowcases. 'Douglas messaged this morning. Sorry! It's the main reason I came in here, but then I started thinking about the sheets...'

Standing stock still, Samantha searched Nicole's face, trying to determine if this was good news or bad. 'And?'

'He's contacted Ian Farley's daughter. Well, sort of. He has an email address for her, so he emailed and is waiting for a response.' Nicole stopped, her face suddenly sad.

'What is it Nik?' From the look on her face, it wasn't good news.

Shaking her head, Nicole lifted another stack of linen from the cupboard. 'It's not you, Sam. It's his wife, Frances. She's had a setback and needs treatment in Sydney. Douglas will go too, and stay with their daughter, so it takes him out of action for a few days. Maybe more.' Sniffling, Nicole added, 'Frances is a very special person. Watching her decline is just, well, it's just awful!'

'I'm sorry Nik. And for Douglas and his family. He is such a gentleman, I can only imagine how special his wife is.' Samantha internally chastised herself, for obsessing about her own situation. Even lovely people like Douglas have sadness and challenges. 'My stuff can wait. I appreciate all he's done so far.'

'Oh, but that's just it, Sam. Douglas seems to have the bit

between his teeth, his words not mine, and he will continue to work on your matter while he's in Sydney. He just can't see you until he returns. It might be a week, possibly two.'

Flustered and somewhat embarrassed, Samantha managed to murmur, 'Thank you, Nik. For everything. You and Douglas, Jamie and Judith. Everyone I've met here. I'm just so grateful, really I am.' She began to cry, and swiped the tears away sheepishly. 'I'm not used to being cared for, Nik. Not since I was seventeen.'

'Silly goose.' Nicole drew Samantha into a hug. 'Of course we care. We all care about you and Evie.' They stood like that for a few moments, until Evie breezed in, her little face pink with cold, despite the beanie she wore.

'Mummy, is it time to feed the horses? Can we go and check their water?'

Samantha nodded and reached for her coat. 'I think we need to do just that Evie, then we'll take some of the muffins we baked up to Nik's for morning tea.'

31

—————

Driving across the bridge on his way to pick Warwick up, Jamie thought about Samantha and Evie. About the night he found them by the side of the road. It had been two months since then, and although he'd heard Douglas was helping, he understood Samantha was no closer to getting her licence. He wished it would all move a little faster for her.

He'd had dinner at the pub with Rose and Angus, and Meggie and Max, two nights ago, and there was something about the way Rose looked at him when he mentioned Samantha helping with the cattle work recently. She seemed to be searching his face, or voice, for clues. It was strange. Clues to what, he wasn't sure.

Rose told him she'd asked Nicole to bring Samantha and Evie for a play date with wee Charlie and Harper, and would he and Woz like to come too? He agreed. Charlie and Warwick were great friends, although Charlie had started school this year.

So here he was, with Warwick in the back seat, heading to Barrington Homestead. He hoped Angus would be there, then Rose, Nicole and Samantha could chat while the men wrangled the kids.

It was late afternoon, and cold. Jamie helped Warwick out of the car and chuckled as he ran up the steps where wee Charlie waited with his cattle dog, Woof. Jamie couldn't see Nicole's car, so they must still be on their way.

Rose was standing at the front door with Harper in her arms. 'Hello Warwick, kick your boots off there, that's the way. Charlie, bring Woz inside, it's freezing out here.' She smiled as Jamie toed his boots off. 'Hello Jamie. I've got the fire going in the lounge and a batch of scones fresh out of the oven.'

Leaning over, Jamie kissed Rose on the cheek, then held his arms out for Harper, who happily allowed him to take her. 'Hello Rose. Scones, eh?' He stepped into the hallway, and then the lounge. Charlie and Warwick were beginning a game with building blocks and toy cars on the floor, so he followed Rose to the kitchen, still carrying Harper.

'Angus is feeding the horses, but he'll be here shortly. Nicole is on her way too.' Rose busied herself at the sink for a moment. 'Oh, here's Nik now.' Jamie walked to the front door with Rose. Nicole waited at the car for Samantha to extricate Evie from the car seat, then they hurried up the front steps.

'Come in, come in. It's so cold out there.' Rose held the door open and Jamie stepped back to give them room.

'Hi Rose.' Nicole brought Samantha forward. 'This is Sam, and little Evie.'

'Hello Sam, hello Evie.' Rose's voice was warm and Samantha gave her a shy smile.

'Thank you for having us, Rose.' Samantha turned to Jamie. 'Hi Jamie.' She set Evie down on the floor. 'Say hello to Jamie, and Woz is just over there.' Despite Samantha's urging, Evie stayed by her side, but gave Jamie a cute little wave of her hand.

Kneeling down, Jamie placed Harper on the floor. 'Evie, this is Harper.' Evie almost ran to Jamie, and with one hand on his arm, gently touched Harper's curly red hair.

'Baby Harper.' She whispered and touched Harper's hair again. 'Pretty curls.' Then she smiled up at Rose, and Jamie saw his friend's face instantly soften. 'Like her Mummy.'

'Oh, you're a sweetheart, Evie.' Rose held out her hand. 'Would you like to help me put jam and cream on the scones?'

Evie nodded. 'Harper come too?'

'Yes, Harper too.' Rose grinned at Samantha. 'Can you bring Harper in please, Sam? I'll put her in the highchair and Evie can kneel on a chair at the counter next to her.'

Samantha's expression lightened. Jamie realised she must have been nervous, meeting new people. She scooped Harper up and followed Rose into the kitchen, Nicole walking behind. Jamie wasn't sure if should follow, or supervise the boys, but a shout from Warwick answered his question. 'I'm driving the red car, Charlie!'

'No Woz, you have the blue car!'

'Red car!' Warwick's voice wobbled and Jamie strode into the lounge, sat on the floor and redirected their attention to piecing together a wooden race track. Their squabble was forgotten as they rushed to find pieces for Jamie to click together. During the melee, Angus arrived. He poked his head into the kitchen, then retreated to the lounge, sitting on the floor with his long legs stretched in front of him, towards the fire.

'Mate. I got here just in the nick of time.' Angus grinned at Jamie. 'Any longer and you'd be making butterfly cakes in the kitchen.'

Jamie nudged Angus. 'Shut up. Mate. I was hoping you'd offer me a beer.'

'Nah. It's coffee or tea only for this one. Apparently beer isn't suitable for a play date.' He used his fingers to indicate quotation marks. 'I have my orders. And we'd have to stand out the back with a beer, and it's too bloody cold.' Angus wiggled his eyebrows and Jamie snort-laughed.

'Too bloody cold.' Charlie, with one eye on Angus, repeated the words. 'Too bloody cold.'

'Charlie.' There was a warning in Angus's tone, but Charlie ignored it, dragging a plastic box of cars and race track pieces closer to his father. Jamie caught Angus's eye, but he just shook his head, mouthing, 'my son.'

Leaning against an armchair, Jamie could hear the women talking in the kitchen. Not what they said, but the tone of their chat. It was friendly and relaxed. So he relaxed. *Of course Rose and Samantha will get on. Why wouldn't they?*

Nicole popped her head into the lounge room. 'Afternoon tea at the kitchen table please lads.'

Standing, Jamie scooped Woz into his arms and galloped into the next room. He sat on the bench seat on one side of the table, with the two boys beside him. Angus was at the head of the table, and Rose at the other end with Harper in her high-chair beside her. Samantha and Nicole were on a bench seat opposite Jamie, with Evie between them.

Rose gestured to Jamie as he licked a splodge of cream from one finger. 'Sam is going to come out another day, when it's not so cold, and visit my horses.' Rose screwed her nose up as she spoke to Samantha. 'You think Jamie's horses are well-bred. Wait until you see mine.'

'Stop boasting Rose.' Angus winked at Samantha. 'She believes she has the best horseflesh in Barrington. Maybe the State.'

'I won't be able to judge that, until I see them, Angus.' Samantha kept her face impassive as she spoke, but a tiny smile tugged at the corners of her mouth, and Rose laughed out loud, delighted.

'Oh, you'll fit in around here, Sam!' Rose wagged a finger at Angus. 'I've already told Sam about Topper, my grandfather's old stallion, and his breeding.' She turned to Jamie, her smile sugary-sweet. 'It's not a competition, but I do believe a couple of yours are descended from Topper?'

'You got me there Rose.' Jamie was pleased to see Samantha relaxed and teasing. It was a side of her he'd only previously glimpsed. 'Actually Sam?'

'Yes?'

'Misty, the horse of ours you rode, is a grand-daughter of Old Topper.' Jamie saw Woz reaching for another scone and grabbed his hand. 'How many have you had, son?'

'Couple.' Warwick wasn't telling.

'Three, Jamie. Woz had three scones. Like me.' Evie called out across the table, holding up three fingers.

'Hmmm. Three.' Jamie gazed at Evie. 'And how many has Charlie had?'

'Three, same as us.' Evie was quick to answer and Jamie raised his eyebrows, tying not to laugh out loud. He was about to say something, but Evie hadn't finished. 'But Charlie's Daddy had four. Big ones. With lots and lots of cream.'

'Really?' Rose arched an eyebrow at Angus.

'Lovely scones, Rose darling.' Angus didn't care.

'I think three is enough, Woz. How about you wash your hands, and then you can play with the others.'

Nicole stood up. 'Come on Woz. You too Evie. We'll all wash our hands.' She scooped Harper out of the high chair and held her close, whispering to Rose, 'I could cuddle this one all day.' The older children followed Nicole to the bathroom.

Rose began clearing their afternoon tea things and Samantha didn't hesitate to help. Nicole returned with the children and Angus joined them in the lounge. Jamie hesitated. *Go to the lounge with Angus, or join Rose and Sam in the kitchen?*

The question was answered for him when Rose called out, 'Bring the teapot in here, please Jamie.'

Samantha was at the sink, washing up, while Rose put the leftover scones away. Jamie picked up a tea towel and dried the dishes as Samantha washed them.

'Gosh Jamie. Nicole's home is stunning, and your parents' homestead. But Barrington Homestead is next level.' Samantha gazed up at him and his breath caught for a micro-second. She looked relaxed, and happy, without the usual air of anxiety, or fear, she carried with her. He hadn't realised how invested he'd become in her recovery, in the possibility of a life without fear.

'It is Sam. It's one of the original homesteads in the district and it is spectacular. Rose and Angus maintain it beautifully too, these old homes need constant upkeep.' Jamie pointed to the ceiling. 'Pressed metal. Stunning.'

Rose chimed in. 'You'll have to visit another day, Sam, when we have more time. I can show you the horses and the homestead too, if you like.' She sighed. 'I know I was lucky to grow up here, and I don't think I appreciated it when I was young.' She glanced into the room where the children were playing. Evie had joined the game with the boys, and they didn't seem to mind. Harper was on Nicole's lap, reading a picture book together.

'If it suits you Sam, I'd be happy to provide some employment from time to time, when we do cattle work. Jamie says you're very handy.' Samantha was about to speak, but Rose continued. 'And don't worry about Evie. Bring her with you. Jamie's mother-in-law, Rachael, often minds mine, here at the house. I don't think she'd mind having Evie too. And if we're moving a lot of cattle, Jamie will be here too, with Woz.'

Samantha's face was flushed, and Jamie wondered if Rose's offer had embarrassed her. But her eyes were shining when she answered Rose. 'I'd like that very much, thank you Rose. And I'm happy to help, anytime. For nothing. Just knowing I can help out is all I need.'

'Nonsense Sam. It's one thing not to accept payment from Nik, and I understand your reasons for that. But honestly, we'd have Jamie helping, and then paying a couple of the Campbell lads too.' Rose took the tea towel from Jamie's hand and hung it on the rail in front of the oven. 'Is this the type of work you'd like to do, Sam?'

'It is. I'm comfortable with farm work. Cattle work, tractor work, hay making. But with Evie to support, I will probably have to look for something more regular, once I have my licence. A town job. That's why I'm happy to just help, as a friend, like Jamie does. I love it so much, you'd be doing *me* a favour.' Samantha's face was a mixture of serious intention, and outright happiness. 'I'm not looking for a hand-out Rose. Just a hand-up.' Samantha turned her face away, while she rinsed the suds form the sink. Rose caught Jamie's eye and smiled. He could see she liked the younger woman.

'I'm sorry if I worded it badly.' Rose spoke more quietly and placed her arm gently around Samantha's shoulders. Jamie stepped back, not sure if should leave the room. 'But if your offer stands, we'd love to have your help at our next muster.'

Nicole appeared in the doorway, Harper on her hip. 'But no musters, Rose Gordon Hamilton, until this television crew have been and gone.'

'No musters this week, Nik. I promise.' Rose laughed and held out her arms to take Harper. 'This one looks tired, but I really don't want her to have a nap now, it's a bit late in the day.'

'We need to head off Rose.' Nicole nodded to Samantha. 'Evie has the boys playing racing cars on demand in there. It's hilarious.'

'Really?' Samantha looked surprised. 'She's always been quite shy.'

Jamie walked ahead of her into the other room. Evie had the

boys lined up with a car each. She shouted 'Go!' and the boys released the toys onto the racing track. Samantha looked confused at first, then entertained. She shook her head. 'No idea where she learned this. But it wasn't from me.'

'Aw, I dunno Sam. I reckon all women can create a competitive atmosphere when they want to.' Angus chuckled, but Jamie wasn't sure Samantha agreed.

Dropping to his haunches, Jamie told Warwick they were leaving and to help Charlie pack up the game. Evie helped too, and soon it was all back in the big plastic tub.

There was a flurry of goodbyes. No one wanted to stand outside and chat in the biting wind, so they raced to their cars, strapping the children in quickly.

Jamie followed Nicole's car and tooted his horn once, when she turned into the driveway. Then he was home, at his little cottage, with Warwick ready for a bath and dinner. The evening seemed quieter than usual and he slept restlessly.

32

———

'THEY'RE HERE, AUNTIE. ARE YOU ON YOUR WAY?' Kristen's tone, a mixture of excitement and nerves, sent Judith into a spin.

'The television crew?' Checking her watch, Judith gasped. 'They're an hour early!'

'Apparently they had a good trip up from Sydney. I'm not sure. We're making them some breakfast, but they're keen to look inside the bookshop. Something about lighting.' Kristen sounded like she'd been running.

'Alright. I'm on my way. I'll drive down. Five minutes.' Judith clicked the phone off and rushed to the bathroom. She patted a few strands of grey hair into place, and applied a pale tangerine lipstick.

Minutes later she unlocked the front door of the bookshop and hit the light switch and central heating. She tried to spot the television people through the café window, but couldn't see them. No doubt Millie had put them at the back table, for a bit of privacy.

As Judith went through her usual morning opening procedures, including riding up to the mezzanine in the lift to check the bean bags were properly situated and plumped up, she noticed a higher volume of foot traffic than usual, going in and out of the café. *Small towns, big stories.* Judith chuckled to herself. Word must have circulated in record time.

Half an hour later she saw them exit the café with Rachael and Meggie. Three men and a young woman. Rachael waved to Judith from outside, but entered the door in the middle of the building, that led up to the apartment. There was no one staying there until tomorrow night, so they needed to get that footage today. Judith knew it would be booked solid when the festival was on, so early filming was clever. They weren't carrying camera gear, so this must be just a look-through, and they'd come back.

Millie popped into the bookshop, a large takeaway coffee in her hand, which she passed to Judith. 'Did you have time for breakfast, Judith? Can I make you something and bring it in?'

'I didn't, but I'll wait until they've been in, so I know what they need from me.' She sipped the coffee and rolled her eyes at Millie. 'You're a lifesaver, thank you. So, what are they like?'

'Very down to earth, actually. The woman is their production assistant, so she's all over the schedule and so on. The older man is the producer and the other two are camera and sound people.' Millie glanced around the book shop. 'It always looks so inviting in here, Judith.'

'The host? The one we see on TV? Is he coming later?'

Judith had no idea how television shows were produced, but she was keen to understand.

'I wondered that too, but Meggie said they shoot this early footage, then he does voiceover commentary back in the studio. It's mostly for promotion purposes.' Millie shrugged, then giggled. 'Who knew?'

'Who knew indeed.' Judith laughed with her friend. 'Oh, I can hear them coming down the stairs now.'

'I'll nip back to the café.' Millie rushed to the door and held it open, as Rachael ushered the crew into the shop.

'Judith. Hello.' Rachael waited until they were all inside. 'This is Janene and Frank, producers, and Jimmy and Dax.' Judith shook hands with Janene, and answered her questions. But from the corner of her eye she saw Jimmy and Dax conversing with Frank by the front window, and then the three men raced up to the mezzanine.

'Janene. Check this out!' Jimmy's voice was excited and Janene grinned up at him, then excused herself and sped up the stairs too. Meggie followed them up.

Judith raised an eyebrow to Rachael, who laughingly shook her head. 'No idea, Judith. But they absolutely adored the apartment, especially Hanna's little reading room. I think they're planning to bring the gear in after lunch, something about the western sun.'

'It's so exciting.' Judith whispered the words, she wasn't sure why, but Rachael answered with the same tone.

'It really is.'

They clattered back down the stairs and Judith looked at Frank, then Janene, who propped an iPad on the bookshop counter and opened an electronic calendar, or perhaps it was a spreadsheet. 'Your shop is beautiful, Judith. I could almost imagine I'm somewhere in the UK right now.'

'Thank you. But it's not really my shop, although I'm the Manager. It's a not-for-profit, and Rachael here is our very generous landlord.' Judith was thrilled to hear Janene's comment and couldn't keep the smile from her face as she patted Rachael's arm.

'The whole concept is gorgeous. The bookish apartment above the most divine little bookshop, and the café next door is fabulous too.' Janene tapped a few notes into her device, the turned to Jimmy. 'What time do you think we should come back to shoot in here?'

'After lunch. We'll do the bookshop first, then the apartment. The sun will be pouring in through those western windows upstairs by mid-afternoon.' Jimmy waved his arms around as he spoke and Judith was caught up in his enthusiasm.

'Alright. What can I do, to help you?' Judith hastily pulled a notebook across the counter, and picked up a pen.

Frank and Meggie joined them, while Jimmy and Dax ran back up to the mezzanine, conferring quietly with each other. 'The local author, Rose Gordon, do you think we could get her in here for the shoot? We'd like to have her at the desk, signing books and answer a few questions to camera. It's short notice, so we can do it the day after tomorrow, before we leave, if today doesn't suit her.'

Judith shot a quick glance at Meggie as she made a note. 'I'll call her now, if you like.' She turned to Janene. 'Anything else?'

'Yes. Jimmy wants to get some footage up in the mezzanine

area. Some looking down at the shop while the author is here, but also with kids in the beanbags up there, listening to a story.' Janene frowned. 'We can juggle things around, if you like. But we were planning to do the heritage filming tomorrow, the homesteads and the Old Courthouse, where we're staying.'

'Give me a moment.' Judith turned to Rachael. 'Can you please ask Hanna if she'd come in later to read to the kids. She reads beautifully.' With a grin at Frank, she added, 'and she's young and vibrant.' Rachael murmured yes, and shot out of the shop, almost running into the café to speak to Hanna.

'Kids for upstairs.' Judith thought about it for a moment. 'Rose, the author, has a little girl. And Rachael should be able to liberate her grandson from Kindy. That's two. How many do you want?'

'Three or four would be perfect, but we can go with two. It's short notice.' Janene waved to Jimmy, still on the mezzanine. 'Can you make it work with two kids, if that's all we can get?'

'Sure. But three would be perfect.' Jimmy and Dax returned to the main area of the shop.

'Frank, do we have time for another coffee, while Judith makes arrangements? Then, if it's sorted, we'll head out to the Courthouse accommodation, drop our bags, scope it out, and come back into town.' Janene closed her device.

'Yes. Alright team.' Frank turned to Judith. 'We'll grab coffee next door, but we'll pop back in here in around twenty minutes to see if you're set. Meggie, would you like to join us?'

'Thank you, Frank.' Meggie nodded, and Judith felt confident as she watched them head next door. She dialled Rose to lock her in first.

'Yes, I can come in with Harper, no problem Judith.' Rose paused. 'Um, but while they're filming my bit, at the desk, I might need someone to watch her. She's into everything just now.'

'I'll be here Rose, and Rachael and no doubt Meggie too. And Hanna will hopefully have them upstairs for a bit, reading.' Judith heard Rose sigh.

'Of course. All good. We'll be there.' Rose ended the call and Judith looked up as Rachael returned.

'Hanna said yes, but she has to deliver a wedding cake at three. I asked Kristen if she'd fill in if needed, but she's not keen.' Rachael tapped her fingers on the counter. 'What about Nicole and Samantha? Then we'd have Evie too. And Nicole to help wrangle the kids.'

'Yes. Good thinking Rachael. I'll call Nik now.'

33

Nicole clicked the phone off and went in search of Samantha. She could hear Evie's happy voice outside, and followed the sound until she came to them, over by the horses.

'Hi Sam. Brrr, it's still cold out here.' Nicole wrapped her arms around herself.

'I know!' Samantha held her mitten-covered hands up. 'But Evie had an apple inside and we had to bring the core out for the horses.' She rolled her eyes and shrugged. 'And the first horse to come over was Diana, so she's got the apple and now Evie wants to eat more apples so she can give something to all the horses.'

'You're funny Evie.' Nicole lifted the little girl down from the fence. 'But I wonder if you'd like to come to the bookshop today, to hear a story?'

'Yes please Nik!' Evie bounced a bit on her feet and tugged Smanatha's arm. 'Can we Mummy, pleeease?'

Samantha smiled at her daughter, murmuring, 'that sounds lovely.' But she turned to Nicole with eyebrows raised. 'Is there something more to this, Nik?'

Nicole nodded. 'Let's head inside, I need to warm up. But yes, the film crew have arrived and they've been scoping out locations in town. The apartment, bookshop and café. And Judith says she needs our help.'

'Our help?' A line appeared between Samantha's eyes.

Nicole shrugged. 'It was a quick call. But what I understand is, that they're coming here very soon to drop their bags and have a look around, but they'll head back to town to film in the bookshop, and then upstairs in the apartment. Something about lighting.'

'How can we help?' Samantha led Nicole through to the apartment. It was clean and tidy, with a cooling rack covered in shortbread biscuits.

'We baked cookies, Nik.' Evie climbed onto a chair and reached towards the tray.

'Stop.' Samantha held her hand up and Evie paused, her little fingers still almost touching the nearest biscuit. 'Go and wash your hands first Evie. You've been patting the horses.' Evie slid from the chair and skipped out of the room.

'Judith and Rose need a hand. They want to film Rose signing books at the desk, but she needs to bring Harper with her. I can help with the kids.' Nicole sat at the kitchen table as Samantha began making a pot of tea. 'They need three kids in the bean bags upstairs, I think Hanna is going to read to them.'

'I see. So Rose is binging Harper, but not Charlie?' Samantha brought the teapot over and pushed the tray of biscuits towards Nicole. Evie, holding up her still-damp hands for her mother to check, scrambled up on a chair and snatched a biscuit quickly, saying 'please' to Samantha just before she took a giant bite.

'Evie! Slow down.' Samantha moved the biscuits away from her daughter's reach.

'Charlie is at school. Meggie's little one, Dee, is a bit young for this. Rachael will pick Woz up from Kindy and Judith wondered if Evie could be part of it too?' Nicole suddenly wondered if Samantha would say no, to protect Evie's identity.

'In principle, I'll say yes. But only if it's possible to not show Evie's face, maybe film her from behind?' Samantha nibbled a biscuit, her hand shaking slightly as she picked up her teacup.

'Of course Sam! We can tell them that, and if it's not possible we'll just pull Evie out of the shot altogether. I totally understand.' Nicole screwed up her face in thought. 'Maybe we can get Melanie to bring little Bronte in.'

'I would have said no outright Nik, except he,' she emphasised 'he' and Nicole knew who Samantha meant, 'doesn't really watch television. We didn't have one in the house, but I suspect he watched some stuff on his computer in his study. It should be okay and I'm happy to help manage the children too. Evie and Woz always play well together and little Harper is a cutie.'

'Harper is adorable. All that strawberry hair.' Nicole sipped her tea as Samanta gazed at Evie, her expression unreadable.

'Alright Evie. One is enough. You can get your colouring book and pencils, if you like. We're going to the bookshop in a little while.' Samantha turned back to Nicole, her voice softer now. 'I have to start believing we can stop hiding from him at some point.'

Placing her hand over Samantha's, Nicole looked into her eyes for a moment. 'You've had it hard Sam. Harder than most. But I truly believe you're on your way to a new life for you and Evie. Everyone here is looking out for you. You're not alone.'

Samantha put her other hand over Nicole's. 'I know that Nik. And I'm so grateful. I already feel part of this community, in a very small way, and that's why we'll come and help.' She threw her head back and laughed, surprising Nicole. 'It's what we do in Barrington!'

Nicole laughed too. 'Oh Sam, you're the younger sister I never had.' They stood at the same moment and hugged each other, then Nicole cocked her head on one side. 'Is that a car? Gosh, the television people! They're here already!' She rushed from Samantha's place, shouting over her shoulder, 'thank you! I'll check what time we need to be in town.'

34

Despite her confidence when speaking with Nicole, Samantha was still nervous about exposing herself and Evie. But she rationalised her decision, knowing a glimpse wouldn't identify either of them. Her hair was short and dark, rather than long and blonde. And Evie's had darkened slightly too, since it had been trimmed. They both had more colour in their cheeks and Evie had filled out a bit in the weeks they'd been at Nicole's. Samantha hadn't put on weight, but she felt stronger and fitter.

Nicole popped back in. Samantha rarely locked her front door during the day anymore. 'Would you like to have an early lunch at the café, Sam? We can have Harper with us while they film Rose.'

'Oh. Yes.' Samantha was pleased, she hadn't been to the café. Not because Nicole hadn't asked her, but just to maintain a low profile. But there was something about today that made her brave. And confident. She felt *part of it*, this promotion for the festival. 'What should we wear?'

'I just asked Janene that, she's the production assistant. She said whatever we'd normally wear into town to go to the café or the bookshop. Just regular clothes. So I'm wearing jeans and boots and a button up shirt and jumper.' Nicole leant against the kitchen table. 'They seem really relaxed. The crew. Friendly. Janene and Frank, the producers, are in The Stables and the technicians, uh, camera and sound I think, are in The Carriage Shed. Jimmy and Dax.'

Nicole blushed and Samantha chuckled. 'And?'

'Well, they really love the accommodation and can't wait to see inside the Courthouse. That's tomorrow morning.' Nicole did a little happy dance and giggled. 'I'm so excited! It's great publicity for my business here.'

'I'm so happy for you Nik!' Samantha wondered what Nicole had told them about her. She hesitated. 'Nik?'

'Yes.' Nicole stood still but her eyes were still dancing.

Samantha grinned. 'I don't want to be a pain, but I'm not sure what you've told them. About me and Evie. You know, us being here?'

Nicole grinned. 'I lied.'

'You lied?' Samantha raised an eyebrow, but Nicole's smile was infectious.

'You're my niece, visiting from South Australia. You're family and here for a few weeks.' Nicole turned in a circle. 'It feels true. You *could* be my niece.'

Samantha shook her head in wonder. 'Bless you Nik. I couldn't love you more if it was true.' Checking that Evie was still occupied with her colouring book, she added. 'So they don't know? About how you help people. Women. Like me?'

'No!' Nicole shook her head emphatically. 'It wouldn't be a safe place anymore if I advertised that. No, we don't mention that at all.' Pulling her phone out of her pocket, she checked the time. 'We should head in soon, say thirty minutes?'

'We'll be ready.' Samantha locked the front door when Nicole left, then rushed to her room to get changed. 'Evie. We're going out sweetie, come and tell me what you'd like to wear.'

————

'Your café is so lovely, Millie.' Samantha had never been in such a nice café. She'd been to a few in Melbourne with her mum when she was young, but couldn't recall any that impressed her more than this one.

They were sitting at a table down the back and after greeting Millie, Hanna arrived with sandwiches for their lunch. Evie was having her very first babycino and Samantha marvelled at the giant cappuccino in front of her. She couldn't remember ever having one before, but was loving it.

They'd almost finished lunch when Rose rushed in, Harper in her arms. 'Oh Nik, you're here. I hoped you would be. They're all set up in the bookshop and they want me in there now.' She thrust Harper into Nicole's waiting arms. 'Hi Sam, hello Evie.' Rose was clearly flustered, but her smile was warm.

'Hi Rose.' Samantha put her hand on Rose's arm. 'Stop. Just for a moment. Take a breath.' Rose stopped, then patted her hair with one hand. Glorious auburn hair that fell over her shoulders in bold waves. 'You look lovely. Beautiful.' Samantha studied her new friend's face for a moment, then grabbed a napkin from the table. 'You have a smudge of something here, near your eye. Mascara perhaps?' Samantha rubbed the spot gently, and stood back. 'Perfect Rose.'

'Yes. Very author-ley.' Nicole agreed. 'Now go, don't second guess yourself.'

'Okay. You're right Nik.' Rose hesitated, her eyes on Samantha. 'Thank you, Sam.' Her words were simple, yet conveyed a depth of meaning that melted into Samantha's core. She felt *seen* by Rose. Then Rose was gone, striding down the length of the café, her long legs clad in blue jeans, riding boots and a stunning dark green silk shirt, tucked in. *Country and elegant all at the same time.*

Rachael dropped by next, with Warwick in tow. She waved and sent him running down to their table. By the time Rachael got to them, Warwick and Evie were sharing the colouring book and pencils. 'Hello Sam, Nik. They've almost finished filming Rose, but they want to do some from the mezzanine with the kids in the background.' She took a breath. 'Hanna's just getting ready now, and we'll all go over, if that's okay.'

The next hour flew by. Samantha tried to keep out of the way as much as possible, but they wanted to film from upstairs with a couple of people browsing the shelves. With Nicole minding Harper, squished into a bean bag together, and Hanna reading to Warwick and Evie, it left Samantha, Meggie and Rachael to wander around the store. Samantha ensured she kept her back to the camera, but Meggie stood by the desk and had Rose sign a book for her. They were sister-in-law's and Samantha could see they had a genuine friendship.

They gathered at the counter with Judith while the television people huddled together to check what they'd filmed, and if they had enough. The woman, Janene, probably only a year or two older than Samantha, asked Meggie if they could get a couple of men into the store, just for another short piece. Meggie walked outside with her phone for a few minutes, then returned with a thumbs-up.

Less than five minutes later Rose's husband Angus arrived, and Jamie was with him. That surprised Samantha. And Jamie was dressed 'for town' rather than in his farm clothes. Angus grinned at Meggie, then kissed Rose lightly on the top of her head. 'The men are here, where do you want us?'

Samantha giggled and Meggie rolled her eyes at her brother. Jimmy, the cameraman, was back on the mezzanine and directed Angus to carry a couple of books to the counter. Angus mumbled something about, 'don't make me carry kissing books, mate.'

Jamie moved across to the bookshelf near Samantha, while Jimmy continued to give direction. 'When I say action, just pull a book off the shelf and hand it to her.' Jimmy held up three fingers. 'One, two, action.'

At exactly that moment Warwick called out from the mezzanine. 'Daddeee! Daddee! I'm up here!' Jimmy spun around and captured Woz waving to his father, then trained the camera back to Jamie, grinning at his offspring.

'Mate. That's a wrap. It doesn't get any better than that.'

Jimmy began dismantling his gear, while Frank shook hands with Angus and Jamie. 'Good timing. Thanks for that.'

Jimmy looked at his watch. 'Rachael, we'd like to go upstairs now and film in the apartment. Meggie, can you be in this?'

'Of course.' Meggie and Rachael followed the crew out and Hanna and Nicole came downstairs with the three children.

'I've gotta run. Nice to see you all. Cake delivery.' Hanna scooted out the door before it had even closed behind the others.

Warwick tugged on Jamie's hand. 'Nanny picked me up from Kindy, daddy. She promised me a milkshake.'

'I wanna milkshake too!' Evie pouted, looking at Samantha. She was about to refuse, not sure what Nicole wanted to do.

'Oh, I think all the film stars should have a milkshake, or a coffee at least.' Angus had Harper in his arms.

'Alright, milkshakes it is.' Rose turned to Judith. 'Can you join us Judith, we'll all go next door?'

'Sure. I have a volunteer coming in less than ten minutes. Order me a chai latte please.'

And that's how Samantha found herself sitting next to Jamie, their children on their laps slurping milkshakes. The whole group laughed and teased one another and Samantha was right in the middle of it all. She hadn't laughed so much since she was a teenager. Her eyes met Nicole's, who gave her an encouraging wink.

Half an hour later they all began to say their good byes, and Samantha wiped a bit of spilt milkshake from the table with her napkin. She cleaned Evie's sticky hands, then Warwick's, without giving it a moment's thought. When she looked up, Jamie was watching her with an unreadable expression. *Maybe she shouldn't have wiped Warwick's hands.* She blushed, feeling flustered, then met Rose's eyes across the table. They seemed to have narrowed, but then she smiled. *Did she imagine that questioning look from Rose?*

35

—————

Barrington Book Club & Reader Festival Update (Three months to Festival)
Attendance: Judith, Millie, Hanna, Kristen, Rose, Rachael, Meggie, Harriet & Nicole
Apologies: Laura, Melanie
Book: *Letters in Blue* by Heather Reyburn

Rose rushed in, the last one to arrive. Angus had arrived home late, wet and muddy. By the time he'd showered and changed, she'd fed the children and his dinner was warming in the oven. She'd hesitated, wondering if she should stay home and let him relax and have an early night. But he'd kissed her gently and pushed her out the door. 'Go Rose. Enjoy.' Then he winked and whispered, 'say hello to your girl-posse.'

'Don't rush Rose, we've only just walked in.' Meggie lifted a bottle of wine and quirked an eyebrow as Rose almost ran inside, face pink from the cold. 'Wine?'

'Thank you Meggs. Yes please. How's baby Dee?' Rose stripped off her coat and scarf and settled into her usual chair with a grin.

'Oh, you heard about the great pumpkin soup disaster?' Meggie chuckled while Harriet snort-laughed.

'We've all heard about that, Meggie. But exactly how did a whole bowl of soup end up on Max's head?' Harriet tittered behind her hand.

Shaking her head and laughing at the same time, Meggie passed the wine bottle across to Nicole. 'So Dee was in the high chair. The soup, luckily, was only luke-warm. Max put the spoon down for a moment, and she threw it on the floor. It landed almost under her feet and when he bent down to retrieve it, she decided to pass him the whole bowl. Or at least, that's what he said happened.'

Rose looked around the table as they all giggled, chuckled and murmured 'we've all been there, Meggie.'

'I know we have a bit to go through for the festival, but I just want to say how much I loved this book.' Harriet held up a paperback copy of *Letters in Blue*. 'And now I'm trying to talk Drum into a visit to Scotland.'

'Oh, me too. Angus and I went for our honeymoon, but we rushed it because we'd left Charlie at home with his Mum.' Rose's eyes twinkled. 'We should go together Harri! I'm sure I can make my portion a tax deduction if I spend time in Wigtown, where all the bookshops are.'

'Are you talking, like, a girl's trip? Leave the kids at

home?' Meggie tapped her chin with one finger. 'Could we? Really? I'm serious. That would be so much fun!' She looked around the table. 'Judith, would you come? Nik? Hanna? Millie?'

Millie lifted her hands in the air. 'Slow down Meggie. The whole town would close if we all went.' She pointed to Hanna. 'You've been talking about going with Harry, haven't you?'

Hanna nodded. 'Yep. But not until next year. I need to focus on my business now.' She sipped her wine, then blushed. 'We'd probably prefer to go alone. You know, just the two of us.'

'Of course. Young love and all that!' Rose clapped her hands suddenly. 'Let's talk more about this, a trip, or trips to Scotland. But not until after the festival. We get side-tracked so easily here.'

Harriet laughed. 'I'm putting this in the official minutes to make sure we revisit the idea.'

'But this book of Heather Reyburn's was such a heart-warming read.' Judith tapped the book on the table. 'And we all love a dual timeline. One thing is certain, the author has spent significant time on the Isle of Skye herself, to write with such authenticity.'

'And that's just it. Have you ever read her bio?' Rose opened Harriet's copy of the book to the author details in the back. 'I was impressed by that too, Judith. But her knowledge of farming in Australia really threw me. Until I read this. She's the real deal. Lived in Scotland when she was younger and she's farmed in Australia.'

'No wonder the story resonated.' Nicole peered at the open

book from across the table. 'And I think it's the first in a series. Or maybe a trilogy. Can't wait to see what she publishes next.'

'But back to the festival. Only three months to go. I have all the authors locked in.' Rose playfully mopped her brow. 'Phew.'

'Accommodation providers are reporting good bookings. Not just for the weekend, but the week leading up to it as well.' Harriet tapped on her iPad. 'Tickets for the main author talk at Town Hall, are starting to sell.' She looked up and grimaced. 'I was getting a bit worried, sales were slow. But since the first promo aired on the weekend show, they've taken off. I fully expect we'll sell out and I've been talking to Council about seating arrangements to create another fifty or so seats.'

'Excellent. I'm almost pinching myself that we're doing so well.' Rachael held her hand up to the offer of more wine. 'Thanks Meggie, but I'm driving tonight. Judith and I decided it was too cold to walk.'

'And speaking of the television promotion.' Meggie paused and Rose chuckled. Her sister-in-law was an expert at creating excitement. 'I spoke to Janene, the production assistant this morning. They've put together a few different pieces from the footage they shot here last week. She called them *teasers*. They're very short, mostly 15 and 30 seconds, and they'll be showing them in the morning and afternoon news shows from this week. It will ramp up and they'll have some longer pieces as we get closer.'

Rose blushed. She'd seen one small piece in the afternoon news, of her signing in the bookshop and another of the interior of the bookshop with Samantha and Jamie browsing the shelves. *So exciting.* 'I have to say, again, that I'm so grateful for this.' She waved an arm encompassing her friends around the table. 'Since the bookshop opened my book sales have risen. And not just that, I've been invited to speak at three writer's festivals, one of them in South Australia.'

'That's great Rose!' Hanna leaned forward eagerly. 'I think the whole town, and all the businesses, will do well from this publicity.'

'You're right Hanna.' Rose chuckled. 'And some of my indie-author-friends are reporting more interest in their books too. It's a good thing we're doing here and I want to thank you, all of you.' Rose felt a wave of emotion rush over her and leaned closer to Meggie for a moment.

Meggie playfully nudged her away. 'Don't make it weird, Rose. It's good for all of us.' Rose laughed. *Trust Meggie to keep it real.*

They talked through some of the logistics, but the whole team was using the shared drive and updating their areas of responsibility on almost a daily basis, so there were no surprises.

Kristen and Hanna cleared the almost empty platters of hot savouries and returned with a cheese, nut and fruit platter for dessert.

'What's in that little bowl with the cover Hanna?' Rachael pointed at the bowl surrounded by several fruits, cut into bite-size pieces. And there was a tiny dish full of toothpicks.

'Chocolate fondue, laced with Baileys.' Hanna winked as she removed the lid and gestured to the toothpicks. 'I think you should go first Rachael.'

'Ooh. Chocolate with Baileys? Yes.' Rachael stabbed a

strawberry with a toothpick and dipped it in the sauce. She swirled it for a moment, then holding her plate under the delicacy to catch the drips, brought it to her mouth. 'Mmm. It's warm and gooey and so, so good!'

Within moments they were all armed with toothpicks. 'You're amazing Hanna. You and Kristen and Millie. You manage to surprise me with something special at every book club meeting.' Rose popped a banana piece, covered in chocolate in her mouth and closed her eyes in reverence. *But it's not just the food here. It's the whole vibe.* She opened her eyes and for a moment thought she must have said it out loud, as everyone was looking at her.

'It's you Rose. You and Harriet and Meggie and Debbie started the book club. It's really special. You're all so fabulous.' Rachael's voice was thick with emotion and Rose felt her own heart ache for the loss of Debbie.

'It's grown from there too, Rachael.' Harriet placed a gentle hand on her shoulder. 'What began as a way to catch up on a regular basis, and share our love of books, has turned into something more. It's my favourite night of the month.'

'It's book club meets business incubator. And it's full of smart women who *do* stuff. We're not just talkers, girls. We're doers.' Meggie had her hands on her hips and Rose smiled inwardly. *Darling Meggie.*

'You're right. All of you. It's my favourite night too.' Judith pointed to Kristen. 'And you have chocolate on your chin.'

'It's messy!' Kristen protested as she wiped it away. They chatted amongst themselves for a moment and Rose was happy to simply bask in their company.

'Hey Nik. How's Samantha getting on? Any more news from Douglas?' Rose turned slightly in her seat, to face Nicole. 'Do you think she'd like to come to book club too?'

'No news from Douglas. He's still in Sydney. And I did mention book club to Sam, but I don't think she's ready to leave Evie with Lucy just yet. But she reads, quite a lot actually. I've been sharing my books with her. So hopefully she might come in the future.' Nicole looked at her watch. 'I'd best go. Thank you all for a lovely night.'

'Wait Nik. Will we pick a book for next month?' Rose turned to Judith. 'What do you have coming in?'

'*Woodstock* by Michelle Montebello.' Judith passed her phone across to Rose. 'I'm really excited to read this one and I already have stock, for those who want the paperback.'

'Good. Done.' Rose turned to Harriet. 'Did you get that Harri. Can you email the links for those who want the ebook?'

The evening broke up and Rose left quickly, wanting to get home to Angus. She was almost out the door when Hanna pressed a container into her hands. 'The leftover fondue, Rose, and fruit pieces. Take it home and share it with Angus, just warm the chocolate up for thirty seconds and it's good to go.'

'Really Hanna? Wouldn't you like to share it with Harry?' But it was already in Rose's hands.

'No. I've been experimenting on him.' Hanna kissed Rose on the cheek. 'Harry's getting love handles.'

Rose laughed all the way to the car. Harry Stewart didn't have love handles, she was sure, but she delighted in the way Hanna teased him.

Angus had the front door open and ushered her inside. 'It's really cold tonight, come in by the fire.'

'I'll just put this down.' Rose placed her overcoat, handbag and laptop on the hall table and left Hanna's container in the kitchen. 'How was your night? Where are the kids?'

Angus put his arms around her, drawing her close. He nuzzled her neck, his words soft. 'Harper is asleep and Charlie is waiting for you to read him one story. Are you up for it?'

'Yes.' Rose kissed his mouth softly. 'I'll read him a story. Then I have a treat for us to share.'

Later, lying in Angus's arms, the taste of chocolate on her lips, Rose sighed in blissful exhaustion.

36

———

About to run downstairs to check the washing machine, Nicole stopped when her phone rang. 'Hello Douglas. How's Frances?'

'She's no worse Nicole, thank you for asking. But she's staying in Sydney a bit longer.' Douglas always sounded measured and kind.

'Alright then. I can let Sam know that.' Nicole didn't want to put him under pressure and she was sure Samantha would understand.

'That's why I'm calling, Nicole. I need to speak to Samantha in person. I have news.'

His words surprised Nicole. 'News. Should she be worried?' Nicole frowned.

'I think it will be good news. But I'm not sure, and that's why I want to deliver it myself. I'm coming home tonight and wonder if I can drop in first thing tomorrow morning?'

'Of course Douglas. Is nine okay? Or earlier? Do you need to get back to Sydney straight away?' Nicole's tummy flipped over. It must be something important.

Douglas paused. 'Nine is perfect, thank you. And I'll stay in Barrington for a couple of nights before heading back. In case I can be of service to Samantha.'

'Okay Douglas, I'll see you tomorrow morning.' Nicole put the phone down and ran the conversation through her mind again. Douglas hadn't given her any clues. It sounded somewhat mysterious. She walked down to the laundry.

Samantha was already there, folding linen still-warm from the dryer. She looked up and smiled broadly. 'Good morning Nik. How was your book club and festival meeting?'

'It was good Sam, really good. Have you been watching the news or the morning show? They're showing little promos for the festival.' Nicole loved that Samantha was taking an interest in the festival.

Samantha nodded. 'I saw one piece this morning. Rose was signing books. It's funny to see the way they put it together, such a short piece from, like, an hour of filming.'

'I suspect they have made more snippets. Actually, Meggie said they're called *teasers*. They change them around to keep it fresh. Or something like that.' Nicole giggled and shrugged. 'Where's Evie?'

'She's watching ABC Kids. It's just too cold to be outside for long. But she's a bit bored with inside activities.' Samantha reached for another sheet from the dryer. 'I told her she could come out here and help me fold the linen, but she didn't seem keen.'

'Kids.' Nicole took the other end of the sheet and they folded it together quickly. 'Douglas just called.'

'Oh?' The hopeful look on Samantha's face reminded Nicole just how patient she'd been.

'He's coming by tomorrow morning at nine. He has some news.' Nicole shook her head. 'And before you ask, he didn't tell me anything except that it might be good news.'

'Might be good news.' Samantha repeated the words quietly. 'I've no idea what that could mean. Maybe he has my birth certificate.' She shook her head, and almost speaking to herself added, 'but he'd tell me that.'

They worked together silently for a few minutes. 'Is he bringing his wife home? Is she any better?'

Nicole stopped, the ends of the sheet in each hand. 'That's just it. Frances isn't ready to come home, but he's coming back for a couple of nights. He said to speak to you, and to stay to be *of service* to you.'

'What does that mean?' Samantha huffed. But a moment later she seemed chastened. 'I'm sorry. He's so kind. And he's leaving his wife, who needs him, to be *of service* to me?' She shook her head. 'I don't know what it means, but I know I'm very lucky to have him working on this matter for me.'

'He is a wonderful human being Sam. But I'm as much in the dark as you are, I'm sorry.'

37

The night stretched on and Samantha tossed and turned. Evie sat up, half asleep, and asked if it was morning. Samantha hushed her and told it was night time. She was still awake long after her daughter had fallen asleep again.

Next morning Samantha was tired, having only fallen asleep somewhere around two. She had butterflies when she wondered what Douglas may possibly have to tell her. Her mood communicated itself to Evie, who was grumpy at breakfast and demanding to pat the horses. Finally, after spilling juice on the table and pushing her toast away, Samantha cut up an apple, telling Evie she could feed the core to the horses if she ate most of it herself.

They were walking back to the house, rugged up in their coats, when Douglas drove in just before nine. Samanta waved, and waited by the car as he got out.

'Good morning Sam.' He seemed to peer at her longer than usual and she wondered if her tiredness was obvious. He turned to Evie and smiled. 'Hello Miss Evie, I have something for you.' He pulled a tiny colourfully knitted kitten out of his coat pocket and held it out to Evie. 'My daughter made this for you.'

Evie looked at it for a moment, but didn't move to take it from his hand. Samantha was embarrassed, and about to chastise her, when she smiled brightly up at Douglas and stepped forward. 'Thank you.' Evie reached out and took the little cat and Samantha picked her up, relieved. But Evie leaned sideways in her arms to pat Douglas on the cheek with her little hand. 'It's a pretty kitty.' His delight was obvious and they trooped inside the courthouse and up to Nicole's kitchen together.

Despite her desperation to hear the news Douglas had for her, good manners moved Samantha to help Nicole serve tea and biscuits. After settling Evie by the toy box, where she proceeded to introduce her newly acquired kitten to the other dolls and animals, Samantha finally sat down opposite Douglas.

'Please thank your daughter for the gift, Evie loves it already.' Samantha moved the sugar jar closer to him.

'Evie is a lovely little girl, Sam.' He gazed at the child fondly. 'You've done very well.'

Douglas glanced at Nicole, who suddenly stood. 'Oh, would you rather I go downstairs? I have work I can do down there.'

Samantha and Douglas answered at the same time. 'No. Please stay.' They looked at each other and chuckled and a little bit of Samantha's anxiety dissipated.

'It's good you're here too, Nicole.' Douglas opened the file he'd withdrawn from his briefcase. 'I was able to contact the daughter of your mother's partner. She ignored my first email because she didn't know who I was, so it took a little while.' He looked up. 'And this is where it gets interesting.' He put a spoon of sugar in his tea and stirred. 'You told me, last time I was here, that your mother, Tracy, passed away in June last year?'

'Yes.' Samantha blinked back tears. Thinking of all the things she wished she'd told her mum always hurt.

'So there was some difficulty, in speaking with Ian's daughter, when I asked if they may have found some documents of Tracy's when they sorted through her father's possessions. I asked if they had already sorted through the house, assuming they may sell it.' Douglas seemed to be watching her reaction, so Samantha nodded.

'That seems logical.'

'They haven't found any of Tracy's possessions, and have only removed a small number of their father's personal items from the house.' He sipped his tea.

'Okaaay.' Samantha had no idea where this was heading.

Douglas leaned back, and spoke directly to Nicole. 'Can you sit beside Sam for me, please Nik?'

Tears sprang into Smantha's eyes as Nicole moved to sit beside her, their chairs almost touching. *This must be bad, this must be bad.*

'Samantha.' His words were soft and kind. 'This will be a shock. The reason they haven't gone through the house,' he paused. 'Is because your mother is still living there. Tracy is very much alive.'

Samantha shook her head, her mind spinning. She felt Nicole's arm around her shoulders, then saw spots in front of her eyes. *Mum is alive! It can't be!* For a moment she felt faint and her ears were filled with a loud whooshing noise, but Nicole's arm around her was firm, and she could hear her saying, 'this is good news Sam. This is good news.'

Finally, Samantha straightened her back and gazed across at Douglas, aware there were tears pouring down her cheeks and completely unable to stop them. 'But I thought. *He* told me. *He* said they'd already buried her!'

Hearing her own words, her hands clenched, and molten anger replaced the shock Douglas's news had caused. With teeth gritted, she hissed, 'the bastard! The fucking bastard!' She would have said more but Evie let out a plaintive whine.

'Mummee!' Evie ran to Samantha and she pushed her chair back, allowing her daughter to climb into her lap. She buried her face in Evie's hair, taking huge gulps of air. Nicole offered Evie a cookie and she moved onto a chair of her own, sitting up with the biscuit on a plate in front of her.

Samantha put her hands to her red-hot cheeks, mortified by her own outburst. 'I am so sorry Douglas. Please forgive me. I am so sorry.'

'Think nothing of it Samantha. When I found out I may have said a few expletives myself.' His tone was sympathetic, but Samantha couldn't imagine Douglas ever swearing.

'So you've spoken to her? Mum? Does she know where I am.' Samantha glanced at Evie. 'Where we are?' Her mind was racing. If her mum knew where they were, surely she'd come. To see them. To take them home.

'Wait, Samantha.' Douglas patted her hand. 'I haven't spoken directly to Tracy and I haven't told your, um, Ian's daughter, that I have anything to do with you. What I do have, is your mother's mobile number and address, and an email address. I wouldn't contact her until I have your instructions, Sam. *You're* my client.'

Finally, with Nicole still rubbing her back, Samantha calmed her breathing. 'What now? Should I call her?' She wanted to, but she was nervous. She hadn't been in contact for such a long time. Hadn't written, or sent photographs of Evie. What if her mum didn't want to see her, or help them?

'Yes, I think we should speak to her.' Douglas had his notepad in front of him. 'But before we do, I want to confirm the details.'

'Details?' Samantha nodded. 'Of course.' She waited.

'Your partner.' Douglas looked up. 'I'm not calling him your husband because we know that's not true.' He continued. 'Your partner told you, in June last year that your mother had passed away. Is that correct?'

'Yes.' Samantha frowned. 'I hadn't had a response to my last three letters. We wrote about once a month to each other.' She covered her face with her hands. 'I had to leave them unsealed. He read my letters before they were posted. It was to make sure I didn't raise alarms, or ask her to come and get me.' She blinked back tears. 'But I mostly lied in the letters. Told her everything was good. Sent photos of Evie. Because he would punish me if I told the truth. And I didn't want to upset Mum either. But in my heart, if I ever escaped, I always thought I could go to her.' She looked at Douglas. 'Until he took that away from me. Told me she had a sudden heart attack. That Ian had called him and that the funeral was already over because I wasn't welcome there.'

'And you believed him, of course.' Douglas was writing quickly. 'And by doing this, you were further isolated, with no way of escaping, and no one to run to.'

Nicole whispered, 'the bastard' under her breath and Samantha suddenly grinned at Douglas. 'But she's alive. I'm just so happy she's alive.'

'Yes and that's very good news, Sam. We won't know for sure, until we speak to Tracy, but I suspect she's been told you didn't want her in your life, that you've moved on.' Douglas had the pen in his hand poised above the paper.

Nicole grabbed Samantha's hand. 'It's possible your last letters weren't even sent. And that her letters weren't given to you.'

Samantha looked at her for a moment, then slowly nodded. 'All of that. He's capable of all of that.' She turned to Douglas. 'Will it be better if you speak to my mum first, Douglas? To see what she knows and what she's been told?'

'I think that's a good idea. If she's in the dark as much as you are, we don't want the shock of your story to cause her any grief.' Douglas straightened.

'Alright.' Samantha put her face in her hands again, shaking her head. 'I just can't believe this Douglas. I really can't. I've been grieving her.'

Douglas began to pack his notes and folder back into his briefcase. 'It's tempting to do this straight away, but Sam, I'd like to give you a couple of hours to process this news.' He peered at his watch. 'Would it be alright to reconvene after lunch? Can we do it here Nicole? Around two?'

'Yes. Yes of course, Douglas.' Nicole patted Samantha's hand. 'Is that alright with you, Sam?'

Douglas was standing now, and Samantha found herself on her feet too. Evie was playing by the toy box, not taking any notice. Walking around the table, Samantha was in front of Douglas, but his arms were already open and she leaned into his chest, her arms around his back, hugging him tightly. 'Bless you, Douglas. Bless you and thank you.'

They walked downstairs, with Evie running ahead holding a couple of carrots Nicole had given her, to feed the horses. Once outside Samantha called out. 'Wait for me Evie. I'll be right there!'

Douglas put his bag in the car, then stood by the open door. 'This will be an emotional phone call. It might be best if Evie is occupied.'

Nicole nodded. 'I can watch her. Take her downstairs.'

Samantha shook her head and reached for Nicole's hand. 'I might need you, Nik.' She nibbled her lip.

'I'll call Jamie, and see if he can come over with Woz. Can we tell him your news?' Nicole glanced at Evie, now standing on the fence. 'Perhaps he can mess around with the horses. Robbie should be home for lunch, I'll ask him to stay too.'

'Thanks Nik. Is that alright?' Samantha sought confirmation from Douglas too.

'Having Jamie here, with the kids, and Robbie too, at the horses works well, Sam. You need to be able to focus on your talk with Tracy. We don't know how long the chat will be, either.' Douglas hesitated. 'Not to impinge your privacy, Sam, but I think we should have you both on speaker with Nicole and myself in the room. I need to make notes, we don't know Tracy's side of the story, and I want Nicole here to support you. It will be emotional for you and your mum, Sam.'

38

JAMIE WAS DOING BOOK WORK AT THE KITCHEN table. It wasn't his favourite job, but he'd fed the cattle quickly, it was cold outside. His phone buzzed with a message. Smiling, he saw it was from Samantha.

> Hi Jamie, are you free this afternoon? I need help with something.

He frowned, wondering what Samantha needed, but replied quickly.

> Sure. How can I help?

> Douglas gave me BIG news this morning. He's coming back at 2pm, can you please watch Evie? Maybe bring Woz?

Jamie read the message twice and blinked. Big news? He hoped it was good news. He realised he hadn't replied and quickly tapped out a message.

> Yes. The Tait men will be there
> before 2.

Thank you Jamie. So much.

It was almost noon. Jamie called Kindy to advise he would pick Warwick up at one-thirty. He made himself lunch, then showered and changed. He took an overcoat for himself and his son's puffer jacket and at the last minute grabbed a second jacket for Evie. He'd put it aside for her a couple of weeks ago, it was too tight under the arms for his boy now.

They arrived at Nicole's early and Robbie greeted them as Jamie stopped the car.

'Hi Robbie.' Jamie opened the back door, letting Warwick scramble down by himself. He reached into the back seat for their jackets, and the extra one he'd brought for Evie.

'Hi Jamie.' Robbie inclined his head towards the house. Samantha appeared, with Evie racing over to greet Warwick.

'Hello Sam.' Her face was pale and Jamie almost placed his arm around her shoulders, but handed her the smaller jacket instead. 'For Evie. I've had to go a size bigger for Woz.'

'Thank you Jamie.' She held the jacket out and looked at it closely. 'This is top quality. Are you sure you can't use it?'

'Too tight under his arms now. He whinges.' Jamie gestured to Evie. 'See if it fits, it will be warmer than the blue one.' The children had run across to the horse paddock. Warwick was already sitting on the top rail. Evie climbed up quickly and perched next to him..

'Thank you.' She smiled at him tentatively and he just gave a shrug, indicating all-good, before walking to the children with her and Robbie. Evie was happy to change into the puffer jacket, it was just like Warwick's. Samantha touched his arm. 'Really Jamie, thank you. I don't expect we'll be too long, but I just need to keep Evie, um, away, until we're done.'

Jamie wanted to ask what it was about, but she didn't offer any more information, so he grinned at Robbie. 'What do you say we give these kids a riding lesson?' From the corner of his eye he saw Samantha hurry back to the house.

'Sure. I've got the saddles ready.' Robbie strode across to the paddock gate and Jamie followed. 'We can lead them around here for a bit. Then we can use Nik's office for afternoon tea.'

Jamie gave him a thumbs-up and they set about saddling the horses and keeping the children engaged. Warwick was happy to be led by Robbie, as Evie would only go with Jamie. Robbie shrugged. 'She's getting to know me, but she has no hesitation with you, mate.'

Watching Evie's face alight with happiness as she chatted to him while he slowly led her around the paddock, Jamie's heart warmed. She was a sweet girl and it took so little to please her.

Moving closer to Robbie, Jamie asked him if he knew what this was about.

'Mate, I'm not sure. But Nik says if it goes well it could have a huge impact on Samantha and Evie's future.' He seemed to hesitate and Jamie glanced at Robbie, his curiosity aroused even further. Jamie looked at him and sighed. Quietly he added, 'there's a chance they have somewhere else to go. That's safe.'

Jamie nodded. 'That's good, mate.' But his mind was racing. *Somewhere else to go? Where?* He thought Samantha and Evie were staying in Barrington. He was pleased for her. Of course he was.

39

Douglas arrived shortly after Jamie and followed Nicole upstairs, where Samantha was pacing the floor. Once Douglas arrived, she settled into a chair at the kitchen table. Nicole had brought her office phone upstairs, It had a conference call facility.

'Good thinking Nik. That should make it easier.' Douglas set out his notebook and a pen, then placed both hands on the table. 'I've been in contact with Tracy, but all she knows is that I am a Solicitor and her stepdaughter provided her number. She is probably thinking it is about Ian's estate.' He gazed at Samantha for a moment. 'As we don't know what she's been told about you, Sam, I didn't want her refusing to take our call.' He checked the time. 'We have a few minutes before we call her. I'll speak first and give her a brief overview, and ask a few questions. If possible, can you remain quiet until I tell her that you're with me?'

Samantha agreed quickly, but she looked close to tears. Nicole moved her chair closer. 'What if she doesn't want to know about me? Or Evie? What if I've already caused her too much pain?'

'She's your mother, Sam. Nothing can change that. And she may be quite shocked, so give her time to process.' Douglas patted Samantha's hand briefly. 'Nicole and I are here to support you, and Tracy.' Glancing at his watch again he moved the phone closer and dialled the number, hitting the speaker button as it began to ring.

'Hello. This is Tracy.'

The moment she spoke, Samantha began silently crying, but she was trying to smile through her tears. Nicole held her hand firmly and slid the tissues closer.

'Hello Tracy. This is Douglas Barlow. Thank you for taking my call.' His words were warm, instilling a quiet confidence in Nicole. She hoped Samantha felt it too.

'How can I help you, Douglas?' Tracy sounded slightly sceptical.

'Tracy, I'm contacting you today on behalf of my client, Samantha Scott. I understand she is your daughter?'

Silence. Samantha opened her mouth, but Douglas shook his head gently.

After what seemed like minutes, but was probably less than thirty seconds, Tracy spoke. 'Samantha? Is she alright? She's calling herself Samantha, not Sarah?' Her tone changed then, it seemed harder. 'Do you also work for Adam Graham, Douglas?'

'Samantha is my client, Tracy. And she has left the home she had, with, er Adam.'

'Oh.' Another silence. 'I wondered.' Her next words came out quickly, urgently. 'Is she safe? And Evie? I think *he's* looking for them.'

'She is safe, Tracy. She is here with me now and will speak to you in just a moment.'

Douglas barely finished, when Tracy cried out. 'Sam? Sam! Is it really you?'

'Yes Mum, it's really me.' Samantha was crying openly now, taking a tissue to blow her nose.

'Tracy, this is very emotional, for both of you.' Douglas took a breath. 'I need to tell you that when your letters stopped coming, in June last year, Samantha was told, by Adam, that you had passed away suddenly. And that your partner, Ian, hadn't wanted her at your funeral.'

'The bastard!' Tracy's voice was strident for a moment, then she was crying too. 'He told me Sarah had fully embraced her marriage and new life and did not want to hear from me. I kept writing, all this time. But I never got a reply. Not once.'

'Oh Mum. I'm so sorry. I believed him. I didn't think *even he* would lie about something like that.' Samantha shook her head and Nicole wrapped her arms around her.

Douglas stepped in. 'Tracy, you said you wondered where Samantha was. That you think Adam is looking for her. Why?'

Tracy blew her nose. 'Sorry, Douglas, let me explain. After not hearing from Sarah, I mean Sam, or Adam for more than a year, he called out of the blue. Asked how I was, and how Ian was. He was friendly, so I was friendly in return, thinking you may have changed your mind about.' Loud sobs could be heard, away from the phone. Tracy spoke again, closer this time. 'About cutting me out of your life!' She cried again on the last words, then seemed to get control of her emotions. 'Sam, he said he'd have you call me soon, but you didn't. And I started to think about it and re-read your letters. They were so stilted, I always thought it was because you were angry with me. About Ian. But then I started to wonder if there was more to it. If something else was keeping you away, or angry.'

Nicole met Smantha's gaze, her eyes wide. Her voice was small, almost childlike. 'Mum, I couldn't tell you the truth in my letters.' She coughed, cried and pushed the phone towards Douglas.

'Tracy, Samantha has been under, what we legally call, coercive control. Worse than that, she has been imprisoned.' They heard Tracy gasp. Douglas gave Samantha a gentle look, and she nodded. 'If she broke the rules, she would be punished. If she had told you the truth, she would be punished.' Tracy sobbed quietly as Douglas continued. 'She is a very brave young woman, Tracy. She has protected Evie through all of this, and managed to escape more than three months ago.'

'Oh god Sam! Sam, I had no idea. I'm so sorry!' Tracy sobbed again. 'I would have come. I would have come for you. I thought you were living the life you wanted. I thought you were happy.'

Samantha straightened in her chair with the determined look she wore when Nicole first met her. 'You couldn't know,

Mum. And thinking back, when *he* told me you'd died, it was when I first tried to leave.' Samantha shook her head. 'By removing you from my life, permanently, I had nowhere to run to.' She wiped her eyes with a tissue. 'I'm so sorry about Ian, Mum. I would have liked to apologise to him.'

Tracy murmured something, but Nicole couldn't catch what she said.

'Sorry mum?' Samantha was distraught, but trying to hold it together.

'He'd be happy to know we're speaking today, Sam. He was sad when you left, but never blamed you for it.' Tracy's tone was gentle and Samantha squeezed Nicole's hand.

Douglas leaned closer to the phone. 'Samantha's happy to hear that, thank you. But Tracy, the only way we discovered the truth about you, is because Samantha needs some of her personal documents and I tried to contact Ian. His daughter told me the true circumstances.'

'Personal documents?'

'Samantha needs identification documents such as her birth certificate, to get her licence again. Even if you don't have any of these items, you can apply for them, as her mother. Can you help us Tracy?' Douglas smiled across the table at Samantha and Nicole.

'Of course. I have a folder of stuff. I'll go through it.' Tracy was subdued now and Nicole frowned at Samantha. Something was wrong.

'Mum?' Samantha sounded unsure.

Nicole looked from Samantha to Douglas. She needed to

step in here. Nicole cleared her throat. 'Hello Tracy, my name is Nicole Stewart. Sam and Evie are in my care. I've been sitting here with Sam, holding her hand, while you talk. But I'd like to say, from where I'm sitting, that your reconnection with Samantha means everything to her. We haven't called, just for your help with those items, but to bring your family together again. I want you to know that Sam's been grieving you, for more than a year. Today has been a shock for you. And Samantha only learned this morning that you are alive. I'm looking at her now, and she's grinning through her tears. She's overjoyed to speak to you.'

Tracy sniffled. 'Thank you Nicole. I am in shock, you're right. And thank you for taking care of my girls.' The way Tracy said *my girls* warmed Nicole to her core. 'Can I ask where you are? Can I come to you there? Or would you like to come here? I want to hug you, Sam. And little Evie. I want to meet my granddaughter!'

Samantha was nodding, but Douglas spoke. 'They're not entirely safe yet, Tracy. We're building a case for Samantha to have sole custody of Evie. But we don't want to show our hand too soon. *He* might be able to get an order to have Evie, even just for visitation. And given his history, we don't trust him.' He cleared his throat. 'Has Adam only contacted you the once?'

'Mum?' Samantha sounded stronger. She was no longer crying. 'Mum, it's possible Adam, or one of his people, have been to your house to see if I'm there. Maybe hung around town. Do you think that's possible?'

'Um. Maybe. There were two men at Ian's funeral, at the

gravesite, that I didn't know. They stood back from everyone else, and when I went to speak to them, they'd left. I thought they might have been people he worked with, but they wore suits. Not many of Ian's friends wear suits. Just a jacket and tie, you know. But that was three months ago.'

Douglas tapped his pen on the notebook in front of him. 'Okay. That's good to know. They must realise by now that Samantha and Evie aren't with you. But it doesn't mean he's given up altogether. We need to be careful.' Douglas turned to Samantha. 'Sam, would you like to give Tracy your mobile number? You can have another chat later, and Tracy, I'll give Sam your number now.'

'Alright. Yes, that's good.' Tracy sounded more settled. 'Message me, Sam, when I can give you a call, okay?'

'Tonight Mum. After Evie goes to bed.' Samantha giggled for the first time then. 'And tomorrow, if you want, I'll introduce you to Evie. You'll love Evie.'

'I've loved Evie since the day she was born. And I can't wait to speak to her.' Tracy chuckled too and Nicole felt a wave of relief sweep over her.

'I'll speak to you too, Tracy. About the identification documents and next steps for you and Sam to be together.' Douglas was making notes as he spoke. 'Samantha has a good support network here, we're in New South Wales. Would it be possible for you to come here to visit, Tracy, while we're getting the legal situation sorted?'

'Yes. Yes. I'll come tomorrow if you want!' The excitement in Tracy's voice had them all laughing and talking.

'I'll talk to you tonight, Mum and I can't wait to see you!'

Samantha hugged Nicole, crying again. Tracy said goodbye and Douglas ended the call.

'Well?' He looked at Samantha.

'I never would have known, Douglas. Without you, I never would have known!'

40

With her head spinning, Samantha didn't know whether to laugh or cry. Speaking to her mum after grieving her death for fourteen months, was almost beyond belief. Better still, her mum wasn't angry and wanted to see her. Not just her, but Evie too. She would have liked to go back to her rooms and think about the conversation, but she could hear voices downstairs. The men had brought the children in from the cold. Nicole was already making afternoon tea in her beautiful big kitchen.

'Sam, nip downstairs and tell them to come up here for afternoon tea. It's warmer.' Nicole chuckled. 'They can bring the biscuit tin up here, too.' She winked. 'If there's anything left in it.'

'Sure. Thanks Nik.' Samantha turned to Douglas. 'Will you stay Douglas, for a cuppa?'

'Of course Sam, I'd love to.'

Samantha ran lightly down the stairs. She felt so happy in that moment, she even hummed a little tune as she went. Opening the door to Nicole's study, she stopped and took in the scene. Robbie was sitting in Nicole's desk chair, but turned to the room, not the desk. Jamie was on the rug on the floor, his back against another chair, with Evie in his lap and a handful of playing cards in his giant paw. Warwick sat opposite and as she watched, he placed a card on top of the pile on the rug between them and shouted 'snap!' Evie giggled and tapped Jamie's arm. He placed a card down, then Warwick did. In a flurry of card placements and much laughing, Evie shouted 'snap!' Jamie laughed loudly and tousled Evie's hair just as Samantha stepped fully into the room.

'Mummy!' Evie scrambled up and ran to her. 'We rode the horses and Jamie said I'm a cowgirl like you, Mummy.'

Samantha grinned at Jamie, and bent down to scoop Evie into her arms. 'Did he? Well if Jamie said it, it must be true.' She smiled at Robbie. 'Nik is doing afternoon tea upstairs. It's warmer, she said.'

'Excellent.' Robbie reached for the empty biscuit tin on the desk and replaced the lid. 'Horse riding is very hungry work.' Samantha giggled.

Jamie pointed to the cards by Warwick's legs. 'Pick up all the cards, Woz. We'll pack them away now.' He looked at his watch.

'You can stay too, can't you Jamie?' Samantha didn't want him to leave. She wanted to tell him about her mum.

'Are you sure?' Standing, he towered over her. 'We don't want to intrude.'

'Yes. Please stay. We have news.' She set Evie down on the floor. 'Run upstairs Evie.'

'Me too!' Woz dumped the playing cards on Nicole's desk and charged after Evie.

'They sound like baby elephants, running up there. Best I go to.' Robbie was out the door in two strides, the biscuit tin still on the desk.

Without conscious thought, Samantha was suddenly in front of Jamie. His face, gazing down at her, was a mixture of curiosity and care. Her eyes were fixed on his. She tried to smile, but silent tears leaked out. His hand, so big, and roughened from outdoor work, reached across and he gently thumbed a tear from her cheek.

'Was it a good phone call, Sam?' His gently spoken words brought more tears, although she tried to nod and smile at the same time.

And suddenly she was in his arms, her face turned into his shoulder, her breath against his collarbone. It seemed like the safest, warmest, place to be and she relaxed into him. Both arms were around her now, holding her securely. One large hand rubbed her back in gentle circles. He kissed the top of her head softly. 'I'm pleased for you Sam, really pleased.' His voice was full of emotion and she wrapped her arms around his waist, squeezing her acknowledgement.

After a minute, he relaxed his grip, and she leaned back in his arms to look up at him. Their eyes met. 'My mum, Jamie. She's not dead. She's been alive this whole time.' Samantha gulped. 'And she's not angry with me. She wants to come here. To see me, and meet Evie.'

'Your Mum? Really? Coming here?' Something changed in his face. Relief?

'Yes. Douglas doesn't want me leaving here until we have the legal stuff sorted.' She leaned into him again, suddenly realising that eventually she would return to Victoria, to her mum, once her matters were settled. 'So Mum will come here to see us. We're going to talk more tonight. It was a shock for her, that I'd left, er, my situation. But she's happy, Jamie. Really happy!'

'I'm pleased for you Sam. And your mum. And Evie too, she has a grandmother.' Jamie stepped back, breaking the embrace.

'Tracy. That's mum's name.' Samantha felt cold suddenly, the door to the hall was open behind her. She wrapped her arms around herself. 'We should go up, have a cuppa.'

'Tracy.' Jamie reached over and scooped up the biscuit tin. 'I look forward to meeting her.'

41

Jamie chatted with Douglas, Robbie and Nik and wrangled Woz when he bellowed about wanting another lamington, but all he could remember from the afternoon was that Samantha and Evie would return to Victoria once it was safe to do so. *He was happy for them. Really he was.*

While he delighted in her joy, there was something else about discovering Tracy was alive that was playing on his mind. It wasn't until he was driving home, Warwick quiet in the back seat after his big afternoon, that it hit him. *That bastard, her ex-partner, had allowed Samantha to believe her mother was dead.* The implications wrenched him, somewhere deep in his guts. Tracy had been effectively *killed* by the man. Lost to Samantha forever. And not just her mother, but the possibility of a safe haven, had been cut out of her life.

Jamie shook his head. How strong Samantha was, to take

the opportunity to run when she did. To not lose herself to that man, that terrible life. He was amazed. She was so young, so small, but so courageous.

Warwick woke up when he stopped the car, and the next couple of hours was a whirlwind of bath and bedtime stories. They'd had such a big afternoon tea that neither was very hungry. In the end Jamie made toasted cheese sandwiches and they ate them by the fire while watching the last half of a kids movie they'd started the night before.

Later, after his son was asleep, Jamie sat by the fire enjoying a small glass of port, reflecting on his day. It came back to him in a jumble of images and conversations and he tried to re-order it all in his mind.

Firstly, that Samantha asked for *his* help with Evie, really moved him. That she trusted him was precious, given what she'd been through. And he didn't know the details of the abuse she'd suffered in her sham-marriage. His mind wanted to head off in *that* direction, but he pulled his thoughts back. To Evie. *Sweet little Evie.*

He's told Evie the truth, about being a cowgirl. She had a gentle way with the horses, whereas Woz tended to shout and wave his arms around, putting them on edge. *The difference between boys and girls.* But more than that. Evie sat nicely in the saddle, held the reins lightly and listened to every instruction he gave her. She was a mini-Samantha and he admitted to himself that he was very fond of her. Robbie could have looked after Evie, *but Samantha had called him.* He knew she'd have total trust in Robbie too, and she'd said it was because Evie was still shy with Robbie. But Jamie hadn't seen that. Evie chattered away to Robbie without fear, but gravitated to Jamie. With the horses, then inside. She'd plonked herself down on his lap as if it was the most natural thing in the world.

His thoughts skittered to the embrace he'd shared with Samantha in Nicole's office. Then veered back to the reason he'd been asked to help. So Samantha could speak to Tracy, the mother she'd been told had died, more than a year ago. He was beyond happy for them, all of them. But Samantha had implied she'd go to her mother's, in Victoria, to raise Evie once Douglas had the legal side of things completed. *How long will that take? A few months? A year? Longer?*

Somehow, he had assumed she'd stay in Barrington. That Nicole and Robbie and all the people who had supported Sam and Evie would become her family. That she'd stay in the community. That Evie and Woz would go to school together next year. He shook his head and finished his port. Samantha was young, almost a decade younger than him. She would learn to trust again and eventually re-partner. Maybe have more children.

While he, Jamie, would mourn Debbie for the rest of his life. He went to bed thinking about Debbie and the life they'd planned. He'd almost lost her, when she was pregnant with Warwick, and her second pregnancy wasn't risk-free either. But once Scarlett arrived safely, he'd stopped worrying. They both had. And they'd begun planning. He rolled onto his back, a wave of deep emotion threatening to choke him. He half sat up. For the first time, ever, he admitted he was angry with Deb.

Angry that she'd been so careless when driving, that she hadn't seen the cattle when she knew they were often there. Angry that she died and took Scarlett with her. He would never love another like he loved Debbie. But sometimes he hated her too. When he felt like that, only Woz kept him going.

42

———

Judith looked up as the little bell over the book shop door tinkled. 'Hello Nik.' There was no one else in the shop, she'd only just opened.

'Hi Judith. Samantha and Evie are next door. I just thought I'd pop in for my copy of *Woodstock*. I love the cover so much, I want the paperback version, you know, to keep.' Nicole placed her purse on the counter.

'It's here. I've kept the book club copies separate, as this one has been selling. Like crazy.' Judith placed the book on the counter, then leaned closer to Nicole. 'I follow Michelle Montebello on Facebook and she has a special edition hardcover too. I've ordered one for myself.'

'Ooh, special edition? Like the one she did for The Quarantine Station? Rose has that one.' Nicole looked keen.

'Yes, but even prettier. And she's bringing all her special

editions for the signing at the Festival.' Judith rang up the paperback and Nicole touched the device with her card.

'I'll grab one then. I can't wait to meet all the authors.' Nicole looked up as Trudy arrived.

'I'm here for my shift, Judith. Hi Nicole.' Trudy slipped behind the counter, next to Judith. 'What do you need me to do?'

'I've started pricing this box of stock. Could you finish that and put them on the Top Ten display near the front? Thanks Trudy.' Judith moved beside Nicole. 'Are you going next door for a coffee, or are you in a rush, Nik?'

'Next door. I've ordered.' She touched Judith's arm. 'Come and join us. Sam has news.'

'Good news?' Judith hoped so, Samantha didn't deserve any bad news.

'Yes, wonderful news. She'll be keen to tell you.'

Leaving Trudy to man the book shop, Judith entered the café with Nicole. She waved to Samantha, at the table at the back, then ordered a coffee from Millie. Judith joined them, choosing a chair across the table from Samantha. She said hello to Evie, who was colouring in.

'Have you heard my news, Judith?' Samantha's was bubbling over with excitement and Judith chuckled.

'No, tell me. It must be good news, you look so happy.'

'It is.' Samantha paused as Millie brought their drinks to the table. 'Millie, have you heard my news? I thought Harry may have told Hanna.'

Millie smiled kindly and shook her head. 'Even if Harry did

tell Hanna, which I suspect he hasn't, she'd not tell me without your permission.'

Samantha half stood. 'Can you join us? And Hanna?' She waved an arm gesturing to the café interior. 'It's not busy just now.'

Judith was intrigued. Millie dashed back to the kitchen to get Hanna, and brought coffee back for themselves as well.

'And you can tell Kristen too.' Samantha giggled. 'But someone has to serve the customers.' She paused. Judith was almost on the edge of her chair. 'So. I think you all know I lost my mother last year? That's why I had nowhere to go when I, er, left, my situation.' Judith agreed, but she caught Nicole's eye. She was beaming. Judith returned her attention to Samantha.

'Well. She didn't die. At all. It was a lie. Intended to keep me, um, trapped.' Samantha reached across to Nicole. 'Bless Nik for getting Douglas involved. He found out. And we called her two days ago.' Samantha bounced in her seat and clapped her hands. Evie clapped too.

'That's wonderful news, Sam.' Judith reached over and hugged the younger woman. 'It must have been a shock for you.'

'It was. And for mum too. She'd been writing, but her letters were kept from me, of course. And she'd been told that I wanted nothing to do with her.' Samantha suddenly stopped, her hand over her mouth. 'Oh!'

'What is it Sam?' Nicole leaned around, her face full of concern.

'Mum. She kept writing, even after *he* told her I wanted

nothing to do with her and she never received a reply. She wrote every other week.' Sam shook her head, her eyes distressed. 'She was never angry with me, was she Nik?'

'No Sam. I don't think she was. But she's angry with whats-his-name now!' The way Nicole referred to Samantha's ex made Judith laugh, and Hanna and Millie too.

'That's such good news, Sam. I'm so happy for you.' Hanna nudged Samantha with her shoulder. 'But does this mean we're going to lose you? Will you go to your mother now. Victoria, isn't it?'

Samantha shook her head. Judith was surprised. 'No. At least not for a while. I need to be here so Douglas can help me with my legal stuff. Which needs to be handled in New South Wales.' She grinned at Hanna. 'But Mum is coming here. Today. She flew to Sydney yesterday and is on this morning's train. We're going to meet her in an hour.'

Judith sipped her drink happily. 'Such good news. I can't wait to meet her.'

'Tracy. Her name is Tracy. She's going to stay with me at Nik's for a few days. Douglas had to go back to Sydney, but he'll be back soon and will talk to us together.' Samantha wriggled in her seat. 'Mum has my documents, the originals, for identification. I'll be able to get my licence, and a Medicare card. She's going to help me set up a bank account too.'

'This is brilliant news, Sam. The start of a new life. An independent life.' Millie looked at Hanna. 'And independence for you, too. You'll be able to work, even part-time.'

'And rent a house.' Hanna laughed.

'Or buy one, one day.' Millie added.

Nicole giggled. 'Get a car.'

'Hold on, hold on.' Judith raised a hand. 'You know what you need to do first, Sam?'

'What Judith?' Samantha tapped the table, grinning. 'I feel like I should be writing this down.'

'Join book club. Help us with the Festival.' Judith looked over at Nicole. 'I'm sure Lucy and Robbie can look after Evie for a couple of hours.'

Samantha looked at Nicole. 'I'd love to, but I'm not sure what I can do to help.'

'We'll find something.' Judith was determined. 'You'll never want to leave.'

43

———

As the train approached the station with a strident whistle and screech of brakes, Nicole took a step back. Samantha held Evie, rocking from one foot to the other. *Excitement and nerves.*

Nicole realised, as they waited for the train to come to a complete stop, that she no idea what Tracy looked like or even how old she was.

Several passengers stepped down, three nicely dressed older women smiled as they passed Nicole, and a group of young people wearing backpacks followed them. Samantha called out, 'Mum!'

Nicole stood on tiptoes to peer over Samantha's head to the end of the platform. A woman, much younger than she expected, strode toward them wheeling a small suitcase. She wore jeans and boots, with an overcoat just like the ones most people in Barrington wore at this time of year. She smiled and

245

Nicole saw the likeness immediately. Trim like Samantha and about the same height, her dark hair tied back in a low ponytail.

Samantha met her halfway along the platform, almost running as she held Evie's hand. Tracy dropped the handle of her bag and held her arms wide, embracing Samantha with a fierce protectiveness. By the time Nicole reached them, Evie was in Samantha's arms, squashed between them as they hugged.

Tracy looked up, catching Nicole's eye. She moved away from Samantha and reached her hands out. Nicole took them in hers and Tracy seemed to be holding her emotions in check while she found the words she wanted to say. 'Nicole? You must be Nicole. Thank you. Thank you so much for keeping my girls safe.'

Cutting her off gently, Nicole leaned forward and kissed Tracy's cheek. 'You're very welcome Tracy. We love Sam and Evie and we're so happy to have you here.' She reached for the handle of Tracy's bag. 'But it's cold here on the platform. Let's get you home where it's warm.'

With Tracy in the front seat, Nicole caught her expression when the Old Courthouse came into view. She turned to Nicole, her face aglow. 'Really? This is your home Nicole?'

'Please, call me Nik.' She parked her car beside Robbie's work vehicle. 'Yes. I bought it cheap a few years ago, and we've renovated it. There's always work to do on a building this old, but my husband is a builder, so that helps.' Nicole suppressed a laugh, but caught Samantha's smile in the rear-view mirror.

'We're staying in an apartment downstairs and Nik and her family live upstairs. She has bed and breakfast accommodation too, I can show you later. It's really beautiful. Nik's really clever Mum.' Samantha's tone carried a hint of pride.

'Stop it Sam.' Nicole waved the compliment away, but Samantha's words warmed her. She really would miss her, and Evie, when they left.

They dropped Tracy's bag into Samantha's apartment. They'd never used the second bedroom. Then they trooped upstairs where Robbie waited. He warmly welcomed Tracy and Nicole saw he had the heat on under the large pot on the stove.

'We've got soup for lunch, if that suits you Tracy. Sam and I thought we'd have lunch up here, then give you some time to settle in downstairs and take a walk around the property, if you like.' Nicole set out soup bowls while Robbie sliced homemade sourdough. 'Lucy is at school and Harry is at work, but you'll meet them later.'

'So beautiful.' Tracy turned around in the large living space, then walked to the window, looking out over the driveway.

Samantha moved to stand beside her, an arm around her waist. 'If you look to the left, Mum, you can see the Barrington Tops in the distance. They get snow sometimes. It's almost cold enough this week.'

Nicole noticed Evie was a bit unsure of her grandmother and Tracy was being careful not to overwhelm the little girl. 'Evie, you can open the toy box if you want, and show, um.' Nicole looked at Tracy and Samantha. They'd turned around. 'What should Evie call you, Tracy?'

Samantha giggled. 'You're not really old enough to be Grandma. Nanny?'

Tracy's eyes were overlarge as she considered the question.

She sat on the floor beside Evie, who had lifted out the farm set she liked to play with. 'Evie?' Tracy spoke softly but Evie looked at her straight away. 'I'm your grandmother. Mummy's mummy. Would you like to call me Grandma?'

Evie shook her head firmly. 'No. Woz has a Granny. You can't be Granny.'

'Alright.' Tracy looked at Samantha, unsure.

'Woz is Jamie's little boy. I told you how he helped me, that first night.' Samantha blushed. 'Woz and Evie are great friends.'

'That's lovely.' Tracy passed a cow to Evie. 'I'd like to meet your friend Woz. And his Granny.'

'And Jamie. He's the Daddy.'

'And Jamie.' Tracy agreed. 'Evie, my name is Tracy. You can call me Tracy if that's easier?'

'My name is Evie. It starts with E.' Evie set a family of pigs into a pen.

'Tracy starts with T.' Tracy pointed to the cow. 'I used to have a farm with cows, a bit like this one.'

'Tracy starts with Tee?' Evie looked up.

'Yes.'

'Can I call you Tee?' Evie gently lifted the cow from Tracy's hand and stood it just outside the pigpen.

'Of course. I like that. You can call me Tee. That will be my grandma name.' Nicole snort-laughed and Samantha looked delighted.

'The soup is ready.' Nicole brought them all to the table.

'I wanna sit beside Tee.' Evie pouted, a small frown line between her eyes.

'Of course. And I'll sit on your other side.' Samantha arranged herself with Evie between them.

But Evie wasn't finished. 'Woz will call you Tee as well.' And with an emphatic nod of her head, Evie picked up her soup spoon.

Robbie threw back his head, laughing loudly. 'That's the way Evie.' He winked at Tracy. 'Maybe I'll call her Tee, too.'

44

Samantha was grateful to have her mother stay and after Evie went to bed that first night, they sat up talking for hours. Samantha apologised for leaving the way she did, and for her treatment of Ian.

Her mum waved her words away. 'You were seventeen, Sam. You'd lost your Dad and I wasn't able to keep the contract on the farm.' She shook her head sadly. 'Then Ian came into our life. And while I wasn't looking to replace your father, Ian was kind and caring and offered us a home.' Tracy hung her head. 'I'm ashamed to tell you now that I didn't love him, when we first moved in. And I knew it was too soon, for both of us. But Sam, we had nowhere to go. I hadn't found work and we needed to move out of the house we were in.'

'Oh mum.' Samantha patted her shoulder. 'I kinda knew that. I understand now, but I didn't then. I'm sorry.' She considered her next words, ensuring they were gently spoken. 'But how did it end up for you, with Ian? You stayed with him.'

'He was a good man, Sam.' Tracy shook her head, her face anguished. 'He supported me through everything and I'm so grateful. But it wasn't until he died that I realised I'd loved him the whole time. He never asked me, he was always just happy we were together. But when he was gone, my heart hurt so much that I realised.'

'I'm sorry Mum.' Samantha touched Tracy's face gently. 'But perhaps he knew you loved him? Before you did?'

Tracy reached for a tissue and blew her nose. 'I think he did. His kids said as much at the funeral. I was grateful to hear it.'

'And the house Mum? Is it yours now?' Samantha didn't want to pry, but she needed to know if she and Evie were going to live there, later.

'It's half mine. Ian's half belongs to his children, but they only inherit if I sell it. Or when I die.' She looked up then, smiling. 'Did you know I've been working?'

Samantha frowned. 'You didn't mention it in your letters.'

'No. I don't think I did.' Tracy sipped her hot chocolate, the mug steaming. 'It was casual at first, at the dairy factory in the office. You know I always did the farm bookwork?' When Samantha nodded, she continued. 'Then it became part-time and it was good for me. Gave me a sense of independence. I helped Ian pay off the house mortgage a bit quicker. And I've got a bit put away.'

'I'm proud of you Mum. So you're, like, on holiday from your job to be here?' Samantha hadn't realised there might be a time limit for her visit.

'I've taken a week off, but it's no problem to extend it.' Tracy gazed at Samantha, so closely that she blinked. 'I was hoping I'd be able to bring you back with me. But I understand it may take longer. Maybe even months, before you can come to me.'

Sighing, Samantha fiddled with the little jar of sugar on the table. 'That's why I need to get my licence Mum, and find work here. And I really should move out.' She shook her head. 'Nicole has helped a lot of people. Women and children, like me and Evie. But we've been here over three months and I worry that I'm taking a room away from someone else in need.'

'She's a lovely woman. A good woman.' Tracy gazed around the apartment. 'It's cosy here, and you've been well looked after.'

'And I haven't paid for anything. But now that I have my identification documents I should be able to get my licence and maybe some government support while I look for work.'

Samantha felt her mouth turn upwards, she couldn't stop it if she tried. 'I've been helping with the bed and breakfast accommodation Nik has. You know, cleaning and laundry, so I've saved her some wages. She wanted to pay me, but I couldn't accept.'

'But if you had somewhere else to live, and transport, could you work here, for Nicole?' Tracy rubbed the side of the cup. Samantha could almost see the cogs turning in her head.

'I could. I would. And anything else I could get where Evie could be with me.' Samantha chewed her bottom lip. 'If I knew for sure she was safe, I'd even let her go to Kindy a couple of days a week, with Woz.'

'Ah, yes Woz. And his Granny. I'd love to meet them, while I'm here. And Douglas.' Picking up the empty mugs, Tracy moved to the sink, rinsing them quickly. She looked at her watch. 'It's been a long day Sam. I think I'll turn in.'

'Of course.' Samantha jumped up. 'Gosh, it's after ten. You must be exhausted.'

'May I have a peek at Evie before I go to bed? I'll be quiet.' Tracy was already tiptoeing to the bedroom door.

'Once she's asleep it would take a cannon to wake her.' Giggling, Samantha opened the door. The light from the living area fell across the bed. Evie was sleeping on her side, her hands under the pillow and long dark lashes on her soft cheek, her hair tumbled about her shoulders.

Tracy gazed at her, for what seemed like minutes. 'She's so beautiful', she whispered. They backed away and Samantha closed the bedroom door. Turning, she placed her hands on Samantha's cheeks. 'Just like you. After hearing how you were treated, all these years, I'm amazed you're so, I don't know the right word, together? Brave and strong, certainly. I'm proud of you. Your Dad would be too. And Ian.'

Hearing that, Samantha felt her chest expand. Happiness, and perhaps some pride in her actions, in spite of the disastrous decision that began it all. But her answer was simple. 'I had no choice. I'm a mother.'

———

SUNLIGHT FILTERED in through the blinds the next morning, letting Samantha know it was later than usual. She turned over, expecting to find Evie snuggled beside her, but the bed was empty. She hurriedly sat up, head cocked on one side, listening for her daughter. Then she heard it. Evie's giggles and her mother's softly spoken response. Samantha relaxed, then slid out of bed, following the sounds.

The other bedroom door was closed, but Evie's happy little voice was coming from within. Samantha cracked open the door and laughed out loud. Evie was in bed with Tracy, who was holding a picture book version of Black Beauty, reading aloud.

'Mummy!' Evie waved. 'I'm reading a book with Tee.'

'I can see that.' Samantha stepped closer and smiled down at both of them. 'That looks very cosy.'

Wriggling closer to Tracy, Evie patted the bed beside her. 'You can get in too, Mummy.' Samantha almost said no, she'd have a shower. But images of other mornings, when she was small, snuggling in bed with her mum. Reading and talking, waiting for her father to find them after milking the cows. Life was simple then. She was loved and feared nothing. In one gigantic bound Samantha leaped onto the bed and burrowed under the blankets too, smiling at her mother, with Evie between them.

———

THEY'D BARELY HAD breakfast and a walk around the property when Douglas arrived. They met for more than an hour and completed the application for government support, Medicare and Samantha's licence. Once she had a social security identification, Douglas could file for custody. They discussed going to the police to press charges for the abuse Samantha had experienced at her ex-partner's hands, but she wasn't keen and did not want to antagonise him.

Tracy wanted Adam to pay for what he'd done, but Nicole supported Samantha, and quietly suggested they take it in stages. And Douglas said they could 'keep their powder dry' in case they needed to do that later.

45

Samantha's mother had been here for two days, and Jamie wondered how it was going and what decisions they were making. He told himself he only had Samantha and Evie's best interests at heart, but deep down, he hoped they'd stay in the area. Sometimes, before he was fully awake in the morning, he imagined he could see something shining, just out of reach.

Inside his kitchen for a mid-morning cup of tea, Jamie checked his phone. No messages. Sipping his tea, the phone face up on the kitchen table, he ran through the jobs he needed to get done that week. He and his father had planned to move stock to new paddocks closer to Jamie's cottage. While it wasn't a muster and they didn't really need help, he had considered asking Samantha to come over. He thought she'd enjoy it. Actually, his mum had suggested it only yesterday, but when he'd told her about Samantha's mother coming, she'd given him a look and then shrugged. 'Oh. Well that's that, then.'

He wasn't really sure what she meant, but suspected it was about Samantha and Evie having somewhere to go. Back to Victoria.

Without giving it much thought, he picked up his phone, writing the text and hitting send.

> Hope it's lovely having your mum
> here. J.

He didn't expect an immediate response. He was sure she'd be busy.

> It's brilliant!! So much to tell you!
> We're at the café!

Jamie chuckled at her overuse of exclamation marks. She was excited. And rightly so. He was happy for her, and Evie. He was about to respond when another message popped through.

> How are you? Busy?

> Yes. Always. I'm a farmer, lol!

He hit send, then typed another message.

> Moving cattle tomorrow, was going
> to ask if you want to come? Not a
> big job.

There was no response and after twenty minutes he put the phone in his pocket, washed up his cup and went off to check the fence of the paddock by his house. He didn't want the heifers pushing through any weak spots.

By lunchtime he had checked the whole fence, and tightened up the wires in a couple of spots. His father had come by on his motorbike, inviting him to come up to the house for soup and toast. Jill was in town at a Council meeting.

Driving the old farm truck with the fencing gear in the back, he followed his Dad back to the homestead. Toeing off his boots on the back veranda, he stopped for a moment to pat the dogs. His phone beeped, but he left it in his pocket until he'd washed up in the laundry. Jamie walked through to the kitchen in his socks, the phone in his hand.

'Pumpkin, chilli and sweet corn soup, lad.' Ross held a ladle in one hand and a bowl in the other.

'My favourite Dad. Thanks.' Jamie busied himself buttering toast and helped carry everything to the table. He'd almost finished the soup when he remembered the phone. He picked it up, cocking an eyebrow at Ross.

'Go ahead son. I might put another slice in the toaster?'

'Yes please Dad. Thanks.' Jamie opened his phone.

> I'd love to help. Mum will watch Evie. Can you pick me up?

> Great. Thankyou. Is nine ok?

> Perfect. C U then.

Jamie grinned, just as his father plonked a plate of buttered toast between them. He jerked his chin, the question unspoken.

'Sam. She can help tomorrow. I'll pick her up at nine.'

Jamie picked up a piece of toast and made a show of taking a huge bite, not meeting his father's eyes.

'Good-o.' They ate in silence, until Ross cleared his throat. 'Um, your mother said something about Sam's mother coming here. Back from the dead.'

'Yes.' Jamie deliberately brightened his voice. 'It's great news. She'd been told her mother passed away. More than a year ago.' Jamie shook his head, his voice dropping. 'I can't begin to imagine what she's been through. But I know she was grieving her mother. Who does that Dad?'

'Bloke needs a good kick up the arse.' Ross had as much trouble understanding it as Jamie.

'More than a kick up the arse, Dad. He should be in jail.' Jamie carried the plates to the sink. 'And we don't know the half of it, I'm sure.' He wanted to say something else. Praise Samantha for her courage, at least. But didn't want his father to read too much into it.

'She's a good girl, that Sam. And Evie, well, she's a bright little button too.' Jamie was surprised. High praise from his father.

———

JAMIE DROPPED by the homestead next morning before driving over to get Samantha. His mum met him at the back door.

'Just Sam today, Jamie? Or her mother and little Evie too?'

'Just Sam, mum. We should be done by lunch time.' Jamie leaned across to kiss Jill on the cheek.

'Do you know how long her mother is staying? Would you like to invite them for morning tea tomorrow? No Kindy for Woz, we'll all be here. Nicole and Robbie too, if they're free?' Jill said the words casually enough, but Jamie wondered at her motivation. He knew she liked Sam, and Evie, but did she need to meet her mum? Especially if they'd be returning to Victoria soon enough.

'What's this about Mum? I don't know how long Tracy is staying.' His mother gave him a steely look and Jamie ducked his head. 'But I'll ask, okay.'

———

HE SAW them over by the horses as he drove in. From a distance Samantha and her mum looked alike, although Sam's hair was shorter. Evie saw him and waved madly from the top rail of the horse paddock. 'Jamie, Jamie!'

As he strode across to them, Evie scrambled down and ran to meet him, her arms up. He scooped her up and settled her on his hip. 'Hello Miss Evie. It's lovely to see you too.'

He felt a bit awkward, holding Evie, while her mother and grandmother looked on. But Samantha just grinned. 'Mum, this is Jamie Tait.' She nudged him. 'My mum, Tracy.'

Jamie wrangled Evie to his other hip and held his hand out. 'Lovely to meet you Tracy.'

Her hand was small, but her grip was firm. 'I'm delighted to meet you too, Jamie.'

Samantha took Evie from his arms, passing her to Tracy.

'You're having some time with Tee, Evie, while I help Jamie move his cattle.'

'I wanna help Jamie too.' Evie pouted.

'Um, not today Evie.' Samantha spoke soothingly, but Evie began to cry. Tracy patted Evie's back, mouthing to Samantha, 'just go, she'll be fine'.

Jamie cleared his throat. 'Evie?' She turned to him, tears on cheeks. 'Um, my um, er, Granny, wants you all to come tomorrow for morning tea. When Woz is there too.'

Sniffling, Evie seemed to consider this. 'No Woz today?'

'No Evie. He's at Kindy today. But if you come tomorrow, he'll be there to play with you.' Jamie tousled her hair, loving the way her face lit up when he mentioned Woz.

She snuggled against Tracy. 'And Tee can come too?'

Grinning, Jamie echoed her. 'Of course Tee can come. Granny will be there. And Nik and Robbie too, if they're free. It'll be a big morning tea at the homestead.'

Tracy took over. 'That sounds lovely, doesn't it Evie? Do you think we should bake something to take to Jamie's house tomorrow?'

Evie nodded vigorously. 'Cake. Chocolate cake.' She wriggled to get down, waved perfunctorily at her mother and Jamie, and tugged at Tracy's hand to lead her inside.

Samantha called out. 'Just check with Nik if we don't have all the fixings for cake, mum.' Tracy waved back, laughing over her shoulder.

Opening the passenger door of Jamie's car, Sam pointed to him, her face alive with mischief. 'To the horses, Jamie.'

'To the horses.' He chuckled as he slid into the driver's seat.

———

THEY CHATTED as they rode side by side along the far laneways. Ross had gone ahead on the motorbike to open gates. The dogs trotted beside them. Jamie noted how Samantha had knelt by each of the dogs before she mounted Misty, cradling their heads gently in her hands, speaking quietly to them. She had a gentle touch.

As they rode, Samantha caught him up on the news. About her mother and how she'd been lied to. At one point she stopped, her voice rough, choking back tears. But she continued and he built a picture of just how trapped and isolated she'd been. How her ex had controlled every aspect of her life. His admiration for her courage grew, and he told her so.

She blushed, very prettily, and he felt his heart give a lurch. *Stop it Jamie. Think of Deb. And after everything Sam's been through, she doesn't need complications.*

'I was thinking about that too, Jamie. Mum said something similar, um, about my fortitude.' She raised her eyebrows and he chuckled. 'And I think it was this.' She waved a hand towards the paddocks in front of them and the hills beyond.

Jamie was confused. 'This?'

'Growing up on a farm. Living this kind of life. It's embedded, you know? Part of our DNA maybe. Don't you think it gives us something others don't have? Like an inner strength?' She crinkled her nose. 'I'm not explaining it properly. But farming isn't easy. The weather, the threat of disease, the farm-gate prices fluctuating. It's not the life for everyone. You've got to have a certain, um, toughness.' She touched her chest. 'In here. And I think that's what kept me going.'

Jamie heard what she said, but his mind was racing. *She gets it. Sam really gets it.* After a moment he gazed at her steadily. 'It's all that Sam. You're all that.'

He didn't recall much of the conversation after that. They moved the cattle along the laneways, Ross going ahead at times, using the dogs to keep the mob together. They got to the larger home paddock and the cattle spread out, there were green shoots of grass everywhere. But Jamie needed to funnel them to one side, through another gate, and into the next paddock, closer to his cottage.

They had most of them through the gate, until a nearby bull bellowed. A couple of the heifers lifted their heads, sniffing the air. Two turned and pushed past him, racing towards the gate Ross hadn't yet closed. The bull was bellowing on the other side of the fence, his head in the air, weaving back and forth. *Damn. He'll go right though that fence.* Jamie spun Captain in a tight circle and galloped after them, while Samantha kept close to the mob. Ross was at the gate now, closing it.

With the dogs helping, Jamie trotted the heifers back. Samantha, moved out of the gateway to let them through. One ran through easily, Jamie was on her right flank, when the other turned and charged Samantha on Misty. But she held her ground, using her hands and heels to keep her horse steady. The beast spun again, towards the bull, still roaming back and forth along the fence line. Before Jamie could gallop after her, Samantha leaned forward on Misty and shot off, getting in front of the cow and waving her arms and whooping, which turned it around. It trotted back, flanks heaving, with Misty right on her tail.

Jamie dismounted and closed the gate. 'Well done, Sam.' He wanted to say more, but the bull was still causing a ruckus.

They rode across to Ross, who was astride the motorbike. 'We need to move the bull, he has their scent now.'

'Okay Dad. The small paddock on the other side of my place? Just for a couple of days? We can throw some hay in for him.' Jamie stood in the stirrups, looking back towards the paddock. Most of the cows had moved further in and were grazing.

'Yup.' Ross turned the bike, and dashed back the way they'd come in.

'Dad will open the gates to yard. We'll go ahead and put some hay in. He should be able to chase the bull though with the bike.' Jamie nudged Captain into a trot, and with Samantha alongside, the rode through to the shed closest to his home. She held the horses while he spread the hay out, and by that time the bull trotted in quite docilely.

'Time for a cuppa love, before you go home?' Ross tapped Samantha on the shoulder.

'A quick one, thank you.' She smiled warmly at his dad, who rode off on the bike, no doubt to put the kettle on and rummage around for biscuits.

As the rode past the cottage Samantha pointed to it. 'Is that a worker's cottage Jamie? It's well cared for.'

Jamie pulled Captain to a halt. Samantha turned Misty and came alongside him. 'No, Sam. That's my house. Me and Woz.'

He watched her eyebrows raise, and she stared at the front yard of the little house for a moment.

'It's so sweet.' She blushed. 'I'm sorry. I just assumed you lived at the main homestead. You know, being on your own with Woz.'

'I thought about it, after I lost Deb. And Scarlett. It may have been easier. But we'd made our home here, together.' He shrugged his shoulders. 'I'm luckier than some. Mum and Dad are close by. And they rattle around in the homestead now, it's too big for them really.' He nudged Captain, and they continued towards the stables. 'The cottage was built at the same time. Dad says from extra materials not used in the homestead. When I was growing up we had a farm manager living in it. But he retired when I finished school and I took over his job. But I didn't move into the cottage until I married Deb.'

They walked up to the homestead after unsaddling the horses and giving them a quick rub down. Samantha kicked off her boots. *Debbie's boots.* And followed him into the house.

Ross caught her eye as he poured her tea, 'You're very handy on that horse, Sam.'

'Thank you. And you pour a lovely cup of tea, Ross.' Her eyes twinkled and his father's face softened.

46

BEST. DAY. EVER. SHE DIDN'T SAY IT ALOUD, BUT SHE was bubbling over with happiness as Jamie drove her home. He seemed deep in thought, but in a good way. They were almost at Nicole's driveway when a car, sleek and black with tinted windows, drove past too fast, heading toward the mountains.

'They'll soon slow down. It changes to a gravel road a bit further on.' Jamie shook his head. 'Some drivers are…'

'Dickheads?' Samantha's tone was helpful and he snorted.

'Yup. Dickheads.' They looked at each other and laughed again.

Jamie parked beside Nicole's car and Evie skipped out of the house. 'We've made little chocolate cakes!' She had a splodge of chocolate on her jumper and a telltale stain on one side of her mouth.

Tracy followed. 'Chocolate muffins, Evie. They're for tomorrow, at Jamie's house.'

Evie took hold of Tracy's hand, saying seriously. 'But we had to try them. And I licked the wooden spoon.'

Samantha reached out, touching the corner of Evie's mouth. 'I can see some evidence of that, right here.' She spun around at a noise behind her. The black car that had whizzed by minutes before, was now cruising slowly along the driveway to the Old Courthouse. Nicole stepped out of the house, onto the veranda, her hand shading her eyes.

A shiver ran up Samantha's spine and she took Evie's hand, saying tersely. 'Let's wait over here by Nicole. You too Mum.' Jamie frowned at her words, then turned, taking a step towards the driver's side door as the car braked, scattering gravel from its back tires.

The man that stepped out wasn't familiar to Samantha, but he wore a three-piece suit. Just like Adam always did. Her heart began racing. He was large. Easily as big as Jamie. He had a big jaw and a broken nose. *He's found me. Fucking Adam's found me.* Samantha backed closer to the house. Nicole and Tracy stood beside her, and she pushed Evie a little bit behind their legs.

The big man approached, but Jamie stepped in front of him. *He knows. Jamie knows.* Samantha almost cried out then, but didn't want to distract him.

'Can I help you?' Jamie's rough tone was anything but helpful. She'd never heard him speak like that.

The big man nodded towards the women. 'We're here to pick up Sarah and Evie.' He was face to face with Jamie.

'There's no Sarah here. You're trespassing.' Jamie folded his arms across his chest and gestured to the car with his chin. 'Return to your vehicle and leave.'

Nicole opened the front door. 'Get inside Sam. You, Evie and Tracy. Lock yourselves inside.' She had her phone in her hand. 'I'm messaging Robbie. And calling the police.'

They scuttled inside and locked the apartment door. Tracy took Evie into the kitchen, but Samantha watched through the window. The big man hadn't backed off. She was frightened for Jamie. The passenger door opened and Samantha gasped. It was Adam. He walked towards Jamie.

Samantha hissed to her mother. 'Stay here. Keep Evie safe. Lock the door behind me.' She ran out through the door, pausing until she heard the lock click, then rushed out to the veranda to stand beside Nicole.

'Sarah!' Adam called out, his voice commanding. 'Fetch our daughter and come with me. Now!' He tried to walk to her, but Jamie stepped in front of him. Then, almost in slow motion, she saw the big man, standing side-on to Jamie, pull his arm back, his hand a fist.

'Jamie!' Samantha screamed. Jamie ducked, but not enough and the blow caught him on the shoulder. He reeled back, but came back with a punch of his own so fast she almost missed it. Jamie hit the man in the face. He staggered back a step, moved his head from side to side, then fell to the ground with a loud thump. Adam jumped back, shocked.

Jamie stood over the man on the ground, then called out to Nicole, his voice loud, but shaky. 'Call the police Nik. I think I've killed the bastard.'

Samantha gasped, bringing a hand to her mouth. 'Oh no!'

Adam pointed at her. 'This is your fault Sarah. You will be punished!'

He turned towards the car, but Jamie stepped in front of him, his words a low growl. 'Stay right where you are. I don't mind hitting you too.' Adam froze.

As he spoke, Robbie's work truck pulled in and Robbie and Harry leapt out. The police arrived next, with an ambulance behind them. It all happened so quickly, Samantha's head was spinning. Nicole led her to a chair on the veranda and sat with her, holding her shaking hand. One policeman came to speak to them, while another interviewed Jamie.

The paramedics were kneeling by the man Jamie had killed. One called out. 'He's alright. He's coming to.' *Not dead then. Knocked out.* Relief flooded her body. Not that she cared about the thug, but she didn't want Jamie to be in trouble.

And then Douglas was there, talking with the police. She hadn't even seen his car. The large man was loaded into the ambulance, but the paramedics said it was 'precautionary'.

Douglas asked them to move inside, it was warmer. Samantha looked through the window again before fetching Tracy and Evie. Adam was in handcuffs, standing by the police car. Her eyes widened.

It was decided Tracy and Evie would remain in the apartment while Samantha, Jamie, Nicole and Douglas went upstairs with one police officer. Robbie and Harry busied themselves outside, but said they'd stay close by until the police had left. Another car drove in, more police. One of them was a woman in plain clothes.

Nicole tended Jamie's hand, he'd scraped his knuckles and

Samantha suspected a finger was broken. But he refused to go to hospital to have it looked at until he knew Samantha and Evie were safe. *Bless you Jamie.*

After tending to Jamie, Nicole began feeding them. Cups of tea, fresh buttered bread, scones. Robbie and Harry came in, ate something, and left again. Samantha wondered if her mum and Evie were okay. But she knew her mother would make lunch for them, and keep Evie occupied.

The policewoman took Samantha down to Nicole's office, to speak to her alone. It was exhausting, but Samantha tried to keep her voice even and stick to the facts. At one point Douglas came downstairs too, providing information he'd uncovered. Samantha hadn't really been married. Evie's birth was never registered.

Later, when the police had left, Douglas advised there would be more interviews and a closed-door custody hearing, but he was sure it would be alright. To Samantha's delight, the police charged Adam and his accomplice with trespassing and attempted kidnapping. Jamie acted in self-defence and provided protection for the women and children. He would not be charged.

It was dark when Jamie left. He'd spoken to his parents during the afternoon, and they were taking care of Warwick. Samantha walked out to the car with him.

'What a day.' She shook her head. 'Jamie, thank you, for what you did for us. I'll never forget it.' A tear slid down her face. 'I keep thinking, what if we hadn't come home when we did. What if he had taken Evie! He would have hurt Mum to do it. I know him.'

Jamie gathered her into his arms and it seemed the most natural thing in the world. 'I'm glad I was here. You're safe now.' He straightened his arms and kissed the top of her head. 'And it's brought everything to a head. Your situation. Douglas said it's saved months of legal work.'

'Darling Douglas. And Nik. And you Jamie. Bless you.' She looked up at him. 'And Robbie and Harry. They would have backed you up without hesitation.'

'It's not a bad place is it? Barrington?' Jamie's voice sounded uncertain.

'It's the best place, Jamie.' She smiled at him. 'You had better go. Your parents will want to know what happened here, and Woz will be ready for bed.'

'Alright.' He released her, but Samantha sensed he was reluctant. A small knot of worry gnawed at her insides.

Later, after Evie was asleep and she could hear soft snores form the other bedroom, Samantha lay awake. She cried silently. *She was free, but her life was still complicated.*

47

Barrington Book Club & Reader Festival Update (Two months to Festival)
Attendance: Judith, Millie, Hanna, Melanie, Rose, Rachael, Meggie, Harriet & Nicole
Apologies: Laura, Kristen
Book: *Woodstock* by Michelle Montebello

Settling herself at their usual table, Rose reached for the wine. 'Has Samantha made plans to go back to Victoria, Nik? What's the next step for her?'

'Of all the women I've had come through my doors, I've never met one stronger than Samantha, yet she's probably the youngest. Seeing that man in action, how threatening he was.' Nicole shook her head. 'And Jamie Tait is *one good man*. But in answer to your questions, yes, I think she will go back to Victoria. Tracy left last week, she has a part-time job down there. But

Sam and Evie need to stay until their legal matters are sorted, and that might take a couple of months yet.'

'And how is she, generally?' Rose passed the wine bottle down to Judith.

'Going from strength to strength. She has her licence now. And a little bit of government support. Douglas thinks she may get a payout, but that could take a while.' Nicole grimaced and fiddled with the book in front of her. 'But what she really wants, is work. She'd like to move out. Not because she doesn't like it, but she knows there are others needing help and a place to stay.'

'But renting something, short term, is not easy.' Meggie rested her chin on her fingers.

'I know. She knows. But there it is. If she moves out, she'll accept payment to help me with the bed and breakfast business.' Nicole sighed.

'She did another day of cattle work with Jamie, didn't she?' Rose frowned, trying to remember the details.

'She did. *That* morning.'

Rachael cleared her throat. 'I was chatting about it with Jill only yesterday. Jamie's hand is on the mend, although he dislocated a finger. Jill told me that Ross thinks the world of her. Of Sam. That she's a real farm-girl. Handy, he said.' Rachael used her fingers to make quotation marks in the air when she said "handy".

'He's not one for praise.' Rose was surprised. Ross rarely commented.

'I thought she might come tonight to book club?' Judith popped a salmon blini in her mouth.

'I asked her.' Nicole passed the platter along to Hanna. 'But I think she's reluctant to build more friendships, knowing she'll leave in a couple of months. It's the same for housing and work, I guess.'

'I have a question. How did her ex know she was here, in Barrington?' Rose peered at Nicole over her glass.

'Um. It was kind of our fault. The festival.' Nicole wrinkled her nose.

Rose was shocked. 'The festival?'

'Yes. The *teasers* that have been playing on the news. Someone recognised Evie in the bookshop. It was just a quick glimpse of her in the bean bag, but her voice as well, I think. The police had it directly from him, in his statement.'

'Oh no!' Meggie's eyes were wide. 'I'm so sorry!'

Nicole reached her hand over, touching Meggie gently on the arm. 'Don't be, it brought it to a head.'

'But Jamie was injured. And when I think of what could have happened if he hadn't been there.' Meggie looked distraught.

'Darling Meggie. Jamie *was* there. It's okay.' Rose opened her laptop, wanting to change the subject. 'What's first? The book or the festival?'

'The book!' Hanna squeaked, and Rose grinned. She already knew how much Hanna had loved this one, she'd talked about it a couple of days ago when Rose was ordering coffee. 'Michelle Montebello does dual timelines really well. Honestly, this story, you'd think she was American.'

'Steve and I have been thinking about a trip to the States. Not just now, but it's on our bucket list. And now I want to go to the Woodstock site. I know it's just a field. And that whole soundtrack, the Woodstock one, we grew up with it.' Rachael held up the book. 'And the cover is beautiful. This one is a keeper.'

'Wait until you see the special editions she is bringing to the festival.' Judith waggled her eyebrows. 'Get in quick, I say.'

'Well I've been there. To Max Yasgur's dairy farm.' Meggie looked smug. 'And I could picture the festival, in this book. It was a five-star read for me.'

'And me.'

'Oh, me too.'

Rose chuckled. They'd never chosen a book the whole group didn't love. 'Alright team, onto the Festival. Everything is locked in, authors confirmed.' She turned to Millie. 'You and your team have the catering sorted, but I haven't had confirmation from Finn, regarding the bar service at the opening and the author signing event.'

Rolling her eyes, Milie chuckled. 'Oh, he's organised. He and Lucas. And my Matty is coming up for the weekend to help. I'll ask Finn to confirm the details with you Rose.'

'No. He has confirmed.' Meggie turned to Rose. 'Sorry, I've been chatting to him, I meant to email you.'

'All good.' Rose consulted her spreadsheet. 'Rachael, the Council assistance? Is that locked in?'

'Yes it is. And the service clubs helping with parking, bus shuttles from the train station and the market day sausage sizzle. We've got local entertainers and stall holders lined up too, over at the park.' Rachael passed some notes to Rose. 'I'll email these, but in case you need a hard copy.'

'Thanks Rach.' Rose quickly scanned through her To Do list. 'Honestly, we're doing better than expected. Kristen is managing the grant funding documents, she shot me an email yesterday.' Rose looked up. 'Where is Kristen tonight, by the way?'

Rose caught the look that passed between Judith and Hanna. 'Don't answer that, she's up to date with her festival tasks.'

Hanna giggled. 'Callum asked her to an agricultural field day, down near Albury.'

'Oh. The Henty Field Days. Closer to Wagga, I think.' Rose murmured. 'Cute.'

'Yes. Cute indeed. And Harry's a bit put out.' Hanna laughed.

'Harry? Why?' Rose was curious.

'He went with Callum last year. Boys break. Had a great time.' Hanna covered her mouth, still giggling. 'Callum said he'd booked accommodation for Henty and Harry assumed he'd go with him. When Callum said Kristen was going, Harry got the message. But he grumbled and said that Callum should organise a romantic weekend somewhere else with Kristen, not drag her along to a man-thing.'

'A man-thing.' Rose chuckled. 'I dare him to say that to Laura, or Jill Tait.'

Millie brought out a tray of sweets – various slices cut into bite-size pieces, and they chatted generally as they finished their wine and prepared to head home.

'Next month's book? Any suggestions?' Rose turned to Judith. 'You've got your finger on the pulse, Judith.'

'I do have a suggestion. It's a new one by Phillipa Nefri Clark.' She tapped on her phone for a moment, then held it up to show an image of the cover. 'Not her crime series. This is a small-town historical mystery called *The Lost Girl of Seahaven*. I have stock coming in this week.'

'Oh, I love the *Temple River Series* and it can be read as a stand-alone. It's a yes from me.' Hanna picked up her phone, clicked a few times then grinned. 'Downloaded.'

'Everyone agreed?' Rose knew they'd all agree, but she liked to ask. 'Message us all when the paperbacks are in, please Judith.'

Rose strolled to her car with Nicole. Judith and Rachael were just ahead, walking home together. The others were helping Millie and Hanna tidy up. 'About Jamie, Nik?'

'Yes?'

'How he was, when Sam's ex, and company, arrived.' Rose shook her head, frowning. 'I've known him my whole life. I honestly can't see him being aggressive, under any circumstances.'

'I know what you mean, Rose. I feel the same about Robbie. But when he and Harry arrived and saw what was going on, they were ready to jump in too. It's more of a protective mechanism, I think, than any real aggression. But there was no way Jamie was letting them take Samantha and Evie.'

Rose leaned against her car, legs crossed at the ankles. 'Um, I've been wondering, Nik.' She was really uncomfortable, but needed to go on. 'About Jamie and Sam? Do you think?' She couldn't articulate her thoughts and an image of Debbie looking up at Jamie on their wedding day flashed through her mind.

Nicole laid a hand on Rose's shoulder and shook her head. 'There's something there. Friendship on Samantha's part and perhaps a love of the land. Jamie's hard to read, but what I see, mostly, is an eagerness to protect Sam and Evie.' Nicole looked at the sky for a moment. 'There's something else. About Sam.'

48

Nicole was torn. She didn't want to abuse Samantha's trust, but she wanted to ease Rose's mind.

'What about Sam?' Rose had straightened, her voice quiet.

'It's personal.' Nicole breathed in through her nose. 'You know she was abused, emotionally and physically?'

'Not exactly.' The words were whispered, and Rose raised a hand to her face, her eyes anguished.

'He beat her, many times. But he also burnt her, with cigarettes.' Nicole looked away. The thought of the pain Samantha experienced bringing tears to her eyes. She turned, and looked directly at Rose. 'She was recovering from burns. Very personal burns, when she arrived here.'

'Oh god! Poor Sam.' Rose wiped a tear away, whispering, 'she's so lovely and a great mum. I can't bear to think of it.'

'It's one of the reasons I think it will take her a long time, to trust, any sort of intimacy. If ever.' Nicole stepped back. 'I'm pretty sure she's just focussing on starting over and building a safe and happy life for Evie. But I hope Jamie isn't emotionally invested, *in that way*, as I just can't see *that* working anytime soon.'

Nicole sat in her car for a moment, after Rose drove away. Maybe she needed to check in with Samantha about *that*.

———

SAMANTHA HELPED every day with the housekeeping for the accommodation. Now that she had her licence, Nicole offered her car so she could drive into town when she wanted. She'd talked about wanting to take Evie to have a look at the Kindy, but in the same breath talked herself out of it because she was leaving soon.

'I hope I'm still here for the Festival. I'd love to help, if I can.' Samantha peered in the mirror behind the laundry door. She patted her hair, now growing out of the home-made pixie cut. It looked healthy to Nicole, but had no real shape.

'Maybe you should pop into town and get your hair cut Sam? Properly this time, although you did a good job yourself.' Not sure if Samantha was self-conscious, Nicole tried to sound casual.

'I liked it short. But it's growing out a bit wild.' Samantha turned her head from side to side, looking in the mirror. 'Mum put some money into the bank for me, and I've received a government payment too. I can afford to go to the hairdresser.' She hesitated.

'What is it Sam?' Nicole kept her voice soft, wanting to help.

'I haven't had my hair cut. Professionally. Since I left home.' Samantha shook her head. 'At the compound I just trimmed the bottom every now and again. And I had to keep it blonde.' She touched her hair again. 'It was so dry and brittle, from the bleaching. But cutting it short has been good for it.' She grinned. 'And I like it short.'

'It suits you Sam. You're very pretty, you know.' Nicole watched the younger woman's face.

Samantha's eyes grew wide. 'I haven't thought of myself as pretty. For a long time.' She turned away from the mirror.

'Does it bother you, Sam. That someone, a man, may think you're pretty?' Nicole waited while Samantha thought about it.

'It would be nice to be thought pretty.' She suddenly clapped both hands over her face. 'But, oh Nik. I don't want. You know.' She peeked between her fingers. 'Attention. Not *that* sort of attention.'

Placing an arm around her shoulders, Nicole gave her young friend a squeeze. 'What about from Jamie?' She had to ask.

'Jamie?' Samantha looked more distressed. 'But he's grieving. His beautiful wife that everyone here loved!' She shook her head. 'I've seen photos of Debbie. Jamie would never look at me in that way.'

Nicole squeezed her shoulders again, and segued back to the hairdresser. 'How about I see if I can get you in with the hairdresser I use?'

'Yes. Alright, thank you Nik.' Samantha seemed subdued.

Nicole went to her office to call the hairdresser. But what she took away from the conversation was that Samantha didn't want to attract anyone. Except Jamie, who she thought was beyond her reach.

49

———

Jamie stood in front of his mother, flabbergasted by her words. 'You want what?'

'Your father and I would like to offer Samantha and Evie a home here, with us. You said yourself it might take until the end of the year for her situation to be fully resolved. And I heard on the grapevine that Nicole has had to refer a couple of women in similar situations to Samantha, to other assistance.' Jill had her hands on her hips.

'I didn't know that.' He felt chastened. He had no idea there were so many women in need of assistance. What a sheltered life he'd led.

'We have room here, as you know. There are three unused bedrooms and the living area you used when you lived at home. There's a television in there and your father said we could put a small fridge and kettle and toaster in too. And she'd have the main bathroom. We only use the ensuite ourselves. But she'd have to share the kitchen, although I'd invite her to take her meals with us, if it works for her.'

His mother softened her tone. 'Honestly Jamie, it was your father's idea. He's very taken with her.'

'And when her mother comes to visit?' Jamie knew Tracy would be back in a few weeks, and the time after that she'd probably drive up, to take them home with her.

'Tracy is very welcome here too. Of course she is.' Jill was waiting for his response.

'Do you want *me* to ask her?' Jamie looked at his mother incredulously. *Surely not.*

'No Jamie. But I didn't want to extend the invitation without discussing it with you.' She relaxed her stance.

'And do you have a plan? To ask her, I mean?' Jamie reached out, pulling his mother in to a bear hug. 'It's very kind of you. And Dad.' He leaned back and searched his mother's face for a moment. 'But don't be offended if she says no. She's been through a lot.'

'She's coming here this afternoon. Just her and Evie. She's driving Nicole's car.' His mum sounded quite proud of that. In fact, he was too. Sometimes, when he closed his eyes, he could still see her terrified expression, caught in his headlights that very first night. Samantha had come a long way I just a few months.

'Would you like me to be here? When she comes today?' Jamie wanted to make sure staying with his parents was what *Samantha wanted.* He didn't want her to be bulldozed by his mother. Jill could be quite domineering at times.

'Yes. Of course. Can you pick Woz up first? Sam and Evie

will be here at three.' Jill moved away, flicking the jug on. 'That's your father now. Would you like to stay for a cuppa?'

'Thanks Mum. But I've got a bit to do today. I'll see you at three. Do you need anything from town?' Jamie walked through the back of the house, bending down to put his boots on once he was outside. His father was taking his off.

'No thank you Jamie.' Jill smiled at Ross. 'Tea will be ready in a jiff.'

50

THE HAIRDRESSER WAS LOVELY. SHE LET EVIE SIT ON Samantha's lap at the basin, then gave her pencils and paper and her own little chair during the haircut. It didn't take long and looked really good. Better than her own first attempt. The hairdresser said it was a bit *Audrey Hepburn* and Samantha saw herself go bright red in the mirror. Harry Stewart had told her that once, too.

It was only two-thirty and Samantha contemplated going over to the book shop for twenty minutes, but she worried that Evie would resist leaving after such a short time. She was digging her new purse out, the one her mum had bought for her, when the hairdresser glanced at Evie. 'I could give Evie a trim too, if you like. Will only take ten minutes.'

Samantha looked at Evie. It was a bit uneven at the back. But she was being careful with her money too. 'Um, do you think you could do it that quickly? And, er, how much extra?'

'No charge. She's been such a good girl today, and I don't have another client until three. I'd love to just neaten it up a bit.' The hairdresser leaned over Evie. 'Would you like a haircut too Evie?'

Evie moved over to the chair straight away. 'Yes please.' Then she held her little hand up to her shoulders. 'Not as short as Mummies. But to here.'

'Alright Evie.' The hairdresser sought confirmation from Samantha, then began to cut. Evie chatted away the whole time and Samantha loved how she enjoyed the experience. Her very first cut by a proper hairdresser.

Evie's hair was brown-with-honey-flecks and wavy, and sat just below her shoulders in a relaxed bob, with a slightly shorter side fringe. Samantha put her hand to her mouth, then leaned down with her face next to her daughter's. 'She looks so grown up.'

'She looks like you, Samantha.'

Still smiling, Samantha drove them out to Jamie's farm. His mother had invited them and she was more than a little bit pleased. Their property was beautiful. And their horses. And dogs. And cattle. She laughed.

'What's funny Mummy?' Evie laughed too.

'Um, I wonder if Jamie will know us with our new haircuts?'

'Don't be silly Mummy, we're still the same.'

Parking Nicole's car carefully beside Jamie's, Samantha helped Evie out of the back seat.

'Evie! Hello Evie!' Warwick waved from the front veranda.

Evie charged up the steps. 'Hello Woz. Wanna play farms?'

Warwick dragged her over to a long bench seat that may have been an old church pew. 'Take your boots off.' Evie sat down, pulled off her boots, then ran around the veranda behind Warwick, heading for the back door, no doubt.

'Hello Jill.' Samantha felt a bit shy. 'Thank you for inviting us.'

'You're very welcome Sam.' Jill put Samantha's arm through hers and led her around the back. 'Your haircut suits you. Evie's is lovely too.'

'Oh. We've only just.' Samantha was a bit tongue tied. 'Evie's very first cut, you know, by a hairdresser.'

Jamie and Ross were at the back door, taking their boots off. Ross smiled at her warmly and murmured, 'nice to see you, lass.'

But Jamie. He stared at her for what seemed like minutes, before clearing his throat and saying hello. Jill followed Ross inside, but Samantha waited for Jamie. 'I really like your hair, Sam.' He found his voice. 'It's very pretty.'

She blushed, put her head down and walked inside. He was so close behind her that she imagined she could feel his body heat. She knew it was nonsense, but felt flustered.

The children were already playing with the farm set on the rug. Ross was at the head of the table and beckoned Samantha to sit beside him. She was surprised and pleased to see Jamie helping his mother with the tea things in the kitchen. Jill let the children have their biscuits on the rug. She laughed, and told Samantha, 'that rug's seen worse than a few biscuit crumbs.'

'It's had orphan lambs by the fire. We took it in turns to bottle feed them in the night.' Jamie chuckled as he spoke and she could picture him, when he was young like Warwick, helping to feed the lambs.

'And one of our best kelpies whelped right there. It was freezing out and Ross brought her in, knowing she would drop the pups in the night.' Jill laughed and Samantha immersed herself in the strong sense of family that radiated from them.

'Five.' Ross hadn't spoken until that moment.

Samantha looked at him, confused for a moment. Then it dawned on her. 'Five? Five pups. All healthy?'

'All good ones, that litter.' He sipped his tea.

'Samantha, would you like to see the rest of the house?' Jill's words surprised her. But she nodded enthusiastically. 'I'd love to. You have such a beautiful home.'

'Jamie, can you give Sam a tour of the house? I'm going to boil the jug again.' Jill shooed them away and Samantha followed Jamie though a door into a large living area.

'The main lounge.' He stood in the middle of the room while Samantha walked across to an old-fashioned bureau, where dozens of photographs stood in frames of different shapes and sizes. She could see Jamie as a child. And he had a big brother in the pictures. He'd never mentioned a brother. She looked at him, one hand on a frame.

'A long story. Not a good one, really.'

Samantha nodded and moved on. She didn't want to spoil the relaxed tone of the afternoon. She felt sure he'd tell her about his brother, one day.

They moved into a hallway and peeked through a door. 'My parents room. They turned another bedroom into a sitting room and ensuite, years ago.' A long hallway with a study and three more bedrooms, then another lounge.

'This was our games room, back in the day.' It was pretty, she thought. Smaller than the main lounge, and cosy.

Another door led to a bathroom with a shower, basin and enormous claw-foot bathtub.

Samantha pointed to the bath. 'The original?'

'Yup. It's a big deep bath. I've soaked in it more than once after a day mustering cattle.' An image of Jamie in the bath flitted through her head and she quickly drew back.

'It's a big house. I love the high ceilings and timber floors. And all the rugs.' She turned around in the pretty lounge. 'It's a lot of work for your mum, though.'

'It is. And she's a Councillor now too, so she has less time these days. I think they pretty much close these rooms up and just use the ones at the front, most of the time.' Jamie returned to the hallway. 'They have a little bed in their sitting room for Woz, if he sleeps over. But he'll have a room of his own here, when he's older.'

They returned to the table. Samantha accepted a second cup of tea. 'Your home is gorgeous Jill. And very big.'

'Too big.' Ross reached for another biscuit. Jill raised her eyebrows.

'Too much sugar, Ross.'

'Bah.' He ate it anyway.

Jill turned to Samantha. 'We want to ask you, Sam, if you and Evie would like to move in here. With us?' Samantha blinked. *Had she heard Jill properly?* She looked at Ross.

He placed his giant paw over her hand, his voice gravelly. 'We've got room. You can see that.'

Still bewildered, she looked at Jamie.

'Mum and Dad are offering you a place to live, Sam. You and Evie. And Tracy, when she's here. The three bedrooms and living area you just saw aren't being used. And the big bathroom.' Jamie paused. 'Until you have your matters sorted, anyway.'

'As long as you like, love.' Ross reached for another biscuit and Jill gave him a look. He withdrew his hand.

'We know you'd like a bit of independence. We can put a kitchenette, of sorts, in the back lounge. But you'd have to share the kitchen with us.' Jill's words were warm. Samantha tried to smile. She was processing this startling new option.

'You'd eat with us, love.' Ross nodded, as if that settled everything.

Jamie smiled at her from across the table. 'It will free Nicole's accommodation up. And she has work for you too, a couple of days a week, if you want it.'

'How? What?' Samantha was getting her head around being here, on the farm, as an option. She sucked in a breath and started again. 'I love it here. Your farm. The house.' She turned to Ross. 'And I can help. I'll earn my keep. With the cattle, farm work, anything you need.' Then she looked at Jill. 'And share the cooking. Help with the house.' Her eyes were shining. She gazed at Jamie. 'And you too Jamie. Anything you need. I can help.'

'Good.' Ross stood up. 'That's settled.' He leaned over and

kissed Samantha on the cheek. 'I'm going to check the heifers.' And he was gone.

Samantha pushed her chair back and began clearing the table. Jill put her hand out, stopping her. 'You're not here to work. You and Evie are welcome in our home. As family. We all do our bit, but Sam, that's not why we've invited you.'

Samantha waited, glancing at Jamie then back to Jill. 'We like you, Sam. And Evie. Stay with us and see if you like it here.' Samantha nodded and Jill enveloped her in hug, before saying to the children, 'come and help me look for eggs. The chooks have been laying them in strange places lately.'

'Okay Granny.' Warwick and Evie followed Jill from the room and Samantha looked at Jamie.

'Dad doesn't say much. But it was his idea to ask you to come here. But Sam, there's no pressure. If you're uncomfortable in any way...' She held her hand up to his mouth.

'I love your Dad. He reminds me of mine. Thank you. I'll talk to Nicole, and come tomorrow if that's alright.' She grinned. 'But I'd like to see your mum try to stop me from working. On the farm and in the house.'

Jamie hugged her quickly. 'That's the spirit.' Then he let her go.

51

'Hello Judith. Join me.' Steve beckoned her over and Judith happily complied.

'Hi Steve, thank you.' Judith, coffee in hand, slid into the seat he offered. 'How are you? I read in the paper that train services to Barrington will continue, so that's good news.'

'Thanks to you, Judith.' Steve leaned back, and she noticed for the first time that he had streaks of grey through his hair and a lot of fine lines around his eyes when he smiled. 'The Book-Lover packages have been well subscribed and in-town accommodation mid-week bookings have increased. And now we have a new problem.'

She didn't envy his role as Mayor, not one bit. 'What's that Steve?'

'The whole town is booked out for the Festival, even the days before and after. We're opening up the showgrounds for caravans, RVs and camping too.' He shook his head. 'Who knew, hey? We've got planning applications in from a couple of farmers to approve temporary camping facilities, plus an application for resort-type accommodation behind the Barrington General Store.'

Judith frowned. 'But that's good news too, isn't it?'

'It is, but the flow on is that we need to hire another planner and an extra person in the tourism and communications team. We don't have budget, so we're having to juggle things around.' He brought a hand to his forehead in mock exhaustion, then grinned. 'It's brilliant, actually. Barrington is one of the few small towns that's growing. And we're up for a tourism award.'

Relaxing, Judith chuckled. 'I read that in the paper too. That we're up for an award. And I saw it on social media. I voted.'

'Excellent.' Steve sipped his coffee and glanced around the cafe. It was close to lunchtime and already busy. 'Rachael's out at the farm today. Jamie's farm. I'm heading out there this afternoon.'

'Oh? Rachael swapped her shift at the bookshop, but didn't mention that.' Judith waited.

'Samantha and Evie are moving into the homestead with Jill and Ross, you know, to free up Nik's place. For others, if needed.' Steve twitched his lips. Judith had never seen him look unsure.

'I hadn't heard that.' Judith felt there was more to it, but didn't want to speculate.

'It was Ross's idea, Rachael said. He likes them, Samantha and Evie. She helped with the cattle a couple of times. A real farm-girl, he says.' Steve tapped the table with his fingers.

'Is there something bothering you, Steve? About this?' Judith sipped her coffee.

'Not exactly. I haven't met her. Sam. Or Evie.' He sighed. 'Jamie has featured large in their lives since they came here. From that first night.' He gave Judith a questioning look 'You met her that night too. What do you think of her, Judith?'

'I like her. A lot. For a bunch of reasons, Steve.' Judith thought about her next words. 'She's young, but courageous. I don't know the details, but she's been through a lot, and protected Evie all the way through. The child is a delight. A bit shy to start with, but I suspect she's almost forgotten her earlier life. But the thing that strikes me most, with Sam, is her sense of right and wrong. I expect that was instilled from a young age, but she's not looking for handouts. She is grateful for the help she's received here, but she's determined to be independent and support herself and Evie.' Judith leaned forward, her elbows on the small table between them. 'What does Rachael think?'

'Honestly? She was guarded at first, but she's met her a few times now and likes her too. Very much.'

Judith finished her coffee, but said her next words quietly. 'Is it Jamie you're thinking of? And Warwick?'

Steve grimaced. 'Am I so obvious?' He sighed heavily. 'I have trouble seeing Jamie with anyone but our Debbie. I'm wondering if Samantha.' He stopped suddenly and blew his nose, turning away from Judith slightly. When he looked at her again his eyes were shiny with unshed tears and Judith placed a hand gently over his for a brief moment. 'If Samantha, may, one day, replace our girl.'

'No one will ever replace Debbie. And she'll never be

forgotten.' Judith shook her head, her tone gentle. 'And there's a chance Samantha has experienced, um, too much, to trust again. But if she did, wouldn't Jamie be a good choice? He's young Steve, he'll always grieve Debbie, but that doesn't mean he can't live a full life with someone else, if it works out.'

Steve stared at her, taking it in. He slowly got to his feet. 'Thank you Judith. I need to reserve judgement and meet this young woman today with an open mind, don't I?'

Judith pushed her chair back and smiled. 'May I give the Mayor a hug?'

He laughed and his face relaxed with all those tiny laugh lines on display. 'Hug away, Judith.' He squeezed her quickly, whispered 'thank you', and left.

52

Jamie saw Nicole's car arrive at the homestead mid-morning, but he decided to keep away and let Samantha settle in with his Mum's help, and Nicole's. With Woz at Kindy, Jamie was able to work on the bull paddock fence. Most of the wires needed straining, and the top wire needed to be replaced. He'd only just started when his father arrived on the motorbike, with BlueDog sitting on the tray behind him, tongue lolling out in the wind. Jamie straightened and called the dog to him.

'Replacing the top wire. The others just need straining.' Jamie always spoke to Ross in shorthand. His father grunted a response and lifted a roll of new wire from the back of Jamie's work truck.

They toiled in silence for more than an hour, the spring sunshine warming them. The old top wire had been removed and Jamie walked the length of the fence, unrolling the new wire on the ground as he went.

'Cold drink Dad?' Jamie wiped an arm across his forehead and poured water from his cooler, handing it to his father before he gave a response. He poured another for himself and leaned against the vehicle.

Ross jerked his head toward the homestead. 'A gaggle of geese up there.'

Jamie chuckled. Too many women in one place for his old man. 'I imagine Nicole will leave soon.'

'Rachael's picking Woz up today. With Steve, they'll be here at three.'

Jamie was surprised. Steve coming too. Why? He gave his father a look, the question unasked.

'Jill said he hasn't met our Sam yet. Thought it best.' Jamie chuckled inwardly at his father's easy affection for Samantha. *Our Sam*. He'd really taken to her.

'Okay. Because she'll be around Woz?' Jamie still didn't get it. Surely Steve would know his parents wouldn't invite just anyone into their home. Their grandson was safe.

'Because she'll be around you, son.' Ross stared at him hard and Jamie swallowed. *Around me? What? Do they think he and Sam are something?*

'She's been hurt, Dad. Before.' Jamie looked away, wondering, not for the first time, exactly how she'd been hurt. He couldn't imagine. 'I don't expect, um.' He stopped. 'She just needs to be safe. Get on her feet. And she'll probably be back in Victoria by the end of the year.'

'She's a strong lass, son.' His father lifted the wire and jerked his head toward the fence. Jamie said no more, and they worked until his father announced it was time for lunch. 'Coming up to the big house?'

'Nah, Dad. I'll have something at mine.' Jamie watched his father ride away before he walked the short distance to his cottage. He prepared a toasted ham sandwich and thought about his father's words. Yes, he liked Samantha, and adored little Evie. But he hadn't thought beyond their safety. And she had a home to go to, when the time was right. He shook his head. Even if there was spark of interest there, it wasn't simple. He still thought of Debbie every day. *He'd always love Debbie.*

JAMIE AND ROSS arrived at the house a bit after three. They'd finished the fence but needed to clean themselves up before going inside. They kicked their boots off and shared a bar of soap over the laundry trough. Jamie could hear voices inside.

Warwick appeared in the doorway from the kitchen. 'Daddy! Evie's here! There's cake.' He disappeared and Jamie cocked his head at his father.

Ross nudged Jamie with his shoulder. 'There's cake.'

'I'm all for cake.' Jamie followed him inside, trying not to laugh out loud. He said hello to his Mum and Samantha, kissed Rachael on the cheek and shook Steve's hand before sitting at the kitchen table. Samantha bustled around, helping Jill carry cups and saucers and cake plates to the table. She wore one of his mother's oversize aprons over jeans and a blouse. *So cute.* He thought it, but wouldn't say it.

He'd barely sat when Warwick and Evie appeared at the table. 'Where will I sit?' Woz had his hands on his hips.

'You can sit on the rug, Woz.' Jill had two small chairs already set out.

'No.' He climbed up on Steve's lap and made himself comfortable. 'I share with Poppy.'

Steve looked delighted and tousled his grandson's hair with one hand. 'Carrot cake or chocolate cake, Woz?'

'Chocolate.'

Evie looked uncertain and Samantha hadn't sat down yet. She sidled around to Jamie and looked up at him. He couldn't refuse her big brown eyes. He slipped an arm around her and lifted her lightly onto his lap.

'Carrot cake please Jamie. With cream.' He reached for the cake and cut a piece, sliding it across to the plate in front of him. All conversation had stopped and he could feel their eyes on him. Especially Steve's. But Evie was a child and had no idea about the complex relationships in the room. He passed her the cream dish and let her scoop two huge spoons of creamy goodness onto the piece of cake. She reached for the little cake spoon, handing the cake fork to Jamie. Blinking up at him, she said 'go!'

Jamie laughed out loud and dug in with his fork. Evie wrangled a big piece onto her spoon and into her mouth, leaving a drip of cream on her blouse. Rachael leaned over and wiped Evie's shirt-front with a napkin and suddenly they were all speaking again. Jamie looked along the table, to his father, who gave him an almost imperceptible nod of approval. Jamie relaxed.

As soon as the piece of cake was finished, Evie scrambled down and ran across to the small table and chairs. 'Come on Woz!' she called out. 'Bring the puzzle.' Warwick joined her, after Steve wiped his mouth, and they began working on puzzle together.

'Evie hasn't been to kindergarten, has she Sam?' Rachael poured another cup of tea for herself. When Samantha shook her head, Rachael continued. 'But she's a bright little thing.' She pointed to the children. Evie was directing the play and Warwick seemed happy to go along with it.

'Actually, I worried she didn't have any social skills at all. She was always just with me.' Samantha's face went pink. 'But since we've been here, she's come out of her shell. She's always loved books, and I used to make up games we could play together.'

'She's a credit to you, Sam.' Steve placed his hand over Rachael's, on the table.

'Would you consider starting her at the kindergarten, where Woz goes? He's there three days a week now, but you could try her just for one, to begin with. Or just mornings.' Rachael glanced at Jamie. He wondered where she was going with this.

'I've thought about it. I know it would be good for her.' Samantha shook her head. 'But we'll likely be gone by the end of the year. And, um, getting her there, you know.'

'Well, Sam. That's why I'm asking.' Rachael spoke firmly, but kindly. 'Jill or Jamie drop Warwick in to kindergarten, but we often pick him up. We'd be happy to pick Evie up too.'

'Logistically, we have several child seats between us.' Jill gazed at Jamie, then responded to Rachael. 'There's no reason we can't put two in one of our cars, say Jamie's, and you and Steve do the same.'

'Good idea. Steve and I each have a child seat, but we can put both in my car. It's generally me that does the pick up.' Rachael smiled at Steve, who readily agreed. Jamie's head was spinning. He wondered if they'd talked about this already, his mum and Rachael. *The meeting before the meeting.* He tried not to chuckle.

'What do *you* think, Sam? Would you like to try Evie at the Kindy?' Jamie didn't want her to feel pressured.

'I would, yes. But it seems like you're all doing a lot of juggling, with cars and seats, to make it work. We don't want to put anyone out.' Samantha's voice had an edge to it.

Jill gazed at Evie and Warwick again, then looked at Sam. 'Honestly Sam. It's not putting anyone out. It's our pleasure. And it's good for Evie. She'll be in school next year and this will help her get used to more children, all in one place.'

'Okay then. Thank you.' Samantha agreed, but Jamie made a note to himself to talk to her later. He wanted to make sure she didn't feel she had to go along with it, although in his heart he knew it was a good plan for Evie.

Rachael and Steve left soon after and Ross took the children outdoors to lock up the chickens and dogs for the night. Jamie, Jill and Samantha cleared the table and he stayed to help with the dishes.

They continued the conversation as they worked, until Jill turned to Jamie. 'You have two vehicles Jamie. The work truck you use around the farm. But it's registered. And your car, with the car seat in it for Woz.'

Jamie could see where Jill was going with this, and it was a good idea. 'Of course.' He looked at Samantha. 'I'll move the car seat out of Mum's car, to mine. It will be set up for both kids then. And Sam, it can be yours, to use, while you're here. Run the children to kindergarten or pick them up. Run errands, do shopping. Go to Nik's for work. Whatever you need. I'll use the truck. And if I need to get the kids, I can take the car, or Mum can.'

'We each have a set of all the car keys. But they're hanging here, on these hooks.' Jill pointed to a corkboard above their home phone, where several sets of keys hung.

Samantha drew in a breath, her hands shaking, then burst into tears. Jamie stepped forward, but his mum stopped him. She put her arms around the younger woman and hugged her hard. 'You're part of the family, Sam. You and Evie. This is not charity, or a gift. It's just family helping those we love.' Samantha cried harder and Jill waved Jamie away.

He wandered out to the chicken shed. Evie and Warwick each had a half-grown chicken in their arms while his father changed the hay in the laying boxes. Jamie shovelled the old hay into a compost pile behind the chicken run. Ross jerked his head towards the house and Jamie simply said, 'she's with Mum, having a cry. It's overwhelming, I think.'

'Sam's a good lass. She'll be alright.' Ross helped the children return the chickens to their home and they walked back to the house together, while the little ones ran ahead, racing each other.

Jamie was a bit disappointed that his mum didn't invite them to stay for dinner. He got it. Warwick needed a bath and

Samantha and Evie needed to settle into a routine in their new home. But his tread was heavy as they returned to their cottage. It felt strangely empty.

53

'Yes, I can come to book club Nik. I'm almost finished the book you loaned me. It's great, I'd like to read more by this author.' Samantha handed Nicole another set of folded towels. 'Jill doesn't mind looking after Evie.' She giggled. 'But I think Ross enjoys her even more.'

'That's lovely, Sam.' Nicole lowered her voice. 'I've got a mum with two kids in the apartment. They arrived last night, but they're leaving tomorrow morning. They have family, an aunt I think, diving down from southern Queensland to get them.'

'Oh.' Samantha looked over her shoulder. 'Can I do anything to help?'

'No Sam, thank you.' Nicole turned the washing machine on. 'Actually, yes you can. Once they've gone tomorrow we need to clean the apartment. Sheets, towels and so on. I like to have it ready. You know. Just in case.'

'You're such a good person Nik. I'd like to help others, like you do, one day.' Samantha bent her head, concentrating on the sheet she was folding.

'You are helping Sam. You're the best worker I've ever had here. I don't know what I'm going to do when you leave.' Nicole took the sheet from her hand, adding it to the pile on the table. 'Let's do the changeover for The Stables, then have morning tea.'

Samantha picked up the towels, while Nicole took the sheets, walking across to the gorgeous bed and breakfast apartment together.

'So today will be Evie's third day at kindergarten?' Nicole unlocked the door, holding it open for Samantha to walk in.

'Yes, she's loving it. But she's not as confident as I thought. They told me she stays close to Warwick. But she did play with some of the little children yesterday.' Samantha opened the bedroom doors. 'Oh, they only used one room. That makes it quicker.'

They stripped the king bed together, then began remaking it with clean sheets. 'Evie likes the little ones? That's a girl thing.' Nicole chuckled. 'Lucy is still like that.'

'Actually, it was little Harper that she played with most.' Samantha stopped for a moment.

'Rose's little one?'

'Yes. She's met her before, but I wasn't sure she'd remember. But after we got home she was talking about *baby Harper* in the bath.' Samantha smiled. *Evie would be a good big sister. But could I ever go there again?* She shivered.

'Are you cold, Sam?' Nicole wiped her forehead. 'I have no

idea what the real temperature is. I think I'm menopausal. I'm having a tropical holiday over here. Ugh!'

'Oh Nik. You poor thing. But no, I think someone walked over my grave.' Samantha gave Nicole a sympathetic look. She'd noticed her mother seemed hot at unexpected moments when she was staying. *Oh, she's probably going through menopause too.*

As if she could read her mind, Nicole asked about her mum. 'How's Tracy? Does she know you've moved out to the Taits?'

'Yes, and she's really pleased. Firstly, to make your place available for anyone else who needs it, but also because I'm such a farm girl. Ross has given me half a dozen poddy calves to look after. Evie loves coming with me. She wears a pair of gumboots that Woz has outgrown. Mum will be here for the Festival, she's excited about that too. Only five weeks to go.'

'And your matters? Douglas mentioned there might be other charges for your ex. He's still on remand, which surprised me.' Nicole flicked the top sheet over the bed. 'Here, grab the other side of this, Sam.'

Samantha pulled the sheet across, smoothed it out, and tucked it in with perfect hospital corners. 'And this is what I didn't know. The cult,' she used her fingers for quotation marks on the word cult. 'Has really been a hotbed of crime. Douglas's words, not mine. Money laundering for a crime gang. And human trafficking. Young women. Some children.' She shook her head then. 'I never really saw anything myself, but I can see how they got away with it. All the security and secrecy. And while Douglas doesn't have all the details, it's my matter that has brought it to light. Investigating him for the attempted kidnapping.'

'So he may go to jail for a long time?' Nicole sounded hopeful.

'I hope so. And I hope anyone else that felt trapped there, like me, has been able to leave. But Douglas says its best I don't know, and to focus on starting over.' Samantha sucked in a breath.

'Wise words. And good news Sam.' Nicole pulled the quilt up, then straightened it while Samantha did the same on the other side of the bed. 'But it was your courage, your escape, that has opened this up. You should be proud of yourself.'

54

Barrington Book Club & Reader Festival Update (Five weeks to Festival)
Attendance: Judith, Millie, Hanna, Kristen, Laura, Melanie, Rose, Rachael, Meggie, Harriet, Samantha & Nicole
Apologies: nil
Book: *The Lost Girl of Seahaven* by Phillipa Nefri Clark

'Welcome back Laura.' Rose passed her a glass of red wine. 'How was Europe? You've been gone ages.'

'Oh it's a lovely place to visit. But I wouldn't want to live there.' Laura said it with such a straight face that Rose almost spat the wine from her mouth. 'Ben was keen to come back through the United Kingdom, add on a few weeks. But I told him he'd be doing that with his *next girlfriend*. So here we are.'

Rose laughed and shook her head. 'You never change, Laura.'

The others arrived all at once, and they greeted each other warmly, all talking over each other, as they moved to the table at the back of the café. Last to arrive were Nicole and Samantha, the younger woman standing back while Nicole made sure she knew everyone.

Introductions over, they settled into their usual spots. Rose noticed Samantha declined the wine, but accepted a chai latte. Rose still felt unsure about Samantha living at the Tait farm, but she seemed to be the only one, so she kept her own counsel.

'I know you want to jump to the festival agenda, but Rose, I just have to say that this book,' Melanie held up her copy, 'made me cry. Like buckets of tears.'

'Me too! So heart-warming, though.' Judith pulled a tissue from her sleeve. 'Just thinking about this story brings tears to my eyes.'

'But it was sooo good!' Hanna grinned. 'I love her books. This series and the Detective Liz books. I can't decide which I like better.'

'Oh, the Temple River series for me.' Meggie chuckled. 'I vote we start a class action against Phillipa Nefri Clark. She needs to pay for our tissues.'

'Oh you girls.' Laura rolled her eyes. 'Soft-hearted, the lot of you.'

Rose leaned forward, pinning Laura with her gaze. 'You haven't finished it, have you Laura?'

Samantha snort-laughed, then covered her mouth with her hand, but Rose was delighted. She grinned at the newcomer. 'Laura acts all tough. And I'm pretty sure she can make a grown man cry. But she likes a good book with a twist. And this one has it, in spades.'

'Oh stop it, Rose. Pass the wine to me.' Laura ignored the giggles around the table, filling her glass to the brink. 'Melanie's driving tonight.' She sat back, more than a little bit smug.

Rose ran through her list of items for the festival, but she was confident they had everything covered. Her only problem was Harper. Angus could wrangle Charlie, and take him even if he was called out. His mother was coming, but only for the weekend, and Rose had a lot to do the day before, on the Friday. All her usual childcare helpers, like Meggie, had just as many duties as she did. She wished now she'd asked Angus' mum to arrive sooner.

They'd finished the meeting, and were back to general conversation. Rose thought about Lucy then, as a babysitter for Harper. 'Nicole, I need a babysitter for Harper on the Friday. Helen won't get here until late that evening. Do you think Lucy would do it?'

Millie raised her hand. 'You can't steal my staff for your own ends Rose Hamilton. Hanna and I have Lucy booked.'

Rose laughed. 'Of course. Silly of me. All good, maybe I can get Helen to come earlier.'

Samantha said something, but everyone else was talking too. 'Sam? Did you say something? Sorry!' Rose shushed the group.

'Um, I'd be happy to have Harper, if you're alright with that Rose.' She smiled shyly. 'Evie loves her, at kindy.'

'Oh? Yes.' Rose frowned, thinking about something Harper had said when she picked her up. She brightened. 'Does Harper call her Vee?'

'Giggling, Samantha nodded. 'She does. I noticed yesterday when I picked the kids up. She's a lovely little girl, Rose.' She stopped for a moment. 'Um, mum will be here. She's going to help with Warwick too, over the weekend. Jill has Council duties, so we thought we'd bring them into the book shop for some of it.' She glanced at Judith. 'I have a shift upstairs, to read to the little ones. And on Saturday we planned to take them to the market in the park. There's a jumping castle and Evie's never been on one.'

Hearing that, about Evie, reminded Rose just how sheltered their lives had been. Yet here was Samantha offering to help *her*. And Harper had been talking about Evie this week, although Rose hadn't realised who she meant. 'Gosh Sam. That would be wonderful, thank you.' She looked around the group, some still chatting quietly, others starting to clear the table. 'I'll make arrangements with you beforehand, but let's catch up shall we, after kindy one afternoon. With the kids?'

'I'd like that. Thank you Rose.' Samantha spoke quietly and Rose felt she was being thanked for more than just the offer of a catch up. She berated herself. *She should be thanking Samantha.*

———

THAT NIGHT, as she climbed into bed with Angus, Rose lay on her back, thinking about the meeting. Angus rolled over, one arm across her waist.

'Everything alright Rose? You look worried.'

'I think I've been a bit silly.' Rose blinked a tear away, and Angus leaned over her, kissing her mouth softly.

'You're rarely silly, Rose. What is it?' He drew lazy circles on her tummy with one hand.

'I've had this, *thing*, about Samantha.' Rose blushed.

'What thing?' Angus stilled his hand, his eyes searched hers for a moment.

'It's silly. Really. But it's about Jamie. I've been thinking that she, you know, might be after Jamie.' Rose wiped a tear away. 'But she's not like that at all. She's lovely. And very genuine, I think. And Jamie, well, he's Jamie. He's kind, and good.' She sniffled.

'You can't see Jamie with anyone but Debbie.' Angus got to the point, so quickly.

Rose shook her head. 'It's not that I can't. Maybe I can. But I just don't want to.'

'But Rose, darling Rose. You love Jamie, and I know you think you're protecting him. But Rose, he can't grieve forever, although I suspect he will. And I don't think anyone can replace Debbie, in his heart.' Angus kissed her again, his mouth lingering on hers. She felt heat pooling in her tummy. 'But the heart is an amazing organ.' He put one hand over her breast. 'I know. I'm a Vet.' He kissed her again and she sighed. 'The heart can make room for many people. I don't know if Jamie has feelings for Samantha, or if Samantha will overcome her past trauma to enter another relationship. But I think we should leave it up to them to work out. Their hearts will know, in time.'

Rose put her hand behind his head, bringing his lips back to hers. 'You're very wise, Angus Hamilton. Did you study for a long time to learn this, um, heart stuff?' His hand was still on her breast, and he kissed his way down to it.

'Many years Rose.' He murmured.

Rose wanted to speak, but couldn't. *I love you Angus Hamilton.* She arched her back, letting out a tiny moan.

55

T HEY'D SETTLED INTO A ROUTINE WITH JILL AND Ross, at the homestead. By the time Evie was awake and Samantha had showered, dressed and tidied their rooms, it was breakfast time. Samantha and Evie joined them at the age-worn breakfast table where Ross was generally on his second cup of tea.

Evie always asked Ross if he had collected the eggs. He'd tell her no and they'd go outside together, returning with Evie carefully carrying the eggs in a special little basket he'd found, just for her.

On busy mornings, when Jill had to go to a Council meeting and Samantha was working at Nicole's, they'd have tea and toast. But on kindergarten mornings she liked to make scrambled eggs – Evie's favourite breakfast and apparently Ross's too. The first week Evie joined Warwick at Kindy, Samantha drove around the roadway and up the other drive to Jamie's house, to pick Woz up. Jamie was always ready, although sometimes she wondered if Warwick's hair had been brushed. He'd secure Warwick in his seat, place his backpack beside him and wave them off.

Rachael generally dropped the children home. Evie first, then Warwick to Jamie's cottage. Samantha wondered if they had afternoon tea together and if Rachael helped him with household chores.

At the end of the first week, Samantha was washing their bedlinen and towels, when Jill popped into the laundry. 'Good morning Sam. Will you be here all day?'

'Yes, Nik doesn't need me today.' Samantha paused, one hand on the start button. 'Can I do anything for you?'

'Not for me, but for Ross.' Jill checked her watch. 'I've been called to a meeting at short notice, and I haven't left anything for his lunch. He can usually manage a toasted sandwich, but he's moving the irrigation system this morning with Jamie and I think he'll need more.'

'Oh, no problem. I bought mince yesterday, I was going to make pasta tonight, Bolognese. But I can make it for lunch instead, if he'd like that?' Samantha wondered what they'd have for dinner, but decided she could work that out later.

'Perfect. Thank you. I'll sort dinner out.' Jill rushed out and Samantha returned to the kitchen, just as Jamie pulled up with Warwick in tow.

'Hey Sam.' Warwick flew past her and plonked himself down on the rug with Evie, who was sorting out several decks of playing cards. Jamie came in at a more leisurely pace.

'Morning Sam. Dad.' He filled the kettle and turned it on,

cocking an eyebrow at his father who jiggled the pot in front of him.

'Best make a fresh one lad.' Ross folded his newspaper up. It was a rural paper, weekly. Samantha's father used to read it.

'Sam?' Jamie rinsed out the teapot, then opened the tea cannister, a teaspoon in his hand.

'Sure. I'll pour juice for the kids.' Samantha sat with Ross and Jamie at the table while they drank their tea. 'Do you need help moving the irrigation?' She wasn't sure what was involved, but loved an opportunity to be useful outdoors.

'Not really.' Jamie scratched his chin. He hadn't shaved, and she thought he looked different with a short beard. A bit rogu-ish, perhaps. She lowered her eyes. *Reading too many romance books.* 'I didn't realise Mum had to be somewhere. I was hoping she'd have Woz.'

'Leave him here, son. Too many moving parts.' Ross drained his cup and pushed his chair back.

Jamie turned to Samantha, and she smiled quickly, not wanting him to have to ask. 'Woz can stay here with us. It's washing day. And I'll have a hearty lunch ready when you come back.'

'Thank you Sam, very much.' Jamie carried their tea things to the sink. 'Washing day, huh? How often does this washing day take place?'

She knew he was teasing, but she answered anyway. 'Twice a week. It's linens today. Everything else on Tuesday.'

Jamie leaned against the counter with his ankles crossed. 'Every day is washing day over at the worker's cottage. And I only do the linens when I see Mum's on the line. It reminds me.'

Samantha laughed, and was on the verge of offering to help with his washing, then decided it might send a *signal*. 'You and Woz always *look* clean, Jamie. Maybe I should do a sniff test?' He looked startled for a moment, then grinned. Samantha blushed. 'Not like that, Jamie Tait!' She slapped his arm lightly. Ross eased past them and was putting his boots on at the back door. 'Go and help your father.' She turned her back, not wanting him to see her face, although what it might give away, she wasn't sure.

Once the men left, the children whined about having nothing to do. Samantha shook her head, but set up a blackboard easel with two sides Ross had found for Evie, on the veranda. They had a basket of chalk and she called out items for them to draw as she went about her chores.

Samantha prepared the lunch and let the children have theirs at twelve. By one she was getting a bit anxious, Ross usually came for lunch around midday. Shortly after she heard the motorbike arrive at the back door, and then the slam of a car door. She breathed a sigh of relief. She knew how easily accidents could happen on farms.

Hi Sam!' Jamie followed Ross in. 'Has Woz been okay? Not too much for you, having both of them?'

Raising her eyebrows she laughed. 'Two is easier than one, I think. They mostly entertained each other.'

'We haven't spoiled your lunch have we love?' Ross touched her shoulder lightly as he padded through to the table in his socks.

'Not at all. It's spaghetti Bolognese, so I'll just heat a bowl for each of you.' As she stepped over to the stove, she heard Jamie snigger. She turned back, brandishing a wooden spoon. 'What, Jamie?'

Jamie's grin broadened, if that was possible. Samantha frowned. Jamie looked down the table at his father. 'Spaghetti, Dad.' He waggled his eyebrows.

Suddenly she got it. *Ross doesn't like pasta.* Her hand flew to her forehead. Jill should have said something when they discussed it, before she left. She wondered if there was something else she could throw together.

Turning to Ross, she opened her mouth to apologise. He looked her square in the eyes, ignoring Jamie. 'I'm looking forward to that, er, spaghetti meal. It will fill the hole.' He patted his tummy.

Samantha blushed, still wondering what she'd do if he hated it, but she served up two big portions for the men, and a smaller one for herself. Jamie sprinkled parmesan cheese over his, then offered it to his father, who shook his head. Sam sprinkled some on her own and scowled at Jamie. He concentrated on his meal.

They ate in silence until Jamie had all but scraped his plate clean. 'That was delicious, Sam.'

'Would you like more, Jamie?' She reached for his plate but at the same time Ross pushed his plate over to her. She was surprised to see he'd eaten it all. 'Yes please, Sam.' Ross gave Jamie a look and she giggled, then served them each another small helping.

'I had spaghetti once. On a camping trip as a young bloke. Came out of a tin.' Ross moved his empty bowl aside. 'Didn't taste like this. Not even close. You can make this anytime you want, Sam.'

Jamie snort-laughed then shook his head. 'All the times Mum has tried to get you to eat spaghetti and you've refused.' He beamed at Samantha. 'You're a miracle worker, Sam.'

'Didn't come out of a tin.' Ross opened his paper and ignored them.

'The cherry tomatoes I used were out of the garden here. And the basil.' Samantha, feeling chuffed, cleared their lunch things away while Jamie went in search of Warwick.

'We'll be off then. Thanks for lunch Sam, it was tasty.' Jamie nudged Warwick. 'Say goodbye to Pa. And Evie and Sam.'

Warwick waved his arms about. 'Bye Pa! Bye Evie! Bye Sam!' And they were gone.

56

—————

J AMIE LOADED HIS SHEETS INTO THE MACHINE AND thought of Samantha. In fact, almost everything he did lately, at home, on the farm, made him think of her.

At first, when he'd lost Debbie, his mum came over and did things in the house while he was working on the farm. Fresh groceries in the fridge, the beds changed, house cleaned and clothes washed. A few weeks after her death his parents sat him down and asked if he and Warwick would like to move back into the homestead, and he realised then, the burden he'd placed on his mother. She was effectively running two households. He had thanked them, but declined. From that moment he'd taken over the running of the house himself and gained a new appreciation for all that Debbie had done, working long hours in the business and keeping their home running smoothly.

But he and Warwick ate dinner with his parents a couple of

time a week and he often joined them for lunch when Warwick was at kindergarten. But now, with Samantha there, he found himself finding excuses to be there more often. Just this morning he'd driven over with Warwick well before she had to leave on the kindergarten run, and enjoyed a second breakfast of pancakes and maple syrup. He'd said it was to save her time, not having to drive around to his house, but when his father peered at him from the end of the table, the game was up. *His father knew that he liked spending time with Sam and Evie.*

But the thing that really bothered him was learning this morning that Tracy would be here next week, for the festival, and to take Samantha and Evie home afterwards. To Victoria. The realisation hit him, that he didn't want them to leave. And while he was enjoying having them so close, just across the paddock at the homestead, *it wasn't close enough.* He wanted more, but he knew it was way too soon for Samantha to contemplate anything. And was he truly ready to let Debbie go? He sighed. *He could never really let Debbie go. But perhaps he needed to start living again.* What to do about Smantha then? Let her go but stay in touch, in the hope she'll be ready one day?

He was working with his father on the hay baler, greasing all the moving parts. Jamie chuckled. *He* was working. He was under the damn thing, covered in grease and oil, but his father was as clean as whistle, relaxing on an upturned bucket, passing him tools when requested.

'Damn!' Jamie slipped with a wrench and scraped his knuckle for the second time in five minutes. 'The cloth, Dad. Pass me the cloth!' He was irritated, and now bleeding.

'Here, son.' Ross handed him a clean rag, but sounded terse. *Damn, it's not his father's fault.*

'Sorry Dad.' Jamie slid out. Ross didn't move, but jerked his chin towards Jamie's cloth-bound hand.

'Bad?'

'Nah.' Jamie reached for his drink, took a swig, and leaned back against the baler. 'Just a scratch.'

'What's got into you, lad?' Ross rarely asked probing questions, and Jamie would normally shrug and keep working. *But who else could he talk to?*

'Sam. And Evie.' Jamie sighed and looked across the paddocks towards his house. 'I don't want them to go.'

'Tell her.' Ross plucked a clover leaf, studying it for a moment. A lazy bee landed on his hand and he just looked at it, bringing it close to his face. After a moment it flew off, landing in the wildflowers nearby.

'Tell her what? That I don't want her to leave?' Jamie shook his head. 'I don't want to scare her.'

'It won't.' Leaning back, his father put his hands behind his head. 'We'll get a good crop of lucerne this year.'

'It won't scare her? How do you know, Dad? We don't know what she's been though.' Jamie wanted to say more and was almost sorry he'd started the conversation. His father was the epitome of *a man of few words.*

'Don't have to know.' Ross straightened. 'I want her to stay too.'

Jamie knew Ross was attached to Sam and Evie, but was surprised to hear him say it out loud. 'Why Dad? What is it about her? About them?'

'I knew from the start. She's the one.' Jamie reeled back at his father's words. *What?*

'Dad! What?' Jamie shook his head, tying to dislodge what he'd just heard.

'For you, Jamie.' Ross stood up and put his hat on. 'She fits. You.' He whistled to BlueDog, and threw his leg over the motorbike.

Jamie scrambled to his feet, but his father was already on his way back to the house. He packed the tools away, he'd finish this tomorrow. Looking at his watch, he saw it was almost time for Samantha to return from town with the children, after kindergarten. He walked across to his cottage, his father's words ringing in his ears. *Tell her. She's the one. She fits you.*

Jamie rushed inside, cleaning himself up quickly. He'd tell her. What did he have to lose? *Everything. But he had to be honest. She'd expect nothing less.*

———

HE ARRIVED at the homestead a few minutes after Samantha returned from town. Woz and Evie were already at the kitchen table with a glass of juice and a biscuit. Jamie sat down, asking them about their day. Samantha moved from the kitchen to the table, laughing and chatting with his mother. It was beautiful. Almost like a ballet, they were so in sync with each other. He'd never noticed that before.

After finishing their afternoon tea, the kids pulled at his father's hands to go and check the chickens and they trooped out through the back door. Samantha ran after them, calling out, 'put your gumboots on!'

Suddenly it was just he and Jill. She gave him a knowing look. 'Your father spoke to me. Talk to her. To Sam.'

Samantha was back, shaking her head. 'Honestly. They were about to run out there in their socks.' She giggled. 'All three of them!'

'Sam, can you come over to my place, er, now? I need help with something.' Jamie was simply winging it. He had the feeling that if he didn't speak now, the moment would be lost forever.

'Okay. Sure. Right now? ' She was surprised, but agreed quickly. 'I'll get the children.'

'Oh, leave them. They'll be out there for a while yet. Baby chicks.' Jill turned away as she spoke and Jamie could have applauded her performance. *Thanks Mum.*

'We can walk cross the paddock. It's quicker.' Jamie set off with Samantha beside him. It was a warm afternoon but she wore a light long-sleeve tee-shirt and jeans. He realised he'd never seen her in short sleeves. He thought about that for a moment.

'You need help with something inside your house?' Samantha was chirpy, and he risked a sideways glance at her. *Does she know something?*

'Er, yes. In the laundry.' He hated lying. Was absolutely no good at it.

'It's just that, I've never been inside your house.' Samantha was excited.

'You haven't?' He frowned. All these weeks she'd been at

the homestead, had he never invited her inside his cottage? *Self-preservation, Jamie.*

'No, but I'm excited to see it.' She gave him a bit of side-eye. 'It's not, like, a real mess is it? Are you luring me over to clean your house, Jamie Tait?' She giggled and he knew she was joking, but he mentally ran through each room of his house. Clean enough. Tidy enough, he thought.

'Ha.' He laughed. 'Pigsty. You've got me.' She laughed loudly and he knew she didn't believe that. He felt a bit breathless.

They took their boots off and he opened the front door. 'A shotgun hallway. Two rooms either side. Three bedrooms and a living area. Then kitchen and dining in one room at the back.' He gave her time to gaze around as they walked along the hallway. She stopped at a collage of framed wedding photos on the wall.

'Beautiful. Your Debbie was beautiful.' She pointed to another picture, of the wedding party. 'Is that Rose? Is she pregnant there? With Charlie?'

Jamie nodded and in a few steps they were in the kitchen. He wondered what she'd think. It had been Debbie's favourite room.

'This room! It's so cosy.' Samantha spun around. 'I love an eat-in kitchen, farmhouse style. There's something about it, isn't there?' He nodded. 'It keeps families together.'

Samantha clapped her hands, startling him. 'Okay. Lead me to your laundry, I assume it's through here. I want to see this problem you need help with.' She took two steps but Jamie reached out, took her hand, and tugged her closer to him.

57

SAMANTHA HAD BEEN CURIOUS ABOUT JAMIE'S HOUSE since forever. She wondered if she hadn't been invited inside because it was, sort of, a shrine to his beautiful wife. Or if it was a messy man-cave.

But once inside, she was charmed by the little house. The high ceilings and warmly painted timber walls were very country cottage, but lived in. Not messy, but not perfect either. There were a few dishes on the drainboard, and toys on the floor in one corner as if Warwick had rushed out before he could pack them away.

She was surprised when Jamie took her hand, pulling her closer to him. She looked up at his face, raw with emotion. She blinked. For a moment she thought it was about his wife, Debbie, but then he whispered her name. 'Samantha.'

He tugged her hand gently and she walked into his arms. Since the day she first met him, she'd felt safe with him. He had a gentleness that she wasn't used to seeing in a man. But the day he'd stood up to her ex, to protect her. Not just her, but Evie, Nicole and Tracy, she knew he was one of the *good ones*, as her mother often said.

Nestled against his chest, she could hear his heart beating, loud and fast. She tilted her head back. 'Jamie.' *Was this what she thought it was?* She became nervous, and stepped back. 'Jamie?'

'Sam. You're safe with me. There's no pressure.' Jamie spoke softly and she relaxed. 'But I have to be honest.'

She nodded, not trusting herself to speak.

'I don't want you and Evie to leave. I want you to stay here. Give this,' he pointed from himself to her, 'a chance. There's no rush, for anything. Ever. But if you leave, well, we'll never know.'

'You want us to stay?' Samantha grappled with the images running through her mind. 'You think, um.' She gazed at another picture of Debbie on the sideboard. A small baby in her arms and Warwick on her knee, smiling. *So happy. So undamaged.* Samantha closed her eyes for a moment. 'You want to give *us* a chance? You and me?'

'And Woz and Evie.' Jamie was watching her. She didn't know what to say. How to tell him that she might never. She couldn't finish the thought. *He's taking a risk, telling me this. He's being honest.*

'Jamie. I have to tell you. I'm damaged. I don't know, if I can, ever, you know.' She whispered the words, watching his face carefully.

'I know.' Jamie pulled her back into his arms. 'Well, I don't know exactly. But I want you to stay. I love you, Sam. And I love Evie. I've only just realised, but I think I've loved you from the very beginning.' He chuckled. 'Maybe not as much as my dad does.'

She giggled. She adored Ross, and Jill.

'Sam, I want to make us a family. But there's no pressure. We can take all the time you need. And maybe you can learn to love me.' He kissed the top of her head.

58

Samantha pushed out of his arms. She began to cry. 'That's just it Jamie. I do love you. I think I have for a long time too.' She cried harder and held her hand up when he tried to reach for her. 'But I don't know if I can ever *make love* to you.'

Jamie heard her say she loved him, and his heart skipped a beat. Her next words didn't shock him, he knew it may be hard for her. But as she spoke she pushed her sleeves to her elbows and he saw the scars. Lots of small round burns. He couldn't speak. His own eyes filled with tears. He was angry, so angry, but he couldn't undo this, what had happened to Samantha.

'Cigarettes.' She whispered. She pulled the shirt from her jeans and lifted it, exposing her tummy. More burns.

Jamie dropped to his knees, put his arms around her waist and tugged her closer. He gently kissed the scars on her belly. She sobbed, standing there with her hands in his hair. Heart-breaking sobs. He sat back on the floor and pulled her into his lap. Jamie kissed her wrist and her forearms and then he just held her until her sobs subsided. It might have been an hour. Perhaps longer. It was dusk outside when she moved, leaning against his chest. 'The children?'

'They're alright.'

'Your parents?' She started to move. He released his hold, he never wanted her to feel trapped.

'They know, Sam. They knew before me.' He smiled at her gently and she relaxed against him again. His heart sped up.

Samantha was startled. 'They know? But my past? And they'd still have me, for you?' She shook her head, trying to understand. 'I'm not Debbie.'

'I'll tell you what my father said to me, Sam.' He used his fingers to indicate quotation marks. 'She fits you. Sam's the one.'

Samantha cried again, but she was smiling through her tears. Jamie moved her to a kitchen chair and found a box of tissues.

'Sam, I'm never going to say this again. So hear me well. I know you've been hurt, emotionally and physically and I know there's a chance you may never want to.' He didn't know how to say it. 'Consummate, us. And I am okay with that. I love you, and I'll wait. And if it's never, I'll still love you.'

She wasn't sure what he expected her to say, but she just nodded. 'We'd better go back.' *She's processing.*

'Alright.' He'd had visions of cooking dinner for her, keeping her all night. *He could wait.*

At his front door, putting their boots back on, she gazed at him. 'Kiss me, please Jamie.'

Jamie leaned down, moving his lips gently against hers. She sighed and he deepened the kiss. Her arms crept around his back. She touched her tongue to his and moaned softly. She pushed herself against him and it was all he could do to hold his body straight, not wanting to frighten her. He lifted his head, and took her hand in his. They walked across the paddock to the homestead, ablaze with light.

———

LATER THAT NIGHT, in bed alone, Jamie thought about Debbie. He'd loved her since he was sixteen. *He'd always love Debbie.* But Sam, well, he loved her too. And it felt just as deep, and just as real.

59

Rose was edgy. Monday night's book club was all about the festival, yet still she wondered if it would be alright. Her biggest fear was having a room full of authors, but no one turn up to see them. Angus had taken Charlie to school, but not before he knocked over his glass of chocolate milk at breakfast. He'd been teasing Harper and she'd growled at him. Harper only cried harder when Charlie cried too.

Angus had swooped in and taken Charlie, and she'd snapped at him too. He had stopped, given her a look, then wrapped his arms around her. 'It's nerves, Rose. It will be okay.'

Even that had gotten her back up. It was on the tip of her tongue to tell him not to patronise her, but his face said it all. She was being unreasonable. She knew it. Rose waved him away. Not quite an apology, but also not an argument.

The car park behind town hall was full. She checked her watch. Samantha would be waiting. *And I need a coffee.* Then she remembered Angus had told her to park behind the Vet surgery, he'd leave room for her car. She drove along and he was right, there was room for her car there. Raising her eyes to the ceiling she whispered, 'I don't deserve you Angus Hamilton.'

Harper was still whining, picking up on Rose's anxiety. She worried her daughter might be a handful for Samantha and not for the first time she wondered if she should have asked Helen to come earlier.

Ten minutes later than arranged, Rose rushed into the book shop, her laptop in a bag over her shoulder, plus another bag with all of Harper's needs for the day and Harper herself, wriggling in her arms.

'Vee! Vee!' Harper almost fell, but Samantha appeared, scooping her up quickly, then setting her down beside Evie.

Evie took Harper's hand and Rose let out a deep sigh in a rush of pent-up energy. 'Sam. Thank you. I'm sorry I'm late.' She smiled, then fiddled with an earring. Harper had half pulled it out.

Samantha chuckled. 'Judith hasn't officially opened, you've got a few minutes.' She stepped over to the counter and handed a giant takeaway coffee cup to Rose. 'I was early, Millie said this was your favourite. Um, caramel latte.' She pointed to a second, smaller cup on the counter. 'I'm trying it. I'm just learning to like coffee.'

'Oh Sam!' Rose flung an arm around the younger woman's shoulders and laughed for the first time that day. 'Bless you. Coffee is the best thing. I have anxiety. What if something goes wrong? What if no one turns up?' She shook her head. 'Poor

Harper. She's picked up on my mood.' Rose grimaced. 'It was a bit, er, turbulent, at home this morning.'

Judith appeared from the back room. 'No one turning up is the least of your worries Rose.' She pointed to the front door where a group of twenty or more people had gathered, laughing and chatting together. 'Samantha, you might want to use the lift, I think you'll fit in with the girls, and go up to the mezzanine. I'm going to open the door.'

Rose helped Samantha and they used the spiral staircase. Evie settled into a pink beanbag, with Harper beside her. 'Go Rose.' Samantha pointed at the group now milling around in the book shop. 'Your fans await.'

Someone must have heard her words, because a customer called out. 'It's Rose. Rose Gordon!' Oohs and aahs and a whole of 'hello Rose' reached her as she almost skipped down the stairs. So many curious faces, but all friendly.

Two of her fellow authors hovered just inside the door and another walked in as she approached. Rose waved them over to the signing table. 'Phillipa, Heather, Michelle. Join me.'

The morning flew by. Rose had never smiled so much and her voice was hoarse from chatting with readers. They seemed to come in waves, but that was because Judith was managing them, with Meggie helping. They were circulating in groups of twenty or so, through the cafe, the heritage walk and the book shop.

It was late morning before she had a chance to check on Harper. She was asleep with her thumb in her mouth, on Samantha's lap. Evie was reading quietly, still in the pink bean bag, but with an older version of Samantha. 'Rose, this is my mum, Tracy.'

'Lovely to meet you Tracy.' Rose spoke quietly, not wanting to wake Harper up. 'Has Harper been a good girl?' She honestly hadn't heard a peep form the children, but it had been noisy downstairs all morning.

'Harper's such a good girl, Rose. She shared morning tea with Evie, then I changed her, and she seemed happy on my lap. She's only been asleep for fifteen minutes.'

'Oh, that's great thank you.' Rose heard her name called and looked downstairs.

'We're going next door for lunch Rose, can you join us?' It was her author friends and Meggie.

Rose was about to say no, that she should go home for a couple of hours with Harper, but Samantha cleared her throat and Rose turned to her.

'I'd like to take Harper home. I have two car seats. And mum is here too.' Samantha seemed uncertain. 'If you're okay with that?'

Rose didn't hesitate. 'That would be brilliant, thank you Sam. I'll call out to the homestead after school, with Charlie.' She grinned. 'And my mother-in-law, Helen, should be at ours by then. She's got them for the rest of the weekend.' Rose waved to her friends downstairs. 'Order for me, girls. I'll have what you're having.' Laughter and chatter drifted out through the door. 'Are you coming to the opening tonight Sam?'

'Oh no, I don't think so.' She gestured to Evie. 'The children. I told Jamie I'd have Woz too. Jill and Ross are coming in with Jamie.'

'Oh.' Rose was disappointed. Samantha deserved to come out for an evening.

'Of course you should go, Sam. I'll look after Evie and Warwick. He knows me well enough.' Tracy tried to get out of the beanbag. Evie was already out, searching for another book to read. 'Of course, I might have to look after them here, if no one helps me out of this thing!' Tracy chortled and Rose held out her hand, heaving Tracy to her feet.

'They look fabulous, these bean bags. Pretty colours and such. But honestly, I don't think adults should ever sit in them.' Tracy shook her head, still laughing softly.

Harper moved in Samantha's arms, then opened her eyes. She peered at her mother. 'Mummy.'

'Would you like to go home with Sam and Evie, Harper? And mummy and Charlie will get you later.' Rose waited. This could go either way. Harper was sometimes clingy after a nap, or she'd ignore Rose altogether.

Reaching up, she patted Samantha's face. 'Vee.'

'That's settled then.' Rose laughed. 'She's all yours!' But she gazed from Samantha to Tracy. 'Call me if you need me, if she gets upset. I'll come straight away.' She had to say it, but she suspected they wouldn't need to call.

60

THERE WAS A STRANGE DYNAMIC AT THE HOMESTEAD, when Rose came in the afternoon for Harper. Charlie immediately joined the other children, watching Bluey on the television in the main lounge.

Ross sat in his usual spot at the large table and Rose sat beside him. Jill was still in town and Tracy had gone through to check on the children, so Jamie was in the kitchen helping Samantha with the afternoon tea things.

They hadn't spent any time alone since that afternoon at his house, but Samantha felt they were building something together. Like a house, brick by brick. She loved the way Jamie sometimes touched her hand with his, or kissed the tip of her nose when he said hello. Little gestures demonstrating his affection, but not at all demanding.

But she felt Rose watching them, that afternoon. Jamie teasing her gently as she poured milk into a small jug, the way

Ross responded to Evie when she ran to the table to ask him something. Tracy returned and overheard Evie call Ross 'Pa.' Her mother gave her a quick look, and in the same moment Rose did too.

Jamie carried Harper out to the car for Rose, she'd had a big day. Rose seemed to hesitate on the front step, but she turned and hugged Samantha quickly. 'Thank you Sam. I wouldn't have managed today without you. You too Tracy.'

And they were gone. All of them. Rose drove out and Ross went to check the heifers. Jamie took Warwick home for a bath. But he was returning to pick up Sam and his parents for the evening function.

Tracy ran a bath for Evie and Samantha washed up the afternoon tea dishes. Evie was allowed to watch a show on the ABC after her bath, and Samantha made sure her mum was okay with watching Evie and Warwick that evening. Jamie had insisted she come out with them.

'We haven't talked about it Sam, but you know I'm heading home on Wednesday. I have to work next week.' Tracy folded up the tea towel she was holding.

'Yes. Um, it's been so nice to have you here.' Samantha still hadn't decided if she should stay or go. She considered going home for a couple of months, and then coming back to visit. And maybe Jamie and Warwick could visit her. Douglas had been working diligently in the background and Samantha had full custody of Evie. Adam was still on remand, for a few months more at least. She rarely thought about him. And Evie never mentioned him.

'This town has something Sam. You've been here almost six

months, but you have quite a community around you.' Tracy turned her face away but not before Samantha saw her eyes fill with tears.

'Oh Mum.' Samantha rushed to Tracy and hugged her hard. 'I've been lucky, finding Nicole and Jamie that first night. And Judith. They've welcomed me. A stranger with a lot of baggage. But you're my mum. No one can replace you.'

Tracy patted her back. Her voice was soft. 'I know love. But I'm just one person. Here, you have more.' She leaned back, looking into Samantha's face. 'Jamie?'

Samantha wiped her eyes with the back of her head and nodded. 'But mum. I don't know if I can ever.' She looked at the ceiling, blushing. 'Be *everything* to him. And it would be wrong, I think, not to. He's young enough to meet someone else.'

'I understand. And you'll always be welcome to come home. But I think, Sam, that maybe you should try, with Jamie.' Tracy touched her face. 'Beautiful Samantha. I'm so sorry. What you went though.'

Sniffling, Samantha leaned into her mother's shoulder. 'If I can't, with Jamie, then I won't with anyone. I know that mum. But I don't want to rush.' Blinking, she smiled through her tears. 'And I feel a bit, you know, Jane Austen.'

Tracy frowned. 'Jane Austen? The writer?'

'Yes. They fall in love in her stories, without, ever, um, you know.' Samantha giggled. 'It's a touch of the hand, a look, a gesture. They used to fall in love without even kissing, some-times.' She rolled her eyes. 'It's like that with Jamie. So romantic.' She giggled again, whispering. 'But we have kissed. And he's very good at it.'

Laughing, Tracy wrapped her arms around Samantha. 'I've always thought you could tell by the kiss.' She waggled her eyebrows. 'You must stay Sam. You and Jamie take your time. I'll come back at Christmas, if you'll have me.'

'Really? You're not disappointed?' Samantha blew her nose loudly.

'No darling girl. I'd be disappointed if you didn't give it a try, with Jamie.' Tracy cocked her head on one side. 'I can hear a car, that must be Jill. And Ross will be back any moment.'

———

THE NIGHT WAS FUN. Samantha was happy it wasn't a very fancy event. *I must buy a couple of outfits, for going out.* But she fitted in with the crowd in capri pants and a long-sleeved blouse.

The event was in the town hall. Jamie whispered that there were at least two hundred people in attendance. Rose and the authors she'd met earlier were joined by a couple of others on the stage, for a chat about 'all things books.' Harriet was the MC and Samantha thought they were all very clever. And funny. She hadn't laughed so much in a long time. There were lots of questions from the audience. At least three from Hanna, and one from Harry, which surprised Sam. *So Harry Stewart reads romance books.* She caught Jamie's eye at that and they shared a grin.

Afterwards, there was a supper catered by Millie's team and a bar run by her boyfriend Finn. She saw Harry behind the bar too, and Samantha was introduced to Finn's son Lucas and Millie's son Matty.

But the thing that surprised Samantha the most, was that Jamie held her hand. All night. Not just when they were sitting close together, but in front of his mates, like Angus, Drum and Max. He didn't let go when Rose and Meggie joined them, even though she saw Rose eyeing their linked hands, more than once.

Samantha excused herself, to go to the bathroom, and Rose linked their arms and said she'd come too.

Standing at the sink, Samantha waited while Rose reapplied her lipstick. Samantha didn't have any makeup and wouldn't know how to use it if she did.

'Debbie was my best friend. We grew up together.' Rose stared into Samantha's eyes in the mirror. 'And Jamie. We played together when we were young.'

Samantha turned her face away. She couldn't meet Rose's eyes. She knew she could never replace Debbie. *Beautiful, accomplished Debbie.*

'She was very special. To me, to Jamie. The whole town loved her, I think.' Samantha nodded at Rose's words, her shoulders dropping.

Rose touched Samantha's hand, startling her. She looked up, anxious about how she should respond. 'Sam, you're a beautiful girl. Inside and out. And you're not Debbie.' Samantha nodded, trying hard not to cry. *Maybe she would go home with her mum after all.* 'And I see how Jamie is with you, Sam. And I think you are perfect for each other.' Rose's tone was warm and it took Samantha a moment to register what she'd said.

'Perfect?' Samanthas mind was racing.

'You're such a farm girl, you totally *get* Jamie. Yes, he loved Debbie with all his heart, but she wasn't a farm kid. She had a life off the farm, with the café, although she helped when she could. But you Sam, you're his perfect match. Two peas and all that.' Rose reached down and hugged her. 'Don't look so anxious Sam. It had to be said. You don't *need* my blessing, but you have it Sam.'

Rose's words finally registered and Samantha nodded, quickly swiping a stray tear from her cheek. 'Really Rose? You think I'm his match?'

'I really do. And I'm happy for you. For both of you.'

61

NICOLE SLIPPED THE PHONE INTO HER BACK POCKET. 'Another booking, Sam. We're booked out from tomorrow through to the middle of January now. I'm so glad you stayed on, I don't know how I would have managed this without you.'

'And mum will be here tomorrow for the Christmas break, she'll give us a hand.' Samantha wiped over the kitchenette, then stood back. 'There. No streaks.'

'Where's Evie today? Has Jill got her?' Nicole picked up one side of the washing basket filled with dirty towels.

Samantha grabbed the handle on the other side and they made their way back to the laundry in the big house. 'No, Evie and Woz are with Jamie and Ross. They're helping get the hay in.' She shook her head, eyes shining. 'She's so like me. I used to love doing that with my Dad.'

'And how is it going, with you and Jamie?' Nicole glanced

344

at Samantha. She was wearing a tank top today, and had stopped covering her arms up.

'He's so lovely. And romantic.' Samantha blushed.

'Oh?' Nicole giggled. 'Not trying to pry, but Sam, that sounds, um, like you're moving forward.'

'We are. That is. I think we are. But now I have another problem.' They set the basket down and Samantha began sorting the towels into the two commercial washers.

'Oh?' Nicole was curious. But she'd learnt that Sam liked to tell her things in her own time.

'Well.' Samantha stopped, and leaned against the machine for a moment, arms folded. 'Can I tell you this, Nik?'

'Of course.' Nicole giggled. 'I'm so curious, but you know I'd never ask.'

'I think I can. You know.' She waggled her eyebrows up and down and Nicole tried not to laugh.

'But you're not sure?'

'No, I'm sure. I really want to.' Samantha's face took on a dreamy look. 'Jamie's so lovely. But, well, he's become so used to *not* doing anything that I might construe as pressure, that now we've slipped into something else. A sort of kissing-cousin friend-zone.'

'The friend-zone.' Nicole shook her head. 'That's never good.' She straightened. 'I'll turn this one on.' After setting the machine Nicole continued. 'Robbie and I were nearly in the friend-zone. I didn't think I'd never re-partner. But we sat up watching a litter of puppies one night, and well, he kissed me. Really kissed me, if you know what I mean.'

'Really? That's funny Nik.' Samantha put her hands on her hips. 'Any idea where I can get a litter of puppies?'

Nicole snort-laughed. 'No. But Sam, I think you're going to have to make the first move because Jamie never will. He's too scared he'll hurt you.'

Samantha didn't comment, and they began folding clean sheets from the dryer, working in companionable silence, until Samantha said out loud. 'I'll do it. I'll make the first move. I'll be Elizabeth Bennet.'

62

Samantha asked Jill to keep an eye on Evie after she put her to bed, and marched across the paddock to Jamie's by torchlight. She knocked quietly on the door, not sure if Warwick was already in bed.

Jamie opened the door, his expression surprised. 'Sam.' He opened it wider. 'Come in.'

'Is Woz asleep?' She slipped off her canvas runners, following Jamie down the hall.

'He is. Had a big day on the farm.' Jamie chuckled. He stopped outside his son's bedroom and cracked the door open. Samantha could see Warwick sound asleep in just a pair of pyjama shorts, one leg out of the covers. She smiled. He looked so like his father.

They moved into the kitchen. 'Cold drink?' Jamie had a half-finished stubby of beer on the counter.

'Yes please.' Samantha watched Jamie pour her a glass of soda water. He didn't drink it, but since she's told him she liked it, he always had some in his fridge.

'I've been thinking.' Samantha wasn't sure where to start. Jamie hadn't kissed her at the door. That had been her plan A, deepen the kiss and get him into his room somehow. 'Mum will be here tomorrow.'

'Yes. It will be a full house for Christmas.' Jamie grinned.

'That's why I came over. What if Evie and I stayed here, with you and Woz, over Christmas?' Samantha knew he had a third bedroom that he used as an office. Evie could sleep in there, but she'd have to share with Jamie. Her tummy flipped over and she wondered if her face was red.

Jamie raised an eyebrow. 'I like that idea.' He held out his hand. 'Come with me.'

This is easier than I thought. He's taking me to his room. But he led her back to the door of the spare room. She'd only seen it once, the first time she'd been in the house. It had a big old desk in it and an ancient armchair and a few boxes stacked in one corner.

Jamie opened the door and turned on the light. Samantha blinked. It was a completely different room. She stepped inside. It was a little girl's room. With sage green walls, a single bed painted white with a soft-yellow gingham cover. The big old armchair had been recovered in a darker green, with pink and yellow gingham cushions on it. There was a set of white drawers and a white clothes cupboard. On the wall above the bed wooden letters in pink, yellow, green and blue spelled out EVIE.

'You did this? For Evie?' Samantha shook her head. 'When? I had no idea.'

'After that first night you came inside. It's been a project I've worked on in the evenings.' He was pleased with himself, she could see that. Her heart was racing and her tummy was doing more of the butterfly-thing, except maybe they'd moved lower. *Oh gosh.*

Jamie turned the light off and closed the door, then stepped across the hall and opened his bedroom door. She'd only seen it once too, and that was just a peek. Dark and masculine, with a big timber bed. He turned on the light. Samantha stepped inside. The big bed was still there, but the cover was a sort of Wedgewood blue. White sheets. The side tables were painted white, and the chest of drawers was white. She hadn't remembered that. The cupboard doors were white too. She remembered them being timber. Red cedar maybe.

Samantha turned, to speak to him, but he was right there, his eyes locked on hers. She knew she was breathing fast, and her face was red. But he seemed to be wound up, like he was holding onto his control as tightly as he could. *It's now or never Sam. Kiss the man.*

Standing on tiptoe, she leaned against him and turned her face up. There was no hesitation, he kissed her. But it wasn't the gentle kiss she was used to. It was raw and full of need. She kissed him back, putting her whole heart, every bit of love she felt for him, into that kiss.

Jamie picked her up and laid her gently on the bed. He kissed her again. 'Sam?' he murmured the question as kissed his way down her torso.

Somehow her clothes had been discarded and she lay there, just in her underwear. Bringing his face back to hers, she kissed him and sighed. 'Yes. Yes Jamie. Just yes.'

Samantha was molten lava, her body soft and yielding but hotter than hell, as she watched him remove his clothes. All of his clothes. He was beautiful. She knew he would be. He lay with her, taking her gently in his arms. He slowly touched her, drawing circles on her undies. She arched. She'd never felt so *needy.* She tugged at the waistband and he had them off her in seconds. Jamie touched her gently, almost delicately. Where she'd only ever felt pain, she felt pleasure. For a moment she thought about one of Rose Gordon's books. There had been a spicy bit that made her feel warm, all the way to her toes. *So this is what they mean. Who knew?* She nipped his earlobe with her teeth and he breathed in deeply. She whispered, 'Now Jamie.'

———

LATER, curled up in his arms, Samantha shed a few tears. For what she'd been through, and what she'd found with Jamie. *You don't know what you don't know.*

His giant work-roughened hand moved to her face, gently wiping the tears. 'Are you alright, Sam?' But he sounded smug. *He knew she was alright, better than alright.*

'The girls were right. Rose, Nik, Hanna. Even your mum.' Samantha giggled to herself, but tried to keep her expression bland.

'Right about what, Sam?' He sounded slightly worried.

'That it only takes one.'

'One what Sam?' He leaned back, his eyes narrowed.

Opening her eyes as widely as she could, hoping she looked innocent. *Even though she was naked and unashamed.* 'One Good Man, Jamie. The girls told me that all we need is One Good Man.'

THE END

BOOK CLUB READING LIST

1. ***The Bad Bridesmaid*** by Rachael Johns
2. ***A Snowy River Summer*** by Stella Quinn
3. ***Cupid Country Chance*** by Cathryn Hein
4. ***Letters in Blue*** by Heather Reyburn
5. ***Woodstock*** by Michelle Montebello
6. ***The Lost Girl of Seahaven*** by Phillipa Nefri Clark

I hope you enjoy this story and take a moment to check out the books read by the Barrington girl-posse.

Please consider leaving a review. It really helps authors build their following and to keep writing. A simple star rating and a couple of words—(loved it!)— are all that's needed. If you choose to write a longer review, thank you very much.

Susan Mackie

ACKNOWLEDGMENTS

Big thanks to my amazing proof-reader, Janene Morgan *@reads_on_the_road* for her eagle eye.

A huge shout-out to my girls Emily and Jasmine for always being on *Team Susan*. Your absolute belief in me lifts me when I'm feeling low. And to Bloke for your unwavering support. Always grateful for all you do.

Thank you to my writing group: Phillipa, Michelle and Heather. Your support, guidance, and friendship are a blessing (and often a source of hilarity!) Without you, I would not have had the courage to give up my day job and do this writing-editing thing full-time.

The generosity of the authors I've met warms my heart. I've had fabulous author gigs with Julie, Cathryn, Heather, Fiona and Rhonda and create the RWAus magazine with Helen, Jan and Tanya every month.

Thank you to the Book Club Authors mentioned in this book: Rachael Johns, Stella Quinn, Cathryn Hein, Heather Reyburn, Michelle Montebello and Phillipa Nefri Clark – my characters loved reading your stories (as did I).

Thank you to my ARC team for your early reviews - you're all so amazing.

To Fiona Hayes for the stunning watercolour painting you created for this book cover (and earlier books) and all the movie dates we go on. You are a talent.

To Trudy Schultz and Angie White for your photography, and to Lorna for your friendship, free accommodation and help at the markets when I'm in your area. And to Debbie, for your fifty years of friendship.

Lastly – thank you book lovers – for reading my words, writing reviews and recommending my books. Without you, there'd be no words.

SUSAN MACKIE

Author of **The Barrington Book Club - 2025 RUBY Award Finalist** *(Romance Writers of Australia award).*

A voracious reader, Susan dreamed of becoming a writer from the age of eight. Career advisors told her it wasn't a real thing and suggested journalism. So she became a journalist, then took a zig-zag path to publish her first book in 2020, via a varied career in publishing, marketing, tourism and small business. Susan even worked in State Government for a few years (but she doesn't talk about that much).

Nervous about the release of Charlie's Will, she told Bloke while sitting on the sofa one night, that she'd be happy if she sold fifty. Charlie's Will quickly reached Number One in its genre on Amazon - motivating Susan to crack on with more stories and take her writing seriously. Finally. Now Susan is a happy Indie Publisher and offers services to other writers (editing, formatting). She is also the publisher of the Love in a Sunburnt Land Anthology series, co-authored with four (quite brilliant) Aussie women.

Susan loves engaging with fellow authors and readers, and she discovered something she thought was kinda funny. A lot of authors tell her they're introverted. It's a writerly thing, apparently. But (and here's the funny bit), Susan isn't. Introverted. Not one bit. Not at all. Speaking and presenting at writers festivals, conferences and libraries is totally her thing.

So it's okay to send Susan a message, ask a question and chat on social media. She thrives on it and will always respond. Send her a photo of one of her books 'in the wild' and she'll share it. Everywhere.

If you enjoyed this book, join our Facebook group - The Barrington Book Club - and visit Susan's website on the link below.

www.susanmackie.com

ALSO BY SUSAN MACKIE

Charlie's Will

A Place to Start Over

The Bee Whisperer

Ragged Mountain Ranges

Meggie & Max

Something in the Water

Coffee is my Calling

The Barrington Book Club

The Secret Reader